WORMING THE HARPY

WORMING
THE HARPY
and other Bitter Pills

Rhys Hughes

Tartarus Press

Worming the Harpy and other Bitter Pills
by Rhys Hughes

First published by Tartarus Press, 1995.
This edition published by Tartarus Press, 2011 at
Coverley House, Carlton-in-Coverdale, Leyburn
North Yorkshire, DL8 4AY. UK.

This edition adds 'The Forest Chapel Bell', first published
in *Tales from Tartarus*, Tartarus Press, 1995.

The author and publisher would like to thank
Jim Rockhill and Richard Dalby for their help
in the preparation of this volume.

ISBN 978-1-905784-31-8

Printed in Great Britain by the MPG Books Group,
Bodmin and King's Lynn.

To My best friend
Adele Whittle

Now for worms: what makes a dog run mad but a worm in his tongue? And what should that worm be but a spirit? Is there any reason such small vermin as they are should devour such a vast thing as a ship, or have the teeth to gnaw through iron and wood? No, no, they are spirits, or else it were incredible.

Tullius Hostilius, who took upon him to conjure up Jove by Numa Pompilius' books, had no sense to quake and tremble at the wagging and shaking of every leaf but that he thought all leaves are full of worms, and those worms are wicked spirits.

Thomas Nashe,
THE TERRORS OF THE NIGHT, 1594

Cat o' Nine Tales

Herodotus, the old grey cat with a mouth full of stories, usually comes into my kitchen in the evenings. I may be sucking soup from a ladle, juggling mangoes, chopping off the tails of mice (good spaghetti is hard to come by these days) but I always have time for him. For Herodotus is not a cat to be trifled with; and when his mouth is full of stories it is wise to let him spit them out. Else he may swallow them and be sick over the lasagne.

Not that anyone would notice. I keep a kitchen so spotlessly dirty that even the drunken pirates and rough-necks who frequent my restaurant are satisfied. They will often remark that my bootlace-and-green-gravy pizza was absolutely disgusting and then pat me on the back for it and throw me a coin encrusted with teeth where other sailors (doubtless scurvy fellows) were foolish enough to test its validity. The teeth I place under my pillow at night; the coins I give to Herodotus. What he does with them is anyone's guess.

He is indeed an unusual cat. As with most felines, he was born with nine lives, though he has done his best to reduce this number. Sometimes I will baste a vole for him, or grill a dogfish, while he relates his adventures with a slow languid wink in the smoky light of the charcoal ovens. Often we will share a bottle of Chablis or dip our tongues into the sherry syllabub and talk about old times and bewail a world that has changed far too much.

My kitchen is small and dark and its warped wooden timbers are a record of all the meals I have ever prepared.

1

The stains form a pattern that is my history. Spices and sweat, the yellowing effect of turmeric and tears. Through the single grimy window I can glimpse the wan phosphorescence of seaweed-draped ghost ships smuggling illicit spirits between the darkened islands of the bay. Against the walls of my kitchen, I can hear the slap of the harbour waters. And always Herodotus comes, snatching words from an unknown place, to scratch the claws of his life on the itch of my days.

My restaurant is now more popular than ever with the buccaneers and privateers of the port, who sing strange songs as they gorge themselves on my food and empty my beer barrels of their muddy contents. We can always hear their jabbering, even above the hissings and bubblings of my pots and pans. They are slimy scoundrels to a man and woman; swarthy, bristly, leering and jeering rogues, scourges of obscure compass points, bright blue with lewd tattoos. But Herodotus remains unimpressed by such patrons. He merely casts a sardonic eye at their antics through a hole in the door which leads to the eating area. And then he turns back and idly licks a paw.

'Giovanni,' he says. 'Why don't you sell up and open a new place in the town centre? There are many tourists there, with bulging purses. But these pirates leave abominable tips. And they smell. It is important to plan for the future. . . .'

'A slow steady business,' I reply, throwing down my cleaver and mopping my forehead with a pancake. 'Besides, blackguards make good customers in other ways. Their tastebuds have all been ruined by rum and tobacco. Where else could I serve worm curry with a side order of nettles and not receive complaints?'

At which, Herodotus always shrugs his shoulders and sighs. As far as he is concerned, I am somewhat lacking in ambition. To forestall further chiding, I attempt to change the subject. I say: 'Tell me about your nine lives and how you lost eight of them. I've always wanted to know the details. You've made hints and allusions, but those don't satisfy any more. How exactly did you die each time and what did it feel like?'

Herodotus yawns and leaps up onto the edge of a huge black cauldron suspended over the fire. Hedgehog and red lentil soup boils and seethes. 'I was about to tell you the story of Tina Wertigo, the gyroscope girl, and her unbalanced liaison with The Mad Twist. In return for her favours he offered her blue rugs, ambergris and onion domes. . . .'

'Come down from there. You'll burn yourself!' I cry. 'Or at the very least, you'll singe your tail.' But Herodotus ignores me and merely yawns once more. He is a stubborn, as well as reckless, sort of cat, which partly explains why he lost eight of his nine lives in such quick succession. 'Besides, I'd rather hear about you.'

'Why don't you keep quiet and listen then?' Herodotus manages to keep his balance on the lip of the cauldron. 'If you really want to know, I'll tell you. But you mustn't interrupt!'

Now it is my turn to sigh. With remarkable dexterity, I begin to wash and stack the dirty dishes at the sink. They quickly pile into a tower that teeters alarmingly every time I add another piece of crockery. Ten dishes, twenty, thirty. My scrubbing brush flicks soapy water into the furthest corners of the room.

'I lost my first life in a mangle. I fell into a washtub and was stirred with a wooden pole, lifted out with a pair of tongs and squeezed between the rollers until my yellow eyes popped. That was in the city of Skour, where every day is washday and the people yearn constantly to erase from their souls the blemish of some half-remembered sin. Thus Skour is a city in a constant state of flux, each day stripped of a surface layer of dirt to reveal another city yet more dirty. The mangles were powered by an elaborate system of windmills and once trapped in their jaws there was nothing I could do. What did it feel like? Oh, like the thought of rain on a sunny day . . .'

All this while, I am washing and stacking dishes and the tower is growing taller and taller. I do not doubt the truth of Herodotus' tales, for I have never known him attempt to deceive me. Indeed, he is usually more restrained than I would like him to be. Adding cups and saucers to my pagoda of plates, I ask:

'Wasn't it more painful than that?'

Herodotus narrows his eyes and stares at me for a long minute. Who can tell what he is thinking? He crouches on the very edge of the black cauldron and his whiskers curl and droop in the clouds of steam that billow from the pot in fitful asthmatic gasps. Swathed in this aromatic mist, he resembles a tired moon sinking slowly into the white madness of a stormy sea.

'I lost my second life in a mirror. That was in the house of an old lady whose hair was piled up on her head with a selection of multicoloured knitting-needles. Her mirror ran slow; it reflected the distant past as the future stretched out before it. Thus she was able to witness herself as a young girl again, unlined but still unloved, moving with the sure grace of a cloud. In this mirror I saw my own origins, my ultimate demise in the womb of my mother. The reality, it turned out, was nothing more than this. Death had claimed me before life. It felt like a sore thumb without the pain. . . .'

At this, I frown and attempt a wry smile, without success. Such an odd, metaphysical sort of death is quite beyond my understanding. I begin to suspect that Herodotus is falling back on metaphors to express what in all probability was a rather mundane death. 'You were appalled at the prospect of losing your youth and the shock killed you?' I suggest. Herodotus blinks and lets loose a dry chuckle, utterly devoid of humour.

'No, the mirror fell on me. . . .'

4

Here I shudder, while Herodotus closes his mouth, as evil as a shark's, and cages the chuckle that had threatened to slip into a huge great guffaw. Abruptly, he raises his tail, curls it round and licks the tip once. When he resumes, he eyes me with a disturbing curiosity, as if he is seeing me for the first time.

'I lost my third life in a market. This was in the Aching Desert, where nomads mounted on camels vainly attempt to catch swallows and where enormous salamanders vainly attempt to swallow nomads. No sooner had I set foot upon this sandy waste, than my guide, a crafty fellow with a blue turban, turned on me and trussed me up. He carried me across the desert for three days and three nights, his unwound turban trailing behind him like a portable river, until we reached a town whose houses were made out of blocks of salt. There was a market in this town which dealt in camel's milk cheese, slaves and fur. I was skinned and made into a pair of slippers for the Sultana of Prune. It felt like a short hop on a long pier. . . .'

'The other way round surely?' I retort, but Herodotus shakes his head. He knows exactly what he is about, this cat, and resents my need to strike a note of sense on the anvil of his nostalgia.

'I lost my fourth life in a river. At the top of a cobbled alley in the port town of Ezbyx, I chanced upon a barrel of yoghurt. I licked my way down to the centre and then became stuck. My frantic attempts to free myself toppled the barrel and it rolled, grumbling and bouncing, all the way down the street, faster and faster, over the side of the quay and into the water. It sank instantly, with me inside, and the fish that poked their heads into my watery coffin were astonished to see an old enemy so caught out by his own greed. That one felt like the taste of lemons at dawn; a sour end before a fresh start. . . .'

I refrain from remarking that this was an absurd lack of foresight on his part. I do not wish to upset Herodotus

5

further at this stage. I merely continue to stack dishes, higher and higher and higher.

'I lost my fifth life in a long fall. In the mighty city of Abarak, home of The Mad Twist, stands the Tower of Unlikely Dimensions. This is a structure so high that those who stand at the very top can see the curvature of the globe. Well, you can guess what happened. I fell and span towards the ground. As I sped past them, people on different levels offered me a stroke or a kind word or a piece of cheese. I eventually died of old age just before striking the ground. It felt like a song played on an untuned piano. . . .'

I lower my head; there is nothing more to say.

'I lost my sixth and seventh lives at the same instant. While working as a sorcerer's apprentice, I learnt the secret of protecting myself by magical arts while I slept. I painted mystic symbols on my eyelids that would kill any assassin who looked upon them. One day, the sorcerer left two crystal balls on the table in his chamber. One could show the past; the other could show the future. When I took a furtive look at them, I died twice. One of the crystals showed me fast asleep the previous day; the other showed me fast asleep the following day. So I was slain by my own cunning. It felt like sitting on a chair warmed by another occupant. It felt like a sneeze in a paper bag. . . .'

I puff out my cheeks and mutter to myself. The crockery is piled so high that it nearly touches the ceiling. But I continue to add more and Herodotus continues to perch on the edge of the cauldron, while the soup blows scalding bubbles and the pirates in the restaurant yell and growl. My mutter is a quiet one; a rustle like the sound of leaves spinning through the air or like sand that is being poured over an original idea.

'I lost my eighth life in a garret. It felt like a criticism of the sun. I moved into a crumbling deserted house and slept right at the very top. This was in a town where all the avenues are treeless but scattered with rose petals. I became a poet, sleeping during the day, as usual, but taking long walks through cemeteries at night. My poems were rejected and I had to pay for their publication myself. Few copies were sold and I began to starve. Naturally, like all good poets, I swallowed a phial of poison and died in my basket. . . .'

At last I have finished. The dishes form a pillar of dripping discs that push against the weight of the ceiling. I am exhausted. I nod to Herodotus and leave the kitchen by the back door. At the jetty, I pause and gaze out to sea, wiping my hands on my filthy apron. I need to breathe some fresh air before turning to my next task.

As I stand, there is a crash and a yowl from the kitchen. I presume that some of the roughnecks must have started a fight. I roll my tired eyes in exasperation and turn around to go back. Herodotus is standing by my feet, hissing and scowling.

'It was very rude of you to leave,' he says. 'I haven't finished yet. I haven't told you about how I lost my ninth life.'

'Don't be ridiculous! How could you have lost that? Cats only have nine. You'd be a ghost now if you had. . . .'

Herodotus does not reply. I peer more closely at him in the gloom. There is something different about him. I cannot fathom it. Finally the truth dawns. I clear my throat nervously.

'Well?'

'I lost my ninth life in a kitchen. I used to visit a warty old fool who owned a disgusting restaurant. I told him tales, but he was too much of a dullard to appreciate them. One evening, I was balancing on a cauldron of boiling soup and the imbecile was stacking dishes into an enormous pile. Abruptly, he turned around and left the kitchen, slamming the door behind him. The vibration knocked the tower of dishes down onto me and I fell into the soup. . . .'

Worming the Harpy

i

His legs are covered in flea bites, but they are both locked away in a little cupboard, side by side like a pair of high boots, so he is not too concerned.

Six clocks strike the midnight hour. Those without clank their chimes like a laborious joke; borne on the breeze together with leaves and brittle moths. Those within tinkle gently, like ice melting in a shook velvet bag.

This ancient town of Umber-Scone, black as a bat, riddled with narrow cobbled streets like holes in a cheese, is a shattered mirror of former urbanity. Houses lean at crazy or jaunty angles, red tiles are moonwashed and broken, the spaces under the protruding lips of gables are dimly lit by multicoloured lamps, rickety wooden stairways lead to musty rooms full of snores and sighs.

There are no snores or sighs where he sleeps. He is incapable of making such sounds; his lungs are worn too thin. He is peaceful now, dragged down in dreams, in hollow conceits. But there is a rustle at the window. He surfaces back into consciousness, like a swimmer in wine, and his throat is dry.

'Coppelia, my child! Coppelia!'

'What is it, Papa?' She rushes into his room, candle-lantern held high, hair tumbling over her anaemic face. Her lips are like scissors as she works the night air with her question. 'What ails you?'

'There is something at the window, child. Hand me my eyes.'

She opens a small mahogany box that stands on the dressing-table and scoops the two marbled orbs up into her sallow palm. She crosses to her supine father and carefully fits the eyes into his crimson sockets. He blinks thrice, raises his huge head and taps his vision into focus with a sharp knuckle.

'What is it? What is there?'

'I see nothing.' Coppelia moves to the window and lets the halo of her lantern drift through the half-open curtains. There is a groan, a rap and a scratching at the warped glass, a thirsty chuckle that fades and spins away over the rooftops. Outlined on the window is a curious mark. 'Only the print of a hand,' she adds.

'A human hand?' His voice is urgent.

'No: the talons of a demon.'

He shakes his dour head. 'This troubles me, my child. Bring me my nose that I might smell my fear and my brows that I might knit them.' He chews his bottom lip impatiently and oil trickles down his chin.

'Troubled Papa? That is unlike you.' Coppelia fumbles with the nose and misses a thread as she screws it down. But he shrugs off her attempts to adjust the ivory object, and hastily blows it on the green sleeve of his nightgown. Coppelia studies his face. 'You have not been troubled since your accident. Shall I summon the Militia?'

'My accident? So many years ago! But I am more responsible now than I was then. Do not summon the Militia. You would be arrested for tampering with the laws of nature. Let us say nothing and count our blessings. At least I no longer grow old, my child.'

'I know Papa. It is fortunate that I am the most highly skilled maker of mechanical toys in the Province. It is a pity, though, that your lungs keep wearing out so quickly. This is the fifth set this year.'

'It is the smogs, my child.' And then, squinting in the unsteady glow of the lantern, presided over by shadows and spiders which drop from their webs on the cracked ceiling, he adds: 'I cannot sleep now. The handprint has disturbed me. I will rise and pace the garden.'

'Of course.' Between her fingers glitters a tiny silver key. She bends towards the rusty flap in his chest, lifts it and then pauses. 'Shall I wind you up now, Papa?'

ii

A pair of gibbets swing softly in the night. Dark air circulates around the cages and from between the bars moths pour forth in a powdery horde. They swoop and flutter as they digest the mummified scraps that constituted their supper.

The gibbets hang from the branches of an enormous gnarled oak that dominates the crossroads. The prisoners within are like gingerbread men: desiccated and stiff with eyes that register little. Their lank white hair straggles their bony faces, their withered arms and legs still show signs of where they have but lately attempted to gnaw upon themselves.

The men who wait below are even thinner, more insubstantial, broken. They stand and watch for solitary travellers. One of the roads leads up into the blue hills, another twirls away into a dense forest, the third courts bubbles in a malodorous swamp. The fourth leads down to the town and its redundant pleasures.

'We really must stop meeting like this. The chills are not beneficial to the health. Tell me Jakob, would you do it all over again if you could?'

'You jest!' Jakob breaks into a grin, showing teeth like dominoes. 'Of course I would! We nearly pulled it off, you know. Did you see the look on Bishop Knecht's face when

I snatched the ciborium from his sweaty hands and raced out of the Cathedral? Astonishment!'

The other sighs. 'The same old questions, stories, jokes. As if we can ever stop memory slipping away! As if we can ever reverse the hourglass whose vermilion grains are moments in time! But I do remember; and that chase through the market? We knocked over stalls selling copper-work, earthenware, imported fabrics. Many over-priced goods stamped their mark on my frame that day. My ribs were sore for weeks.

'And even more sore when the Bishop ordered them broken with an iron bar. He thought we were iconoclasts: heretics! He would not believe we were simple thieves. Tell me Jakob, do you think we should have stuck to pilfering bread and cheese and the odd jug of wine from the taverns of Dask? Ah, but I remember that ciborium, all jewel encrusted as it was! Tell me, was it your idea to steal it or mine?'

'Shhh!' Jakob raises a reedy finger to his chapped lips. He motions his companion to step back into the shadows. 'Be quiet Tomas,' he whispers. 'Someone is coming. . . .'

Along the road that leads down from the hills, a jaunty figure is capering. Jakob and Tomas watch as he bounds towards them; an ill-set, jangling fellow, dressed in faded motley, with a fiery beard and skin as polished as obsidian. Over his shoulder he carries an odd looking, battered brass instrument and his shoes are soft and worn. Neither Jakob nor Tomas make a move to accost him.

'You let him go!' cries Jakob, once the strange man is out of range.

'So did you!' Tomas shudders and pulls his rags tighter about his shoulders. He glances fearfully at the road that curves towards the town. 'I had a bad feeling about that one. I think it was wiser to leave him alone.'

Jakob nods and scowls. 'But we'll be lucky if another traveller comes this way tonight. We might have missed our one chance. . . .'

There is a sudden crash in the branches of the tree above them. Twigs and acorns shower down upon their heads. The gibbets sway and moan. More moths spiral away into a dark scented with wild garlic, wormwood and decay. The stars are blotted out; a whole constellation.

'What is it?'

Jakob shields his eyes and squints up at the sky. 'It has the face of a demon! It must have been lurking there all along, listening to us. It is heading towards the town, spinning and diving. I can no longer see it. I can see only the blackness of sleep; the blackness that plays tricks on the mind. . . .'

'What shall we do? Report it?'

Jakob throws back his head and looses a guffaw into the silence. His laughter is the croak of a toad. He clutches his stomach and his laugh becomes a wheeze and then a gurgle. Finally it is his eyes alone that show mirth. 'Well done Tomas!' he declares. 'A new joke at last!'

Tomas is sitting on the hard ground, knees drawn up in front of him. He has also been laughing, but his joy is salty; the humour of tears. 'It is a difficult existence, is it not? A thorny life, a Stygian reality.' He cocks his head and listens, as if expecting the demon to return.

'Aye, it's no fun being a condemned prisoner.' Jakob pauses and his jaw works silently, as if it is the mouth of a tongueless puppet. But Tomas can read his words from the undulations of his shattered throat. 'Especially when you're already dead!' He grinds his heel into the dust and a single droplet spills down his own cheek. 'Look, the moths are returning!'

Tomas glances up, and suddenly the air is alive with a cloud of the hairy insects, wings bright with owl's eyes.

'Tell me Jakob,' he asks slowly, 'how long do you think it will take for them to eat all of us?'

iii

The ebony musician enters the town with a light step and a pained expression. He is condemned to move as rhythmically as possible. This was part of a bargain he made—the other part was that he carry his soul over his shoulder.

It has been a difficult week, all in all. He has visited several unfriendly towns and walked rutted roads with little food in his belly. He still recalls how the burghers of Hermannstadt once chased him out of the Cathedral Square with curses and stones. In Kolozsvár his cap netted a single groat.

He has travelled westwards, across the Hortobágy Plain, through Pest and Györ, with a longer sojourn at Pressburg and then Wien, and a hard lot of it in the Tyrol. Finally he has reached another border. His strides are irregular, for his rhythm was forced to be complex, as timeless as his quest.

There are moths everywhere and a chill wind. This town exudes a miasma of undeniable decadence—almost of pure evil—but it is as nothing compared with the unpretty pass he has just negotiated. He shivers as he wonders about that crossroads with the monstrous oak and the gibbets and that dark shape which swooped over him as he descended the path.

Here, at least, there is the chance of warmth, food, perhaps a little ale. The streets of the town are quiet and tangled as string. Mice race ahead of him, hugging the walls with tiny feet. He passes under the arch of a ponderous leaning clock-tower, and down a twisting lane of indigo cobbles, until he chances upon a tavern.

Inside the dubious-looking establishment, a skeleton hangs inverted from the ceiling, describing slow circles, a brazier of coals glowing inside its hollow skull. The other sources of illumination are more orthodox: flickering wicks that droop in blue glass bottles behind the bar. The tavern is deserted save for an oleaginous innkeeper who wipes tall glasses with a grimy cloth. The musician makes his way to the bar, unslings his instrument, and feels inside his threadbare pocket for the last of his change. 'A bed and a drink. . . .'

'At once!' The innkeeper draws a tankard of foamy ale from a rotting barrel and slams it down on the counter. He takes a sharp little knife from his belt and skims off the head. 'Welcome to Umber-Scone!'

'Welcome eh? That's what I need. I have fared none too well in the towns I have lately come from.' He indicates the swirling skeleton. 'Is this the usual form of lighting in these parts?'

'Usual enough here. He was one of my best customers—some would say that he still is. He could never bear to leave this place. It was his last request.' The innkeeper mops his forehead with his cloth and draws a glass for himself. 'So you are a musician? A wandering minstrel?'

'That is correct.' And the musician fingers his instrument, both lovingly and with resentment. He downs his tankard and orders another. So they drink together and become a little drunk. As always, anticipating only scorn, the musician decides to tell his story:

'My name is Dizzy Craggs. I play jazz. A century and more ago I made a pact with the Devil—I sold my soul to become the greatest jazz player in the world. But I soon grew scared and sought a way out. Now I wander the world in search of the perfect jazz tune. That is the escape clause in the contract. If I ever find it, I am free.'

'What is jazz?' The innkeeper slides his own fingers over the tarnished brass. He does not seem particularly

14

impressed by the confession. 'I too once sold my soul to the Devil, as have many in this town. But the Devil demanded a refund. . . .'

There is no mockery in his voice. Dizzy nods his head and raps his knuckles on the counter, rhythmically; always rhythmically. He blows the froth of his murky drink from his lips. 'Jazz is a music you will never have heard. While wandering the world, in a garden suspended between dawn and sunrise, I somehow lost my way between reality and dream. I tripped into another dimension, almost entirely analogous to my own, save in some subtle details. Ever so subtle. There is no jazz here. I am unique.'

They giggle in unison, and drink until Dizzy is worthy of his name and can only yawn and request to be shown to his bed. The innkeeper leads him up a flight of creaking stairs, snapped and twisted in the middle like a broken spine, and opens a warped wooden door into a narrow musty room sparsely furnished with an ancient bed, petrified chest of drawers and wormy chair.

'The worst I have,' the innkeeper confesses, and then adds: 'But you don't want to see my best. My best is far more terrible!' His greasy hand reaches out to grip the musician's shoulder in an ambiguous show of affection.

Dizzy closes the door firmly behind his host, places his instrument on the stained chest of drawers, strips off his soiled jerkin and climbs between the mouldy sheets. Something bites his ankles, he scratches and draws blood. But soon he is asleep. His nightmares are full of sounds; the music of a harp, chuckles and sobs, the clang of three public clocks, each out of time and tune with its fellows. Two strikes each: it is two o'clock and all's unwell in the voracious fervour of the whirling worlds.

Finally he awakens and swings his legs over the side of the bed. It is dark; it is still the middle of the night. He can really hear the sweet tones of a harp, very faint and attenuated. He seizes his instrument and throws open the shut-

15

ters of his window. The sound is clearer now; he steps out onto the sagging balcony and leans over the railings.

A song has come to him in his dreams. Perhaps this is the perfect tune at last, the one that will release him from his diabolical pact? He raises his instrument to his damp mouth. Far below, across the rooftops, he can see into a garden bathed in moonlight. Two figures are walking hand in hand around a toppled fountain—a young girl with long auburn hair and a curiously hunched man with a mechanical gait.

Dizzy plays the first note of his song. It is a soft note, the last gasp of an angel; as silent as a lamb thinking, as blue as northern eyes ground in a pestle. It is his intention to take the melody of his dream, contrast it with the song of the harp, and bend them both through a cool harmonic improvisation.

But before he can continue there is a sudden eruption of black, the balcony shudders and there, before him, hovers a horrible visitation. It glares at him for an instant and then flaps away savagely over the chimneys. Dizzy is dumbfounded; he guesses that it must have been hanging from the underside of the balcony, like a bat. It has the wings of a demon. Down below, the couple in the garden have stopped walking and are looking up towards the creature.

Shaking, and feeling as if he has come within a fingernail's breadth of his destiny, Dizzy staggers back into his room. He realises that he must alert the innkeeper. He pulls on his jerkin and winds his way down the stairs to the drinking room where the brazier still glows and the innkeeper still stands, now smoking a clay pipe. 'A drink and an ear!' he cries.

'Certainly!' The innkeeper draws another ale and hands him a full pipe. 'Unable to sleep, eh? Not surprising for one who has sold his soul to the Devil. . . .'

16

Dizzy lights his pipe from one of the lamps behind the bar. 'I stood out on my balcony and saw—' As the innkeeper leans forward with an intent look on his face, Dizzy knows that it will be asking too much to force upon him another unlikely tale. Besides, it is none of his business; he will be out of this town come morning. So he continues: '—a couple walking in a garden. A girl with long red hair and a hunched man.'

The innkeeper frowns. 'You must be mistaken. I know the girl; her name is Coppelia. She is a toymaker, one of our best. But she lives alone. The hunched man sounds like her father, but Dr Coppelius died many years ago in a bizarre accident. . . .'

'Well then, I must indeed be mistaken.' And seeking a subject mundane enough to kill both the night and the innkeeper's suspicions, Dizzy reaches down and scratches at his legs. 'There are fleas in my room. I have been bitten many times.'

'Naturally. Umber-Scone is infested with fleas.'

'And moths?'

'Of course.' The innkeeper yawns, puffs on his pipe and settles down on a high stool, his eyes hooded by fatigue and the oily flames of the sputtering brazier. He draws a deep breath. 'The moths eat the fleas . . .'

iv

The Hospital of St Scudéry, patron of poor fools, weavers' concubines and samovars, folds in upon itself between leafy park and foot of urban hill. Now on the edge of town, where lunatic wails do not echo among populated streets, the wave of housing once swept over and around it, receding during the plague years and, with violent under-tow, dislodging slates off roof, weakening foundations, but not quite dragging the whole edifice back to the dark centre.

Six hundred madmen roam the shell of the Great Hall, whose double doors are locked with a key as heavy as an arm. Plaster is peeling off the walls and ceiling; the chains that bind the inmates to brackets have rusted through and broken loose. So the lost souls hold court together, each delusion in opposition to all others. For every one who boldly asserts he has a body of glass, there is another who will claim he is opaque, that the mummer's antics of a third cannot be perceived through him.

The upkeep of the place is expensive. Rich couples come and pay to view the lunatics, a shilling a head. It is not quite enough—not now, for they come less frequently. The squalor is distracting.

Herr Wyeth, who runs the institution, who cleans the rooms and passages, who doctors the patients and clucks his tongue, has no degree. He wanted to be an arborist but quickly discovered he could not stand the sight of sap. He has heard that lunatics are like trees, that their ages can be gauged by sawing them in half and counting the rings. And once he tried but was vaguely disappointed with the results.

He is the last member of the Hospital staff to remain. As funds run low, his own position grows insecure. One day soon, he will have to follow the example of his colleagues—he will have to walk away from the Hospital forever, abandoning the inmates to their sordid delusions.

He hears their babblings as he plays solitaire in his office. It is an unusual game, invented by one of his charges. The maxims of the philosopher Lichtenberg are rearranged into new pearls of wisdom according to the random positioning of a handful of brightly coloured glass beads on a stave. The first aphorism thus produced aston-ished Herr Wyeth with its pithy truth and woody beauty—

but since then he has struggled in vain to produce meaningful sentences.

He attempts to concentrate, but the voices warble through the walls:

'A body of glass! A lens! I am a closed vessel—ha! ha!—The moon will strike me and set my heart aflame! My burning heart will consume my inner air! Will I not suffocate?'

'No, the moon no longer peeps through the roof. Now there is a face. It has eyes like lodes of fool's gold.'

'A voice that stings like such gold, sparked into the eyes! Or like a foolish goldsmith, scalded by the molten world! I have been one, in my time. Now can I sing. Oh la!'

Herr Wyeth sighs and clears the stave before him with a sweep of the hand. He does not recognise the voices; he has little real interest in his patients, but urgent action is called for, before their hysterics upset the others.

He takes a volume down from his shelf and opens it before him on his desk. It is the latest medical textbook from Geneva. There is a new cure for hysteria: a cage suspended on a centrifuge. The patient is whirled at high speed, the unhealthy humours are pushed to the surface of the body and sweated out. If this does not work, or if the apparatus is unavailable, dunking is recommended.

'It enters through the hole! What does it want?' The voices continue with mounting frenzy. 'What does it possess?'

'The desires of a demon!'

Herr Wyeth takes the key from the cupboard and carries it on his shoulder like an axe. In his other hand he snatches up the lantern. Originally a prison for anarchists, the Hospital is designed like a cochlea, the shape of the inner ear, the spiral passages guaranteed to amplify seditious talk from the Great Hall at the centre to the Governor's office.

There is a crash now, as of some heavy object thrown with force from one end of the Hall to the other. Herr Wyeth quickens his step. Dunking it shall be; for both of them.

'Leave me alone! I am not a man! I am not edible! I am an hourglass; my liver is made of sand. I loved life once! Once!'

'A punishment for your crime!'

Herr Wyeth bawls: 'Cease! The pair of you shall know pain, like salted heretics, peeled and pickled.' The image gives him a mordant satisfaction. It is a metaphor taken from his glass-bead game. Shorn of wisdom, but spicy as Sabellian sweat—which is another. 'Cease now, whoever you are!'

'Tush! It has me by the scruff. Leave me be, fiend! These manners do not suit. Shame, shame!'

'You fly like a bat. Ha!'

There is yet more pounding and then a general uproar. Other voices join in; demented laughter, cries of rage and despair. Above the babble of chaos, the words of the first speaker rise, high and thin now, as if from far away.

'I did not mean to do it!'

Herr Wyeth reaches the double-doors, heaves the key into the lock and struggles to turn it. The door opens like a dread season; it is colder within and illuminated by moon-wash alone.

Normally the fools fall silent when he enters—they well know the price of disobedience. But this time, they flaunt the rules, racing round and round the vast space, crouching low, flapping arms and screeching. 'Stop!' he cries. 'Stop at once!'

One madman alone is immobile. He sits in the centre of the Hall with his face held towards the gaping hole in the ceiling. 'It entered and took him away,' he says. 'He should not have been here. Perhaps it knew that and came to release him.'

'Who?' Herr Wyeth demands. 'What are you talking about?'

'My friend, Cardillac. He was a goldsmith; a virtuous man. One bright morning a toymaker and her father brought him an automaton for his furnace. It was broken and there was gold in its brain. But Cardillac was short-sighted and hurled in father by mistake. It was an accident.'

Holding his lantern up high, Herr Wyeth sneers. 'What stupidity is this? It calls for a dunking, I believe. No-one is missing; you are all here, wallowing in your own filth as always.'

'No, he was taken. By a demon!'

For a brief instant, Herr Wyeth feels a sliver of wonder, as if double-doors are opening in his own head. But he shrugs. To validate this lunatic's story would require the counting of all six hundred inmates, one by one. An absurd way of disproving a delusion!

His words are tinged with cruelty and boredom. Already he is imagining the fool's submersion—it will also be a drowning of his own troubles.

'We shall see! We shall see!'

v

In the very centre of the town, in a large old house in the shadow of the truncated Cathedral, the vampire family Hoffmann are holding a reunion.

There is much feasting by the light of black candles; and the dishes and red-blood wines come and go with unnerving regularity, for the undead are particular about such things. Grandfather Martin—most stately of the brood—breaks black bread and dabs his thin lips with a satin napkin.

'Hans is late again.' He indicates the moondial in the corner of the room. A cunning combination of mirrors reflects the lunar light all the way through the mansion and focuses it here, in the dining room. 'Every year he is late.'

'He has a long way to come!' Greta is always willing to defend her youngest son. 'From Africa—where he is fighting the Hereros.'

Grandfather Martin shakes his long pale head. 'Cousin Wilhelm flew all the way from the jungles of Peru, where he is seeking the orchid of forgetfulness. No, it is half past three already. Dawn will come before he does.'

'He's young!' protests Greta, nibbling the breaded fingers. Despite her size she is quite frugal in her dietary habits. Not for her the whole raw ox that Brother Einar is fond of polishing off at these annual celebrations—or even the skewered limbs favoured by hirsute Wolfgang. Thumbs dipped in rum sauce are enough for her. 'He's full of the joys of death!'

'Reprobate!' sneers Grandfather Martin. He pours Adam's apple cider and sniffs petulantly. 'What will his excuse be this time?' He dips the black bread into the cider, eases it between his jaws, coughs and raises the napkin once more to his mouth. When he removes it, a yellow maggot is squirming in the satin. 'My, what a fat one! Juicy enough to hang from a watchchain!'

Wilhelm picks at a noxious toadstool. 'Did I tell you about that time in Lima when I caught typhoid?' He shrugs. 'Poor typhoid!'

There is a scraping on the roof. Tiles break loose and slide free. An upstairs window is rattled. Greta meets the gaze of all those assembled—Martin, Klara, Wilhelm, Edgar, Sonya, Einar, Eva, Wolfgang—and beams. 'It is Hans. I knew he would come!'

'I will let him in.' Pushing back his chair, Grandfather Martin stands and makes his slow way out of the dining room and up the stairs. Greta nods triumphantly to herself while most of the others sit quietly and Einar helps himself to another bowl of person broth.

There is a crash and a muted scream from above. Greta looks upwards in some confusion, Einar drops his spoon. The others are as frozen as ideas in amber.

Another cry: 'No!'

There is a long pause, an open mouthed hiatus. Finally Grandfather Martin reappears at the door. There is a strange glint in his eyes. He is no longer pale; his face is deathly ruddy. 'It was not Hans,' he gasps.

'Then who?' Greta reaches for the tureen of traveller-soup, snatches up the ladle and holds it like a mace. The others fumble with knives, forks, bottles. Bared teeth glimmer.

'It left something.' Grandfather Martin clutches his chest. 'My heart! I think it has started beating!'

'Sit down.' Greta is by his side in a blink. 'Stay calm.' She presses him back down into his chair and takes his pulse. His breathing comes in shallow gasps. While she cools his forehead with a cloth soaked in the ichor of frogs, he manages to blurt out:

'It had the body of a demon!'

'Eh?' Wilhelm is pounding the table with his fist. 'A demon you say? What did it bring? We must contact the authorities on the instant!'

'Don't be ridiculous.' Greta orders Wilhelm back into his seat. 'How can we possibly contact the authorities? They might want to search the house. Think about that—the cellars! No, we must keep silent.'

There is another commotion at another window—the downstairs casement. A tall, lean, very blonde figure stands there; impossibly arrogant with elaborate frilly white shirt and huge flapping unbuttoned cuffs. He holds his dramatic pose for ten long licks of his ascetic lips and then jumps nimbly down onto the floor, leaving the windows and drapes swinging behind him. It is Hans.

'Sorry I'm late!' He strides over to the table and empties half a carafe of brandy straight down his throat, blackguard style. 'Horrendous journey! Just finished pickling the chief Baviaan's head when I realised I had to fly. So I spread my wings over the Skeleton Coast and followed the Benguela current, with its flotsam of drowning sailors, all the way up to the dark continent's armpit. Over the Aching Desert I stopped to unwind the black turban of a djinn-worshipping emir—and to ask his wife for a date! Then I soared again over the Middle Sea to the Alps. Eventually I approached our own dear Umber-Scone. . . .'

Oblivious of his surroundings, Hans brushes back his magnificent locks and continues: 'But before I arrived, I dallied at a crossroads on the edge of town, to chase two sombre ghosts who were lurking under some gibbets. How they squealed when I dived at them! Something else had already frightened them. I then glided over the town itself. I spotted a couple strolling in their garden, one of them a very passable young girl. Her neck seemed destined for my mouth. But as I swooped she went inside her house and I had to settle for her companion—a hunched old man. My teeth clamped on his throat, but here's the surprise: his neck was made of iron!'

Hans grins, to show the stumps of his two broken fangs. He waits for the usual gasps of astonishment at his exploits but none are forthcoming. Finally he notices the strained expressions of the family.

It is Greta who breaks the silence. 'Your grandfather is very ill.'

With two gargantuan steps, Hans is by her side. 'What's wrong?' He peers down at Grandfather Martin's immobile face. There is no movement in that body, no flicker of undead vitality. A steady trickle of writhing maggots tumbles out of his mouth. Hans crosses himself; an inverted cross. 'He's not alive is he?'

A dazed figure, soiled shirt torn at the shoulders, staggers into the room. It passes a hand across its grimy brow. 'I found the stairs. I did not tumble. I did not break. I am very fragile, you must remember this. My body is made of glass!'

Hans narrows his eyes and studies the new arrival. Despite himself, he licks his lips again. Appetite must always precede family loyalty—he cannot help himself. He reaches out to the figure.

'Seconds anyone?'

vi

The vet is a pinched man with glasses that magnify his eyes into the eggs of a cockatrice. Around him, in cages, grumble the reasons for his being: imps, basilisks, chimerae, perytons and baldanders, manticores and mermecolions, all lame.

Dawn's left hand is scouring the eastern sky; over the rooftops the darkness retreats with claws that wind in the star-flecked cloak of night. Darkness himself shelters in the streets under the jutting gables, where no sun ever peeps.

The vet's house, alone in all of choleric Umber-Scone, is made of rocks embedded with Silurian fossils, from a time when the mountains lay under the sea. Ammonites curl on the outside walls like hypnotic eyes, protective, ever watchful; and on the inside like a mural of spinning galaxies.

The vet regards his patient, and its owner, with cautious disapproval. 'It was not a good idea, bringing her in unrestrained. They always slip away at the first chance.'

A debauched cleric, all stomach and stained purple robes, waves a weary hand. 'I could hardly bring her in a box. She would have been frightened.' Lovingly he pinches the cheek of his pet. 'She's all I have, Dr Krespel. I couldn't bear to hurt her!'

The vet removes his glasses and rubs his bloodshot eyes. 'Up all night! With respect, Bishop, this could only happen here or in Zug—never in Königsberg, my home.'

'I thought I could hold onto her. She wriggled out of my grasp and was gone in an instant! Yet I enticed her back: I played the harp. All night long! She loves the harp, does my Matilda. I played that new piece by Boccherini and she could not resist. Back she came, into my arms. Ah, Matilda!' The Bishop scratches the fur under her chin. 'How worried I was! How happy I am to have you safe again!'

The vet shakes his head cynically. 'You know that the Town Council has an obligation to clear the streets of strays? If she had been spotted and caught, not even your influence could have saved her from the compound. These animals are mistrusted; they can cause a lot of damage. I suspect the moth population has been seriously depleted this night—and Umber-Scone is famous for its carnivorous moths!'

The Bishop stares coldly at the vet. 'No harm was done. It was night, the town was abed. No-one noticed, no-one complained.'

'You were lucky. A single report and you would have lost your licence. These animals are supposed to be kept on leads and muzzled in public. You remember the outcry last year, after that spate of attacks on children? Some members of the Town Council would like to see them outlawed. It's a political issue now.'

'But Matilda . . .' The Bishop begins to shudder with rage; his huge bulk rumbles alarmingly. 'Matilda wouldn't hurt a flea. Come to think of it, you'd better de-flea her as well, while you're at it. . . .'

'That's not the point. Next time you bring her to my surgery, make sure she can't get away! I'll not be so tolerant again. And you'll pay for my time as well. A whole night!' The vet moves to a cabinet and removes a bottle of pills. 'Here, give her one a day before meals. Make sure she completes the entire course. Come back on the last day and I'll make out a new prescription. That should do the trick. They'll work for fleas as well, though it's up to you to keep her fur clean. . . .'

'You are a little arrogant, Dr Krespel. You are like those fools on the Council who accuse me of practising dark arts. They say I animate the gargoyles of my Cathedral with the blood of virgins! I won't forget this. Come on Matilda, let me just put this lead around your neck. I know, darling, but it's for your own good. We'll be home soon. There's a good girl. I'll play you some nice Telemann once we're back.' Shouldering his miniature harp, the Bishop walks his pet towards the door. On the threshold he pauses and looks round. 'It wasn't really that bad was it? I mean, no-one noticed her. Nothing has changed?'

The vet sneers and turns away. 'It's people like you who give harpies a bad name!' he cries. He shuffles some papers on his desk.

For a moment, the Bishop broods. 'Are you married, Dr Krespel?' Then his eyes light up. 'Nice Matilda, you're safe now.' He steps through the door, closes it behind him and they venture out onto the street. Next time, he decides, the vet will come to him. There is a gargoyle on his north tower that will make a fine companion for Matilda. Suddenly he lunges at his pet and plants a ferocious kiss on her cheek. Together they throw back their heads and howl.

The Falling Star

Down in the park, the park of my impotent dreams, a star fell. I saw it streak purple across the sky: it scratched the edge of a lonely pink cloud before greeting the earth with a resounding kiss. I was standing outside the park at the time, making gamelan music on the railings with my umbrella. The sun was rising slowly. It was very cold. The notes of my music clattered through the silence like a tower of dirty dishes collapsing into a sink or like a row of icicles falling onto the heads of a dozen helmeted knights.

The star had crashed into a clump of dense bushes, pounding a hole in the rich soil beneath. A little reddish steam arose and dispersed on the very slight breeze. I was determined not to let this chance slip me by. Although the gates of the park were still locked, I resolved to gain entry. I clambered over the railings, taking care not to impale myself on the barbed points. I had no desire to become the focus of a new urban myth.

Once over, I was on familiar ground. This park, with its little pathways and lake, its grass embankment and bandstand, had been my only source of comfort in an otherwise bleak life. I had known too well the gloom of long days with nothing to do, the aimless shuffle, the empty existence. The park had seemed to offer a salve for my tormented spirit. An empathy of abundance.

This time, however, its attractions seemed minor in comparison with the greater gift that had plummeted from the empyrean. A meteorite I could sell to a museum. There would be funds to fuel ambitions I had thought would never be realised. There would be joy a-plenty, limits a-topple. There would be yoghurt and honey, moons and daffodils, chimes and rhymes.

Almost unable to contain my excitement, I hurled myself into the foliage, seeking the crater of my salvation. Sure enough, there it lay; a shallow hole like the dent of a divine fist, branches and leaves scattered around it in pleasing profusion. But my expectations were to be exceeded beyond my imagination. For at the base of the crater lay not just a few fragments of a nickel-iron meteorite, but also a dozen spherical objects of unearthly lustre and beauty.

I stood enraptured by this sight, scarcely daring to draw breath. Thus it was that I did not notice the approach of one whom I had often sought to avoid in the past. How long he stood there, peering over my shoulder, I can hardly guess. Suffice it to say that when he spoke, I jumped with fright and nearly tottered over the brink of the crater.

'Star pearls,' he said, 'that's what they are. When a piece of dust gets into a star, the star forms a coating around it. Like an oyster. Star pearls are among the most valuable objects in the universe.'

I whirled around. It was Mellors, the park keeper. 'Nonsense!' I replied. 'It was a meteorite that fell here. Meteorites do not contain pearls.'

'Oh yes they do.' He was emphatic. He span his litter-stick like a majorette. The end glinted in the early light. It had been sharpened to a fine point and appeared to be encrusted with dried blood. Mellors was well known as a tyrant: he saw the park as his own and he despised intruders.

'You are an expert?' I demanded with as much scorn as I could muster. He grimaced and then laughed, his cap wobbling on the crown of his overlarge head. With his painfully thin body and crow's legs it did not seem that he could possibly bear the weight.

'It doesn't matter anyway. Believe what you will. With these pearls I will be set free. I will be able to retire and buy a park of my own. Oh, the things I will be able to do!' His eyes twinkled with rare pleasure. 'I'll not let anybody in. . . .'

'All very nice, I'm sure,' I replied. 'But completely hypothetical. A pipedream. The pearls are mine. I saw them first. I'm taking them home.'

'Ho!' Abruptly, he ceased spinning his infernal stick and leered towards me. 'Is that so? Yet it is true, is it not, that this park is mine? And that, therefore, I am responsible for dealing with any unnatural phenomena that occur within its boundaries? The pearls are not yours. They are mine. I will buy a roof garden.'

'No! No!' I cried, waving my arms. 'You are a fool! Can you not see what is under your very nose? I am the discoverer of this meteorite; it belongs to me alone. These luminous spheres also.' And I crouched forward to leap into the crater.

I was restrained by a firm grip on my collar. I felt the hot breath of Mellors on the nape of my neck. He was struggling to control himself. I was reminded of a kettle whose owner had departed for a voyage around the globe, leaving it to boil itself to a frenzy.

'Perhaps we can come to some arrangement?' I suggested. 'Supposing we split the discovery down the middle? Fifty-fifty? Or, to be more apt, six of one and half-a-dozen of the same. . . .' Peering back over my shoulder, I saw that Mellors was shaking his head.

'The pearls must never be separated. Otherwise they lose their magic. Is it not obvious? Together they can unlock the greatest mysteries of life; alone they are useless. Once taken out of context, their inner vitality begins to fade away. Truly, in this case, the sum is greater than the parts.'

I frowned. 'But what exactly do they do? In what way can they unlock the mysteries of life?'

Mellors smirked. 'That is one of the mysteries they alone can demystify.' He paused, realising that he was venturing into the perilous deeps of paradox. 'It is not for us to know,' he corrected, quoting Wittgenstein: 'What we cannot speak of, we must pass over in silence.'

'Well I'm not passing these over in silence!' I cried. 'Although you are quite welcome to do so. It seems that I shall have to take all of them.' And I pulled away from his clutches and tried again to leap into the pit.

This time, Mellors barred my path with his litter stick. He snarled a challenge. The point grazed the nape of my neck and I twisted, shielding my face with my free hand. I raised my umbrella and parried his next thrust. Frustrated and incensed by my refusal to concede the star pearls, he attacked a third time with increased savagery.

I weaved under his inexpert blows and sliced at his shin, handling my umbrella like a sabre. He jumped over my thrust and struck at my head. The vicious spike narrowly missed my face and I bared my yellow teeth. I was determined to enter fully into the spirit of the thing. 'En garde!' I cried. 'Zut alors! Beaujolais Nouveau!'

These taunts merely angered him further, but this was precisely the effect I was hoping to achieve. As he lunged forward, I ducked, drew the real sword concealed in my umbrella, shifted it to my left hand and pierced the lobe of his ear. His fury made him not only careless but oblivious to pain. He whirled round and his ear came off with a rip of fibres.

I opened my mouth to laugh, but now it was his turn for vengeance. His spike came up, pierced the taut skin under my chin and continued upwards, transfixing my fleshy tongue to the roof of my mouth. When he withdrew the spike, a dozen drops of blood came with it, solidifying into rubies in the cold air. Words followed the rubies. Words of more than a little annoyance.

'Scum! Wheelbarrow licker! Ugli-fruit!'

'Now, now!' He clutched his ear and circled me warily. He eyed my rapier and muttered ruefully.

'Very distasteful,' he said. 'If only I'd known! But I have an ace up my sleeve as well. . . .' He smiled a sly smile and aimed his stick at me. 'Would you like to see it?'

I frowned, and as I did so, he depressed a stud on the base of his handle. There was a click and the whirr of a spring. Before I knew what was happening, the tip of the spike was spinning through the air towards me. I felt it strike the centre of my forehead, boring a third eye into my cranium. There was no pain, but more rubies rolled down my brow to join the diamonds of my tears and the emeralds of my nose. The air was indeed very cold.

I tugged at the spike, but it was stuck fast in my skull. I winced. Mellors was rubbing his chin. 'You must have a very thick skull,' he observed. 'Hardly surprising, considering your nature. Ah well! I shall have to beat you to death with the other end of my stick.' He shrugged.

I dropped my sword, fell to my knees and feigned unconsciousness. When Mellors approached, I snatched up my blade and pierced his groin. He screamed and fell back. I twisted the handle and pulled it free, slicing at him again and again. Fingers flew loose, the tip of a nose, an eyelid. I slashed until his skin hung off in shreds and he was crawling in a pool of his own blood.

'Right!' He was furious, albeit in a soprano sort of way. 'That does it! Now you're for it, my friend! I'll have you bound and gagged, boiled in a metal tank, liquefied and then sprayed onto my flowerbeds as plant food!'

For good measure, I sliced his lips off. They slid across the frozen ground like blubbery half moons. With an arrogant heel, I stamped them to putrid jelly. Never again would they swell to the delicious ache of a vindaloo. As if suddenly aware of this prospect, Mellors became petulant. His face wore such a lugubrious expression that I started to laugh. He attempted to point an accusing finger at me, but for the most part they lay on the ground next to his oozy lips.

'I have made my point,' I said, waving my rapier and carving Möbius strips in the fabric of reality. 'And now the debate is over. I will take the star pearls and leave you to mull over the folly of greed.' I turned my back and stalked off in the direction of the crater. Something small landed by my feet. I whirled round. 'What now?' I demanded, my frown of annoyance impeded by the spike that protruded from my forehead.

With his left hand, Mellors was scooping up the severed digits of his right, thrusting them one by one into random nostrils and then snorting them at me. Enraged by this desperate show of contempt, I slashed at the missiles as they span towards me. With singular misfortune, I managed to deflect one away from a relatively harmless course into my left eye. The ugly gnarled nail scratched open my retina and my world partly dissolved in a flood of pain and salty mucus.

I howled and ground my teeth. 'Will you never learn?' I resumed my calculated slashing, but this time he was more careful to evade my blows. Slipping on our displaced fluids, I followed him down the path and up a little rise towards the boating-lake. 'Bum!' I cursed, as he danced out of range each time I lunged.

At the main gates to the park, a few faces peered eagerly through the iron whorls and spirals. They tapped their wristwatches impatiently as we passed. Mellors checked his own, held it up to me and motioned to the tiny crowd. Politely, I lowered my weapon while he removed a heavy set of keys from his belt and unlocked the gate. Grey and covered in wrinkles, the motley collection of joggers and yoga students flooded through to begin another day of mindless ritual.

As soon as he had replaced the keys at his belt, I continued my offensive. Mellors mocked me as he retreated, thrusting his hips forward in a cryptic, though certainly obscene, gesture. Occasionally, he made a counter lunge with his litter-stick. I grew increasingly frustrated as my blows fell short. With a single working eye, I found it difficult to judge distance. Well aware of this, Mellors exploited his only advantage.

Slowly, as we circled the perimeter of the park, the sun began to warm our wounds. The park started to fill up: old couples and single parents joined the joggers and lentil-eaters; students claimed benches for their revision; perverts in anoraks skulked through the undergrowth; dog-owners polluted the environment with a thousand colours and textures of canine excreta; truants dodged school and enjoyed a surly smoke on the rusty-chained swings of the woodchip playground.

When we had completed half a circuit, Mellors suddenly dropped his guard and sighed. Although I was eager to skewer his ignoble heart and have done with him, I could see that he was on the brink of a revealing insight. We stopped beside a clump of bushes where a writer's group was discharging the contents of the previous night's revels. I recognised a host of prolific poets and poetasters, both male and female. Plodders with the pallor and ambitions of tadpoles attempted to outvomit pretentious book-reviewers and voluptuous editors from Sidcup.

'This whole exercise is more profound than it appears,' Mellors began. 'We are living in a parable. Don't you see? Our actions form part of an elaborate allegory. They are the products of conscious decisions but not of decisive consciousness. Our struggles are part of a much wider scenario.'

'Oh really?' I raised a cynical eyebrow. 'And what, pray, is the message of this parable? And what is the key that can unlock its meanings?'

Mellors sat down on a bench, shaded by a twisted cedar and not yet relieved of its frosty rime. He placed his litter stick by his side and spread out his hands, or rather what remained of them. 'This park represents the entire universe. It is a microcosm of reality. The star pearls represent truth, absolute certainty amid chaos. The meteorite was its messenger, a prophet or philosopher. We represent orthodoxy and dissent, two factions who seek a monopoly on truth.'

I grinned. His metaphysics was impressive. 'Very apt, I'm sure. But I always win at monopoly. Indeed, I intend to mortgage your life this very morning. I would very much like to examine your liver, you see.'

Mellors grunted. 'Your overconfidence is truly startling. But you are right about one thing. There is more truth in viscera than in truth itself. I will eat yours with avocado and rose petals.'

'Oh ho!' Before he could regain his litter-stick, I had flicked it high with the tip of my rapier. It landed amid the circle of writers, where the tadpole used it to scratch his six-hundredth tale in the communal puddle of undigested fish pizza and beer. As I bore down on Mellors with malice formidable, he jumped up and seized on my Adam's apple with his rotting teeth. There was a crunch, as crisp as the morning itself, and the apple had been halved. He spat bloody red things, as analogous to pips as length is to breadth, and hooted.

'Glib gargoyle!' I rasped, with great difficulty. 'Rancid rhabdus! Lousy loganberry! Your parable disappears up its own backside as shall the quartered segments of your limbs. Come here wretch! I shall unwind your intestines on a windlass and make black puddings from them.'

'Piffle!' Once more he bounced out of my reach and the absurd struggle resumed with fresh vigour. We passed through the herb garden, tastefully arranged in the shape of a sundial, and breathed in the heady scents of lemon balm and marjoram and the salad freshness of borage and mint. From here we descended a winding path to the boating lake, cobalt waters trapping the stately reflections of black swans. Ice-cream vendors gestured to us with chocolate flakes and canisters of raspberry sauce. Old women, smelling of mothballs and boiled sweets, tripped us up with improbably long leads fastened to dogs no bigger than their fists.

As we skirted the shore, I noticed the large crows that had gathered on the railings and who appeared particularly interested in my ruined eye. Their beaks seemed connected to my weeping orb by lines of dark purpose. I scowled at them, but they did not flinch. Perched on the barbed spikes, their position was advantageous; fixed at a point between the known universe and the other side of knowledge.

We threaded our way through a senile reunion of ex-servicemen who had gathered at the bandstand. On the covered platform, crusty musicians were forcing stale air into tarnished brass instruments. Bumbling tubas and ridiculous euphoniums assailed us with powerful exhortations, while a score of glockenspiels attempted callow counterpoint. The crowd grumbled at our intrusion, but I was loathe to acknowledge their discontent. Further on, we encountered a small group of children playing with exquisitely worked marbles.

When we had reached the other side of the lake, Mellors paused again and I reluctantly lowered my blade. He indicated a shack that stood at the end of a narrow path. 'That is my hut. I need to relieve myself. I won't be a minute.'

I nodded my rather exasperated assent and waited while he walked up the path and vanished inside the shack. I had often seen him glaring out of its window at fishermen and young lovers. I knew that he kept a teapot in there and a telephone, but I knew little else. Curious, I advanced up the path towards the window. I heard a bizarre grating noise and a series of grunts and I scratched my head. As I peered through the grimy warped glass, I gulped. I had suspected a trick, of course, but nothing of this nature.

Mellors was busy sharpening a spade on a grindstone. Sparks flew and illuminated the gloomy interior in ghastly fits. It was a cluttered shack, stuffed full with ancient garden tools and machinery. With only one good hand, Mellors was finding it difficult to spin the grindstone and hold the spade down at the same time. He tried using his foot to whirl the heavy stone wheel and coughed the resulting iron filings out of his lungs. Each time he held the spade up, the edges of the blade reflected more and more silvery light.

I tapped on the window and drew an insulting doodle in the dirt. Mellors glanced up and sneered. I pulled at the door handle, but the door was locked. I rattled it and screamed. 'Open up you sneak! Come out and fight like a man!'

I pulled at the door again and this time it came off its hinges and I fell backwards beneath its weight. My skull bounced thrice on the crazy paving of the path. Frightened woodlice raced from the gaps in the rotting wood and swarmed into my open mouth. I struggled to my feet just in time to confront Mellors, who was rushing headlong from the shack in savage glee, the spade uplifted above his head.

Luckily the door took the full force of the first blow, splitting in twain and showering long damp splinters into my unprotected face. I dropped the two pieces of door and sidestepped the second blow, retreating a few paces backwards. The third blow, however, caught me completely by surprise, and the blade lodged deep into my neck. The pain was unbearable. Mellors yanked and twisted the spade, as if he were attempting to lever my head off its shoulders. My damaged eye popped from its socket and hung there, glistening. But my spinal cord remained intact and I managed to recover my senses enough to pull free and evade the fourth blow.

Twenty blows later, Mellors was exhausted. I had been retreating all the while, reflecting on the irony of this reversal of fortune. The face of Mellors in near victory was even more grotesque than when I had pressed the advantage. He leered and belched, his cap wobbling like a gyroscope, his hips once more thrusting forward in the regular motion he had often observed but never before successfully used. My dangling eye irritated my cheek to such a degree that I pulled it completely out and hurled it away. Instantly crows swooped and carried this myopic prize back to their perches.

'Look!' Mellors bellowed, leaning on the spade and pointing. 'We are back where we started! We have circumnavigated the entire park. We are pioneers of a sort. Trailblazers. Necessity has been the great-aunt of invention, if not its mother. What more can I say? I am delighted. It was a close race, but I have won.'

Glancing back over my shoulder, I saw the clump of decimated bushes. Taking an enormous gamble, I turned and made my way through the papilionaceous shrubs, fitting my shoes into the footprints I had made earlier. Uncharacteristically, Mellors did not seize the chance to attack me from behind, but followed me into the foliage, swinging his spade like a machete.

We stood on the edge of the crater and looked down. The star pearls were gone. It seemed logical enough, but I joined Mellors in gnashing and weeping and pulling my hair. And then we pulled his hair and vented the cleansing grief together.

'But who could have taken them?' Mellors had become a moon-eyed fool, gangling, retching, eaten up with anxiety and disbelief. 'Who? The magic will die in the wrong hands!'

I snapped my fingers. 'The children!' I cried. 'The children with the marbles! Don't you remember? Those weren't marbles after all! They were our star pearls.'

Mellors shrieked a primeval shriek. 'Let us be after them! We can recover the pearls and then roast the brats on a griddle. I have paraffin and matches at my disposal. Come, superbly boring one, let us combine our talents to a common purpose.'

I was ready there and then to join him, but something made me reach out and restrain him. 'I have been thinking,' I said, 'about your parable. If it is true then all our attempts to recover the pearls will be futile. Indeed, our struggles could never have been resolved.'

'How so?' He knitted his brows with the uneasy pride of a lecturer who has been outstripped by his own student. He peered again into the crater and then began to tremble.

'The pearls represent truth and we represent orthodoxy and dissent. In that case, they do not belong to us. Truth is intended for innocence alone. Those children represent innocence. Thus the pearls are rightly theirs. . . .'

Mellors looked down at my hand, which still gripped his shoulder, and then looked me full in the face. Suddenly he was only as ugly as my own reflection. Absolutely disgusting, instead of unspeakably repellent. He gave me a long slow nod and the faintest augur of a smile. 'Then we have been made redundant,' he said, and raised his spade. 'Is that not so? But we cannot retire as individuals. We must leave together.'

'Of course.' I knew at once what he intended, but I made no attempt to avoid my fate. The spade completed the cut in my neck and released me from this life of sorrows. My head lifted up on a superb fountain of blood and bile, twenty or thirty feet into the air, while my body crumpled into the crater. I saw the layout of the park, the little paths and secret places. And as my head descended, Mellors turned the spade sideways and used the flat of the blade to knock it even higher. This time it span in a perfect arc and impaled itself on one of the barbed railings.

As I dribbled and twitched, I watched Mellors return to his little shack. He reappeared ten minutes later, chained by the neck to a rusty lawnmower. Grunting and gasping, he carried this useless hulk of machinery over to the lake and threw it in with a jubilant cry. The chain pulled taut and he was jerked off his feet, vanishing into the deeps of the lake amid soggy breadcrumbs and waterlogged crisp packets. I saw the wavelets caused by his descent and how they lapped the shores like little tongues, but I did not see the bubbles.

By that time, the crows had pecked out my other eye.

Quasimodulus

He dances in the wind on the roof of the opera house. His cloak lifts high behind him in a vast semi-circle, a dark moon. His pale face is framed by the black cloth; he laughs, he capers, he twirls his swordstick.

'Dio del ciel in me raddoppia il coraggio!'

Lapping the shores of his roof, the sea is a phosphorescent green. White stars burn the sky. The water level is still rising; toads and wading birds already occupy the lake in the attic. The other floors are flooded grottoes, the crumbling stone walls of the auditorium tickled by fingers of weed.

A noise grows out of the night, a dull, insistent drone. He stops and squints and listens with his good ear. Visitors? Surely not! He replaces his mask and walks over to the little shelter he has erected on the roof. A battered harmonium stands next to his makeshift bed. Hardly a Church organ, but the best he could do.

He crashes out a sequence of preliminary discords and then lunges into a gothic version of *Moses und Aron*. His opera hat falls at a jaunty angle over his eyes. The skin under his mask begins to itch. *'Ohne Hoffung dient ihr und glaubt nicht an euch, noch an Gott. Euer Herz ist krank!'*

G natural has stuck. Petulantly, he strikes the keyboard with his fist. The bellows wheeze. What can I do? he wonders. His left fingers continue their serial run, flirting with the ideals of atonality. Soon, however, he abandons the Schoenberg for a Saint-Saëns.

41

The mysterious drone has grown louder. He switches off the harmonium, which gives a frustrated grunt, and steps out of the shelter. The drone has resolved itself into a little boat with an outboard motor.

Muttering, his hands clasped behind his back, he watches as the sprightly craft skims the wavelets. A single powerful searchlight sweeps the water as the boat approaches. Bats flit, like inappropriate metaphors, around the wake of the vessel. The light strikes the sloping side of the roof, hovers unsteadily and then slides upwards to the top, capturing him in a blinding halo.

'Visitors!' Angrily, he waves his swordstick, grasps the scabbard in one hand and unsheathes it, thrusting the blade through the intrusive beam. 'Have you come to mock? Will you not leave me alone?'

'Ho there!' The boat pulls alongside an attic skylight and the engine dies. The light fades to an after-image. A slim, tall figure stands up and gazes at him, hands on hips.

'If you come to mock, then depart!' The surge caused by the boat enters the attic through the open skylight and a huge spray of green foam explodes from a chimney. He whirls away and glides back to his harmonium. Bach's *Toccata and fugue in D Minor* is almost de rigueur at this point, but he finds that he has no will left. His fingers refuse to uncurl.

Halfway there, he pauses and turns back. The stranger has moored his boat to a suitable embellishment and is standing on the roof. 'Why have you come to the opera house? Why do you wish to disturb my peace?'

The figure moves forward. He seems very gentle. His smile is a golden thing, full of honesty and compassion. 'You have been here a long time, alone.'

'I am, as you are doubtless aware, not suited for public life.' He taps the mask strapped to his face. 'They called me the Phantom, they mocked my misery, they turned my grief into a story.' Here he shudders and a single tear springs from the eyehole of his mask, hanging on the shiny steel like a dewdrop. 'They even made my life into a musical! Can you believe it? Hideous, hideous!'

'I meant, on the roof? You have been a long time on the roof?'

'Nearly a year.' The Phantom inclines his great head and sighs melodiously. 'One evening, I felt an urge to see the stars. I climbed up from my secret chamber in the basement and came out onto the slates. It was warm and I fell asleep in the open. Unprecedented! When I awoke, the next morning, the sea was lapping the slates and all Paris was under water. With obvious exceptions!' He indicates, with a flourish, the phallus of the Eiffel Tower in the distance. 'Only the thrusting remains. . . .'

'Yes. The poles melted, you see. Well actually, they just fell apart. A scientist, by accident, happened to discover that ice is fundamentally impossible. Our ignorance alone was keeping it real. The deluge had been expected for some time, but no-one guessed it would happen so quickly. The major cities of the world have all disappeared; the majority of the population of the planet all drowned. Overnight.'

'But why are you here?' A terrible thought strikes the Phantom. 'You are not from Social Services, are you?'

'I have come to recruit you to my scheme.'

The Phantom laughs a shrill, bitter laugh. 'You *do* mock me! You could not possibly be interested in me. I am ugly, malformed, a devil! I am the Phantom of the Opera!'

'Yes, I know. Tell me about your life, and I will tell you about mine.'

The Phantom frowns beneath his mask. He scratches his false nose, and resheathes his blade. 'I know what it means to be despised and feared. I know what it means to be cheated of everything that is worthwhile. I know what it means to have not a single friend in a bustling city, to eke out the existence of a worm or woodlouse in the forgotten chambers of a damp old building. I know.'

The stranger grins and reaches out a hand. 'I understand, for I too was despised and feared. I too have been cheated. I too know what it means to have not a single friend. But I eked out the existence of a worm or woodlouse not in a basement but in a belfry. Once, you see, I was even more ugly than you. . . .'

'More ugly?' The Phantom is aghast. But then his lips curl in a cynical leer beneath his mask and he shakes his head. 'No, you lie.'

The stranger becomes desperate. 'Let me explain! I too fell asleep, next to my beloved bells, and awoke to find the city flooded. For many days I too stared out across the water, afraid, until an empty boat happened to drift past and lodge itself against my tower. It was in good condition and the fuel tank was full. It is the same boat that you see down there. Well, I wandered over the submerged ruins of Europe for many months until I chanced to arrive in Prague.'

'So?'

'In Prague, in Hradcany, in the Mihulka tower, I met one not unlike us. You have heard tell of John Dee? He was a fine magus patronised by Emperor Rudolph II. He was commissioned to turn base metals into gold, the old alchemist's quest. He failed, and the Emperor imprisoned him in the tower. But alchemy is not about gold, it is about the evolution of the spirit. Dee discovered the Elixir of Life and the Philosopher's Stone. His first act was to make himself immortal. He has been there ever since. I was his first visitor. His second act was to turn me from a misshapen grub into the butterfly you now see. And he can do the same for you!'

The Phantom scratches his chin. 'I do not understand.' He attempts to blow his nose with a flamboyant gesture and a silk handkerchief. 'I have suffered so many disappointments, so many. . . .'

'No longer. It is not the meek who shall inherit the Earth, but the dispossessed monsters of the imagination, called forth to amuse a fickle public and then discarded. The modulus that will change our negative aspects to positive ones, our defects to virtues, awaits us! It is a fine irony, is it not? The only ones to survive the flood are those who live in high places, who have been shut away in towers or attics. All over the world, and for all time, writers have placed their most gruesome creations above the rest of the populace. Do you know who else I found in Prague?'

'I have no idea.'

'None other than the Golem. He had lain, in little pieces, in the loft of the Old-New Synagogue, ever since Rabbi Löw removed the mystic shem from his mouth. I took the fragments back to Dr Dee and he fitted them together. The Golem is no longer a shambling clay hulk. He is now a fine figure of a man.'

'*Cara semplicità, quanto mi piaci!*'

'Indeed. Dr Dee and I have formulated a plan. We will seek out all those like us; all the demons and ghouls who have escaped drowning by virtue of elevation. And we will band together. A new age shall begin on Earth! Yes, we shall band together! Count Dracula, high on the battlements of his Carpathian castle; Elizabeth Báthori, the Blood Countess, safe in her walled-up room in Cachtice Manor; Maldoror clinging to his golden tower like a leech. The list is endless. Dr Dee shall transform us into gods. We shall rule over the few remaining humans, just as they ruled over us in their fictions.'

With a sudden, impulsive laugh, the Phantom tears the mask away from his warped face. The tempered steel clatters across the slates. 'I will come with you! But first, tell me who you are!'

The stranger peers into the appalling visage of his host, but he does not waver. His smile is as accepting as ever. 'You do not recognise me? Ha, of course not! Yet you met me once. My name is Quasimodo!'

'Quasimodo? Incredible!'

'Oh yes, I was grotesque, especially in a tutu!' The stranger smiles wistfully, as if recalling the wilder days of youth. 'But I have been transformed, transmogrified, transmuted. I have risen, a phoenix, from the ashes of my past. My body is utterly perfect. I am radiant. I glow with an inner peace and a nimbus envelops my smooth limbs. My eyes are as pure as gems, my hair smells of elderberries. . . .'

'I am convinced. Let us delay no longer!'

Quasimodo extends his hand again. This time, the Phantom takes it. He begins to hum a piece from Berlioz. But then, he turns towards his shelter.

'Before we go, may I take my possessions with me?'

'One only. My boat is small.'

Together, they move across the roof and enter the doorway of the crude shack, constructed entirely from driftwood. The Phantom looks down at his meagre belongings, at the faded photograph of his unrequited love, at his selection of opera-cloaks and walking-sticks. His good eye falls on the harmonium.

'Does it have its own generator?' Quasimodo is doubtful.

'It is powered by clockwork. It is all I could rescue from the flooded orchestra-pit. I dived down with ropes and hauled it to the surface. A dangerous, foolhardy endeavour. But it was a risk I had to take. I cannot live without music.'

With only a little effort, they manhandle it onto the boat. As they sail away, the Phantom plays *Tosca* and *Lucia di Lammermoor*, but then, changes key and pounds out an ironic, ragtime version of Lloyd Webber's travesty. 'The Phantom of the Opera is here!' he wails, and laughs.

46

'Onwards!' Quasimodo also laughs. 'A new world awaits us! A world free of our oppressors, free of readers and writers, ruled only by the former monsters of high places!'

The Phantom stops playing. 'But I am not a dweller of a high place! I usually live in the basement of the opera house. It was purely by chance that I was on the roof that night. How did you know I was here? How did you know I was still alive?'

Quasimodo continues to chuckle. He stretches his new body under the stars. The astral light is reflected in his beautiful eyes. He nods to himself.

'I had a hunch.'

The Good News Grimoire

There are no true Satanists. This was the shocking conclusion at which I arrived as I left the Café Worm at midnight. But I glanced over my shoulder just to be sure. Down the Rubellastrasse I groped and held up my hands to part the fogs that seemed to obstruct my progress. My fingers were yellow, a consequence of growing old, perhaps. I said to myself: 'Harker, this is a rum business for a tailor to be in. Best get out while you can, old fellow, and set a mind to your own affairs.'

I am not a paranormal investigator by choice, nor yet (despite vicious rumours to the contrary) a solicitor or estate agent. I am by day a simple and honest cloth-merchant. I live in rooms, eat mutton broth on Mondays, Gobi Aloo until Friday and grits with sour cider over the weekend. Along with a plush coat, sackcloth breeches, slippers of the same and a rangy greyhound, three-quarters of my entire tailoring revenue is thus consumed.

It was Carnacki who got me into this foul nonsense. Not, I hasten to add, the famous ghost-finder, but that other Carnacki, Alfred. I cursed him long and mightily as I reached the end of Rubellastrasse and continued through lanes as threadbare as a miser's shroud. Winter had descended like a landlord, hail thumping on the town like a knuckle-rap, lightning cracking the air like a demand for arrears. Oh for time to return to my sartorial researches! I had almost perfected a technique for dyeing nightcaps with blackberries.

I took a short cut through the graveyard. Such places remain the safest retreats after dark. Were any ghosts, devils or banditti to espy my passing, they would mistake me for one of their own. 'What normal person would roam a graveyard at this hour?' they would ask themselves. In this manner, I reasoned, I would pass through their midst unharmed. Yet my mind was troubled as I skirted the mortuary church: owls took flight from its eyeless windows, tawny as new coffins. In the dense fog they collided with each other and, spinning in rigid circles, fell at my feet. I pulled free a shoelace and soon had a tasty brace for the pot.

In the oversized pocket of my greatcoat, a musty tome weighed me down. This I had obtained at the Café Worm from an unemployed magus, a stunted fellow desperate for money. More of this later; in the meantime, suffice it to say the book was inordinately heavy. I gasped and wheezed as I plodded onwards. The gentle undulations of the grave-yard were bad enough; when I reached the far side and confronted the steep hill that led up to my own house, I knew I would have to shed some ballast to gain the summit. Delving into my other pocket, I reluctantly discarded my calling-cards, several thousand of them at once. They did not flap like albino crows, nor glide like squares of unbuttered cloud. They merely sank in the fog like tiny marble tombstones in a smoky pool, my identity drowned yet again: HARKER MELMOTH, PARAPSY-CHOLOGIST & TAILOR.

At last, halfway up the dreaded slope, the stunned owls on the lace woke and began to flap together. So I was assisted the remainder of the distance; in gratitude I let them go and went hungry. Yet there were victuals aplenty for my febrile imagination. I crept into the house (more Woodworker's Gothic than Carpenter's) and up the creaking stairs to my own floor. I had a suite of chambers here, all very dusty, very nice, full of glass globes, rusty suits of armour and skeletons, the whole arranged with the niceties of the philosophy of furniture always in mind. More importantly, in the innermost room of the set, I kept my collection of ancient sewing machines, thimbles and yards of black cloth (one for a girl; two for a boy; nine for a winding-sheet) not to mention my operating-table and umbrella, ready for a chance meeting.

Here, I cast off my coat (with much of the relief of a headless nun kicking the habit) and sank into an easy chair. I was frightfully cold as well as weary; I rubbed my hands before the grate, though as no fire was lit it availed me little. I checked my drinks-cabinet to confirm it was truly empty and fell to pondering the bizarre events of the previous fortnight. At the same time, I removed the miniature portrait of Mina from the mantelpiece and lovingly caressed the delicate curve of her chin, the Pre-Raphaelite tresses of her luxuriant hair.

The spooky side of my business, the investigating of things that are perhaps not wise to pursue, becomes necessary only when there is no work for my needle and thread. In the caramel summer, I am usually busy mending green shirts, sewing buttons onto interesting pyjamas and mixing long-forgotten dyes, chiefly Chermisi, once used to stain the robes of Cardinals. I have no truck with the supernatural. It is only when the leaves start turning russet and the wind chatters gates like the jaws of a dreaming cat, that I am compelled to relax my grip on the flywheels of the sewing-machines, remove the pins from my sallow lips and venture out into the cosmic horror of it all. Mon Dieu! (Born in Alsace, I speak my language with a Germanic accent. Mina is Uruguayan.)

By winter, all the work has dried up. I know not why there are no green shirts to mend when the snows lie thick upon the ground; I cannot guess why interesting pyjamas lose no buttons when the water freezes in my pipes and the taps shudder but do not disgorge. And why no Cardinals to be coloured after All Hallows? Whatever the reason, the fact of it is unarguable. And thus I must earn my black bread by other means; I am constrained to take on a case or two.

Generally, I advertise my services in the local paper. This is an efficient method of reaching potential clients. Odd fellows in large Homburgs and pale women in prehensile weeds are forever knocking on my door, trying to solicit my services. Generally these are sad, lonely or simply avaricious people. Less is the number of bones in my body than the times I have heard about the maiden aunt with the buried fortune who promised all to her favourite nephew (or niece) but forgot to mention it in a Will, and also forgot to mention the location of the trove. 'Can you contact her spirit?' they want to know. I state my fee as the exact amount of treasure to be revealed.

Sometimes, however, a case of genuine merit comes my way. There was the thin man who liked to seize passers-by and jump into wells with them. I sealed him in a wishing well; to this day he is punished by the coins of children and lovers. Then there was the beautiful Läis, a succubus who drained men of vitality. I suggested she take up amateur dramatics. It had little effect on her dark nature, but her Ibsen is excellent. And we must not forget the case of the phantom hackney-carriage, which would stop to pick up passengers only to vanish while rushing down the highway at speed. I settled its hash by arranging a meeting between it and the phantom hitch-hiker. There were screams.

But I am digressing. Let me return to the matter in hand. After placing one such advertisement in the *Chaud-Mellé Chronicle*, a rag hotter than any by Joplin, and considerably more confrontational, I received a sinister envelope through the letterbox. Tearing it open and devouring the enclosed note—scribbled on the sort of yellowing paper one associates with abandoned school-rooms—I felt compelled to raise an eyebrow. The author

of the epistle (who styled himself 'The Blue Dwarf')
claimed to have knowledge at his clubbed fingertips which
could forever free me from penury and the marrow of toil.
He was warning me away from trying to seek him out in
an effort to gain his secrets.

I was quietly sceptical, of course; foolish is the man
who spends his doubts as freely as his opinions. But I
decided I would follow up this threat on a perverse whim.
Accordingly, I re-read the note, applied quivering nostril to
ink, determined it was of a composition only to be found
in the Actor's Quarter, and immediately set off for the
affected slums in question. I walked through streets
unknown to me. It was all so strangely still. No breath of
wind came to ruffle the superb cut of my jacket, my hair
stood undisturbed on my head in frozen waves. 'Harker,' I
reminded myself, 'if ever a city held its breath, this is it.
Pray do not suffocate on my behalf, urban monstrosity.'

In damp tenements of my destination, I asked desiccated Thespians for information regarding a short fellow of
blue cast. They directed me to a little park, strewn with
litter and drunks, where I saw him at once. He was standing beside a shattered fountain, playing a lute poorly
tuned. His voice was a passable baritone; his fingers idled
over the old songs of Dunstable, Ockeghem and Josquin
des Pres. But there was an essential spirit lacking in his
work. He had collected a single worn coin in his proffered
cap. I introduced myself without delay. 'Harker Melmoth,'
I said, 'at your service.' He looked up. Less a blue dwarf
than an indigo midget, his smile was cold.

'You weren't supposed to come,' he replied. And yet
there was an insincerity in his tone. I made an elaborate
bow, the tip of my nose gouging the dirt at his absurdly
tiny feet. He screwed up his face and water sprang from his
hooded eyes. 'I admit it!' he wailed. I had known this all
along. To attract my attention, he had sought to discourage

me. I use a similar technique when embroidering waistcoats; designs so repellent that no customer can say them nay.

We chatted awhile. He was a magus, down on his luck, forced to take first to the saw and hoops of the stage conjuror and then—when that too had failed—to pluck for a crust. Evidently a blue dwarf of many talents, all of them unformed. He gave his name as Otho Vathek. 'Though known as the Blue Dwarf, I am really a microscopic giant of cobalt hue,' he said. I should have laughed at this, but something held me back. The hint of tragedy in his eyes was not all studied.

To reciprocate, I told him about my own life and aspirations. I discussed the weave of my professions, the texture of tweed and ghosts. There was scant kinship between us; we had little in common save empty bellies. Yet I took a liking to the small fool. I described my fiancée, Mina Radcliffe, and confessed I missed her dreadfully. He wanted to know where she was. I informed him she had left town some months since. She was away in Ingolstadt University, in her first year, studying Sociology and Re-animation, a sandwich course—but one made with stale bread and spread with bat's cheese.

Finally, I asked him directly about his letter. He blushed bright cyan and admitted he was desperate. 'Otho,' quoth I, 'we are all in the same charnel-house. Now kindly elucidate.' He sighed and proceeded to babble something about a strange book, a grimoire that had recently come into his possession. Unlike other magical handbooks, this one actually worked. I snorted in derision. I knew about grimoires; I owned a dozen. The spells they contained fell into two main categories: charms for attracting members of the opposite sex and charms to force the shades of dead skinflints to reveal their hidden hordes. 'And yet you are both loveless and poor,' I pointed out. At this he shuddered.

As I waited for a reply, his eyes suddenly expanded in terror. He had been glancing around my hip with mounting agitation. Now he let loose a squeak, donned his cap with the coin still inside, strung his lute over his shoulder and gave me a look of profound misery before hurrying off into the distance. I turned to find myself confronting a score or so of black clad figures with twisted countenances who rushed past at a brisk pace. They seemed intent on catching up with the dwarf. They did not look like actors, though their chins were extremely long. I watched as Otho and his pursuers disappeared around a corner where the park gave way to a market trading wigs and greasepaint.

I made my way back to my own segment of the city and troubled no more about the matter. Otho was obviously a condwarf; I would forget our meeting. But three days later, as I was crossing Werther Bridge, heavy with statues and held together by eggs and flour rather than mortar, I came upon him. This time he wielded a flute and all his melodies were shriven things, notes sharp as poniards. He ceased playing and danced a few steps. 'You've returned!' He was jubilant. 'I apologise for rushing off like that. Urgent business, I'm afraid.'

I waved aside his excuses. 'Do not be afraid, little man.' Though he wanted to resume our earlier conversation at the point where it had broken off, I simply wanted answers. 'Why did you tell me about your grimoire and why do you not use it yourself?' He shook his head and explained he had given up the black arts; he was determined to make it as a composer for Musicals instead, the reason why he now lived in the Actor's Quarter. No more invocations and pacts. He touched my arm and solemnly declared he would rather starve.

On the face of it, his tale seemed reasonable enough. Here was a creature who having explored the left hand path had then renounced it, a decision that left him with a grimoire he could not use on principle. Destitute, however, he wished to sell the book. My advert had caught his eye; he had stoked my curiosity by warning me away from the merchandise. Once free of his sorcerous past, he would be able to launch himself body and soul—though mainly soul; there was little of the former—into his chosen profession. All this was normal business practice.

But my suspicions were aroused. I was unconvinced by his demeanour, which remained one of pained expectation. He was a trifle too eager to conduct a transaction. 'Not your usual grimoire,' he added, his tongue rolling thickly in his ulcerated mouth. 'More a key to others, if you know what I mean. A door into a walled garden of delights!' He noticed my frown and sought to reassure me. 'All the familiar demons are there. Asmodeus, Moloch, Baalberith. A good price too. No regrets, I assure you. Well what do you say?' He snatched at my cravat and sought to wind me down to his level. 'Truth is a mirror!'

This time I noticed them before he did. They were threading their way through the crowds that thronged the bridge, attempting to blend in among the commuters. They did not make directly for us, they were clever enough to approach by a circuitous route. Only their chins betrayed them for what they were (whatever that was!). Reaching into one of my myriad voluminous pockets for a pair of serrated scissors (with which I trim the gowns of velveteen marquises) I severed my cravat and separated Otho from my presence. I did not wish to be associated with him in the eyes of the eccentric fellows. He toppled backwards and landed squarely on his haunches. 'Friends of yours?' I inquired mildly.

He saw the figures and bounded to his feet. He was cornered and had to make a quick decision. With the hesitation of a single heartbeat, he clambered over the iron railings of the bridge and jumped into the muddy waters of the river. I rushed to the side and gazed down at the murky wound of his immersion. Then the waters healed the scar, but no body resurfaced. When I turned, the lantern-jawed brood had vanished. All that remained was Otho's tarnished flute. I puffed out my cheeks and continued on my way, strangers commenting most favourably on my original style of neck-wear. From such unhappy accidents are new fashions born. But the snipped cravat did not catch on.

This time I could not so easily dismiss the encounter from my mind. Otho Vathek was in some mighty uncommon trouble, to be sure. There were absurdly-chinned elements out to settle his account in full, or at the very least to reduce the heat of his life to a simmer. I was reluctant to involve myself further but I could feel the nets of his fate closing in around me also. 'Buttons and haberdashery!' I cursed. 'But I will get to the hem of this!' I worked myself into a state of determination. I began to foam at the mouth. I like to take a theme by the scruff of the colon and give it a real exosmotic twist.

To be honest, I was more interested in securing my own future than helping the dwarf. I owed my landlord, Wynkyn de Rackrent, a great deal of money. A grimoire that worked would be a nice little earner: a quick conjuration, an assertion of will over a minor demon and I would be able to pay off all my debts. I assumed the black clad fellows, tenacious in purpose and long in the face, were also desirous of obtaining the book. Why did Otho not sell it to them? I flattered myself he had chosen me alone to benefit from his renunciation of the dark arts. Perhaps I was better dressed than rival buyers. Possibly my scented knees had swung the balance in my favour. I could not fathom it.

At any rate, I guessed I would have to inform him of my intent to purchase the volume before he sold out to another. This meant seeking him out again, rather than waiting for a random encounter. I had picked up his abandoned flute; once across the bridge and into the quieter area of the Old Square, I paused to study the instrument. Although not yet skilled enough to tell anything from a player's saliva, I recognised the make at once. Only one establishment in the city would dare sell this type: Katzen-ellenbogen's on the Rue Discord. I hastened there, arriving to discover the proprietor had shut up shop for lunch. I pounded on the door with my fists until I heard the shuffle of approaching feet and the sound of a bolt being with-drawn. I was admitted with scowls and oaths. The owner was an unctuous wight; he made instruments but could not play a note. 'Harker Melmoth,' I said, *'le style est l'homme.'*

He introduced himself as Irving von Landshort, a distant relation of the blind genius who had founded the shop. Business was anything but brisk. 'What can I do for you?' he groaned. His breath reeked of garlic soup. I presented him with the flute, waving it under his nose like the baton of an insane conductor. 'Yes, I know that,' he said, clipping on tiny pince-nez and studying it for a moment. I asked him if he recalled who had bought it. He nodded. 'A blue dwarf, one of my best customers, though he never pays. I let him have his instruments on credit. Oboes, harps, violins, lutes and flutes. He is always in a hurry.' He scratched his ear and yawned. His spectacles were cracked.

'And when did you last see him?' I inquired. I was tempted to go much further and criticise his crumpled clothes, his poor sense of blend and contrast, but there were more important matters afoot (a foot made of six toes and each an enigma). So I contented myself with fixing him with a morbid stare and hunching my shoulders, as if I were an anarchist who might return with a globular bomb and shatter the whole building if not speedily satisfied. Evidently, however, he had already mistaken me for a member of the Secret Police. While answering my question he took my hand and pressed an ocarina into my palm—a fluty bribe.

'He came in but ten minutes before you. I closed for lunch as soon as he departed. He never stays for long. He was filthy; little mounds of damp clay fell from his limbs in steaming clumps, like grave-earth from the bones of a corpse.' He leant forward and tapped his nose. 'A murder suspect, eh? I thought as much. I knew he'd do it, the tinker. Watch out for the little ones, mother used to say. I gave him a hurdy-gurdy. He promised to pay once he had conducted a deal with a certain sartorial gentleman. A likely story, if you ask me!'

I thanked the proprietor for this news, returned the ocarina and set off once more into the unsatisfactory world. I had the information I wanted and rubbed my hands in anticipation. The dwarf was a busker and whereas lutists are tolerated only in parks, and flautists on bridges, hurdy-gurdy players must needs ply their trade outside theatres. The law is very clear on this point. Thus all I was required to do to find him was cruise the extremities of the city's dozen playhouses.

This reasoning did not pay immediate dividends. It was some days before I could ascertain the exact location of all the buildings in question. One chilly evening (the cobbled streets glittering with ice) I caught the plaintive honks and wheezes of a hurdy-gurdy coming from the midst of a crowd gathered outside the Theatre de l'Orotund. Pushing my way through, I seized him around his thin shoulders. He seemed pleased to see me; he drew me to one side and grinned like a glib fool. He was still encrusted with slime, and his cap had scooped nothing more than a broken tooth; his situation was worsening. I gazed contemptuously at the well-heeled mob. They were queuing to see Caspar Nefandous' new comedy. Dilettantes, all of them; parasites who could not tell amontillado from sherry, or orphrey from sarsenet. How I envied them!

'So you have finally decided to accept my offer?' His relief was a tangible thing; I asked him at once to state his price. 'A single silver florin!' he cried. I showed him my empty pockets and his face fell. I did not have the money on me, but it was just feasible I could raise it. When he learned this, delight reclaimed his features. 'Remember the book is a key,' he added. 'A drop is all it takes. A single drop on the tip of the tongue. Locks will turn, mirrors will spin!'

As we conversed, I kept an eye open for those figures who seemed so intent on disturbing our concourse. Clever I already knew them to be; how clever exactly I was soon to discover. They were concealed in the queue. As the line shuffled forward, the first of the long chinned ones pressed against me. Foetid breath gushed from a twisted maw; fouler even than von Landshort's garlic exhalations. I said to myself: 'Harker, this is no natural halitosis. Good sense to flee.' But I did the proper thing instead; I grasped the fiend around the waist and called to Otho to run. My prey was slippery and strong to boot. He squirmed out of my clutches and knocked me back into the dwarf. As I fell, I hissed into his ear, 'I'll meet you at the Café Worm, a week to the day.' It was the first place that came to mind. He nodded.

Then he was away again, the hurdy-gurdy clattering behind him as he raced into the distance, his pursuers breaking ranks and chasing him wordlessly, in a silence punctuated only by the music of their boots on the cobbles. I wondered what I was letting myself in for. As the whole pack turned down an alleyway, I thought I heard the dwarf cry out: 'No more good sirs, no more. I have done enough!'

I picked myself up, brushed down my soiled sleeves and returned to my rooms. On the landing, I met my neighbour, Monsieur le Purr, who bowed gracefully and wished me good-evening. This was a predetermined code that meant the landlord had been round earlier. And indeed, in the dirt in front of my door, I spied his nefarious footprint. 'Harker, fine fellow,' I muttered under my

breath, 'things shall soon be otherwise. It will be curtains—
nay, billowing drapes!—for Wynkyn de Rackrent when I
have that grimoire. *Coûte que coûte!'*

I needed a whole week, of course, to raise the required
revenue. In these days of negative inflation, a single silver
florin is worth much more than it used to be. That night I
could not sleep; I tossed in my crinoline sheets, hypnagogic
images competing with more conscious vistas for the
territory of my brain. I seemed to see the city spread before
me like a napkin, not entirely flat—one corner curled up
where the town meets and clings to mountains. A million
creases were the implausibly convoluted streets and lanes
of the old Quarters. The city has always seemed ready to
fold in upon itself; I imagined the napkin snatched by the
hand of some metaphysical breakfaster and shaken free of
the toast crumbs that symbolised—rather unsubtly—the
haphazard dwellings and sundry other buildings of our
yeasty metropolis.

No matter! Sleep could wait; there was much work to
be done. Early next morning, I made an appointment to
see my bank-manager. This was the Alfred Carnacki I have
already mentioned. It was he who was responsible for
introducing me to the world of the preternatural in the
first place. Business had been particularly bad; a customer
had defaulted on payment for many sheets of yellow wall-
paper I had supplied him with (this was a special request; I
applied the same technique I use on waistcoats to the
paper, producing a hideous asymmetrical design that
resembled nothing so much as lopped heads caught in
snares, bulbous eyes). Anyway, I had an overdraft at the
bank and Carnacki suggested that I work as a part-time
parapsychologist to make ends meet. I foolishly agreed.

His attitude toward me was one of supercilious irony.
He received me this time into his office as if he knew not
who I was. 'But Monsieur Melmoth!' he chortled. 'How
can I possibly promise a stranger a loan? I would soon be

bankrupt if I humoured all who came through my doors with a similar request. No, it is impossible.' I sighed and offered my glass globes, my suits of rusty armour, my skeletons as security. He would not have it. I even suggested my collection of sewing machines and thimbles. He smirked at this and a cunning light came into his eyes. 'All those items you must stake,' he said, 'and also fulfil one obligation.' When I heard what it was, and assented, he opened a little safe in the back of his office and withdrew the money. The silver florin was cool between my fingers, hard as the buttons of Mina's suspender-belt.

I left the bank with an ambiguous knot tightening in the pit of my stomach. If the dwarf did not deliver the goods, or if the book was not as efficacious as he claimed, I would lose everything. I would be unable to pay the interest on the florin. Gone would be all my possessions, my umbrella and operating-table. More to the point, I would have to fulfil Carnacki's hideous obligation. He had made me sign a form saying that if I defaulted, I would create for him the tallest hat in the world. It was his idea of a sardonic joke.

I was in something of a funk as I awaited my final meeting with Otho Vathek. I neglected all my other work. I even declined Monsieur le Purr's kind offer of a glass of Chablis. A cataphysical tenant, I not so much distrusted him as felt uneasy in his presence. But he was suave; there was no denying his taste and touch, almost as refined as my own. I killed the days by lying on my musty couch, in an attitude of tragic repose, one arm flung over my pale features, my curly locks brushing the carpet. Eventually the assigned day arrived and I made my way down the hill, through the graveyard and along Rubellastrasse to the Bohemian dive known as the Café Worm—an earthy place.

Here I exchanged shot silk handkerchiefs for absinthe (the owner is an understanding chap) and sat in the shadows. The café was full of poets, painters and arty folk, some of them talented, most not, with a dress sense that ranged from nonsensical to offensive. But the girls were wonderful enough, high spirited and savage. I watched them with a measure of self pity; Mina had abandoned me. She still wrote me letters, but these were of a formal sort, cold to the touch. She was so afraid of her prose slipping into the purple that she had firmly bound it on the other side of the spectrum: the sunset of ardour. Bound with locks of her own hair, no doubt! I felt impulsive; I called out for the girls to dance for me. Yet it was the men who clambered onto tables in response to my request. My luck was not holding.

As I sipped the green oblivion, I span the coin on the worm-eaten table before me. It had been monstrously tempting to spend it on food, drink, Hessian cloth or some other of life's essentials. I thought of the things I could yet purchase, were I to leave the café and forget about the dwarf: ripe cheeses, the transient love of a woman, myriad pairs of socks, a telescope. Or I could enter a bookshop and emerge with a proper book. Penny Dreadfuls I had read in my time; Shilling Shockers I had glimpsed. Florin Fantasques were rumoured to be much worse, to venture beyond the borders of the imaginable.

While I debated with myself thus, I felt an insistent tug on my shirt from below. At the same time, the coin struck the side of my absinthe glass with a frosty inhuman tinkle. I shuddered, a feeling of exquisite sadness overwhelmed me. The dwarf was under the table, his finger to his lips. He eased himself up onto the seat opposite mine and heaved the grimoire before me, knocking my glass onto the floor. I gazed at him. He looked even more dishevelled than before, but there was a desperate joy in his eyes. He noticed the florin and licked his lips. '*Borgen macht sorgen, Mein Herr?*'

I nodded sombrely and applied my tongue to the place where my glass had stood, to lap up drops of spilt absinthe. I was not yet reduced to performing this feat on the floor.

The dwarf cleared his throat. 'Your days of sorrow are over now. You have not changed your mind?' I shook my head and he reached out for the coin, but I slapped my palm over it. I did not wish to free him so easily. He bared his teeth and growled. His dirty blue fists clenched tight.

I used my most assertive tone. 'Why are men with chins longer than misery hunting you? Why are they so darkly clad? Why has treacle more substance than their formless figures? How grim can a grimoire be?' I stole a glimpse at the volume while I voiced these questions, but the cover revealed nothing. It was clasped by a rusty old lock and bound in some heavy material, possibly uncured leather, that had been marbled but stank like a sewer. The marbling was grotesque even by my standards. It suggested foul, unwholesome things: putrefying fungus, the growth of a corpse's fingernails, brown shoes worn with a black suit.

He relaxed somewhat and offered me a small smile. 'Most grimoires do not work. This is because they are locks rather than doors. This book is their key. It is not an end in itself. It belongs to a small special category of literature. *Biblia abiblia*, I would say, if I could speak Greek. Listen carefully: one drop is enough.' I did not try to follow his erratic line of thought. We discussed sorcery in general. The basic idea was simple enough. A lonely, inadequate man would attempt to call demons to do his bidding, offering his soul in return for so many years service. Demons were traditionally reluctant to answer a summons. The idea that magicians actually worshipped them was absurd.

'There are no true Satanists,' he continued. 'The sorcerer attempts merely to do business with the Old Fellow or his cohorts. A contract is drawn up, it is very old fashioned and proper. But here is something you may not know: the truth is the reverse.' I frowned at this and pressed him to elaborate, but he remained enigmatic. Just then, I saw one of the long chinned men enter the café.

The dwarf followed my gaze and grasped my arm. 'It's now or never!' he cried. I did not hesitate. I removed my palm from the coin and let him snatch it up. Then he departed with great haste and a ringing laugh. Strangely, the darkly-clad one ignored him. I frowned, thrust the grimoire into the enlarged pocket I had sewn onto my coat specifically for the purpose and followed his example. What had he meant by his cryptic references?

Thus it was in some confusion that I left the Café Worm and did all those things I have already related: the grope back down Rubellastrasse in dense fog, the short cut through the graveyard and the collecting of stunned owls who later assisted me in my struggles with the hill. In my rooms, in my easy chair, I reached for my discarded coat and worked free the book from my pocket. It was a grand tome indeed; the weight of ten thousand forbidden secrets. There was no lettering on the cover but the spine—held a certain way—betrayed a title: the *Good News Grimoire*. I smirked. Good news for whom? By no means for my landlord! I would summon demons to rend him to bloody pieces, to string Tartarean orpharions with his nerves, to make a stew of his liver, neither good nor thirsty (Mem., get recipe for Mina). So I snapped the lock—which was nearly corroded through—threw open the volume on the floor before me and crouched down low for a more exacting perusal.

Imagine my disgust at finding that all the pages had been cut away in a deep square trench! You know the sort of thing: such books are used to conceal jewellery or other valuables. In the centre of this one was a corked flask of some viscous liquid. I was bitterly disappointed. Otho had cheated me after all! And now my life was over: my landlord, Wynkyn de Rackrent, would kick me out; Carnacki would seize my belongings. Mina would forsake me for some rich Swiss student who could create life in a tank. On a whim, I removed the flask, pulled the cork and drained the contents. My head whirled. *Sartor resartus!* I half hoped it was some kind of poison. It did not mix well with the absinthe.

My vision dimmed for but an instant. My senses returned with few complaints. When I looked up, I found that only one thing in the room had changed: the spines of my ordinary grimoires, high on my shelves, were glowing with a steady radiance. I felt attracted to them; I stood on tiptoe and reached for the nearest. It was somehow comforting to the touch. When I opened it at a random page and studied the naked sigils and incantations, I could suddenly understand them; they were no longer abstruse or perverse. The esoteric had been rendered natural. The pages winked at me and I knew then what the dwarf had been getting at. He had described the book as a key. In itself it was nothing, but it had the power to turn the rusty bolts of others.

My attitude toward the Cosmos had changed. I no longer believed in the laddered tights of fate. I could assert my own Will on the World. Common grimoires were obviously coded texts; the liquid was a sort of lens that could focus the fragments of secret knowledge into one crisp meaning. The dwarf had also mentioned that a single drop would suffice; I had consumed the flask entire. I wondered what consequences might follow from this. 'Harker, dear friend,' I cried, 'this is no time for ponderings! To work! Let Wynkyn de Rackrent's bones be used as skittles this night; let his skull be made into a toad's prison. Let his eyes be sewn on tapestries and shoes re-soled with his tongue!'

Without further ado, I selected a spell to call a minor but fairly brutal demon and made the necessary motions with my hands. I was opening a gateway to another dimension, cutting through the fabric of reality like scissors through muslin. I would forfeit my soul, of course, but it would be worth it. Grimoires typically consist of spells to

bind a devil to a conjuror for twenty years; after that time
he loses his soul (terms considerably fairer than those of
Carnacki, who would also feel the bite of my vengeance). I
finished the spell and gazed around for the reward of my
labours, but there was no puff of smoke, no sulphurous
stench or hideous visitation. Had I deluded myself? While I
struggled to make sense of it all, there was a knock on my
door.

It occurred to me, as I answered it, that it might be the
landlord or even Monsieur le Purr. But to my utter amazement it turned out to be one of the long chinned creatures.
'You rang?' he inquired, arching a dark eyebrow. I threw
back my head and laughed. All was now clear. The Blue
Dwarf had used the grimoire after all; his twenty years
were up and his pursuers—who were actually demons—
were eager to claim their part of the bargain. I would not
seek to flee when my time came. I invited the foul monster
in, and outlined my first request: bones as skittles, skull as
toad's prison, tongue as soles. The tapestries I would do
myself. The demon stroked his chin—it would have been
more astonishing had he not—and collapsed into my easy
chair, putting his hooves up on my table. He knitted his
grisly brows.

'I wish you to provide me with a selection of fine
wines,' he said, after a little thought, 'and some éclairs
from Udolpho's pâtisserie. Then I will require a relaxing
bath in black cat's milk and a cigar of purple herbs. Do not
forget to provide nibbles with the wines: diced cucumber,
olives, a few nettles. And milk the cat with circular
motions, widdershins.' He covered a yawn with a gnarled
claw and waved me away. I thought this was a fine joke. I
laughed and laughed and repeated my commands. He fixed
me with a withering stare.

'It is you,' he added, very slowly, 'who must obey me.'
He gazed around the room. 'Nice place. I will be happy
here.' I could do nothing but stand and gape, my throat

making convulsive swallowing motions. He picked up a discarded copy of the *Chaud-Mellé Chronicle* and began to read it, yawning again. I was enraged. I returned to the grimoire and quickly performed another spell, raising a different demon and opening the window to let it in when it arrived. The first long chinned figure sighed and regarded the second as he might an old acquaintance. In fury I directed the second to slice off his chin and beat him to death—or the diabolical equivalent—with it. But the new arrival sauntered over to the mantelpiece, picked up the miniature portrait of Mina and nodded to himself. This insolence was quite incredible.

'I have taken a fancy to her,' he rasped, 'and I would like to spend a couple of evenings in her company.' He clicked his talons under my nose. 'Arrange it!' I tried to wrest the portrait away, but he was too strong. I had known that demons were surly beings, but I was quite unprepared for this. I took the grimoire into my kitchen— filled not with pots and pans but tailor's dummies and cotton reels—and managed to conjure up half-a-dozen at once. They appeared from various cupboards and urns; one emerged from the oven. I ordered them into the other room on the instant; in a bass voice I intoned them to punish their disloyal brothers with the nastiest measures I could conceive. They merely stood their ground and scratched their chins. And then the cacophony deluged me and I fell back. 'A whole jar of pickled shrews for me!' 'No, a snort of Palaeolithic snuff!' 'Well I require a rope of sand!' 'No, a woman made of cheese!' 'Twenty seven kow-tows!' 'Nine league slippers!'

I groaned. What was happening? The demons began arguing; I left them to their Plutonian debate and returned to my living-room. The two original fiends wanted to know why I had not yet carried out my orders. I raved at them; I hurled the grimoire against the wall. I tried to leave, but they blocked my exit. One of them took a step closer. 'You will do as I say!' he bellowed. I retreated before him. Suddenly I found myself against the open window. I stepped out onto the balcony. Far below, the city slumbered. The demons followed.

There was only one way down. I doubted I would survive the fall, but anything was preferable to being a slave of folk with long chins and longer lists of requests. I climbed over the railings. 'There is the city!' I cried. 'Grisly and torn and broken! It languishes like a lover who dreams she is alone. Coquette of loneliness, constellation of dead angel's eyes, how I adore and loathe and desire you! Cleave my body to your bosom, open the coffins of your heart; I am here to sew my bones into the stones of your body. Let my ghost gallop free down your streets and lanes and over your decaying bridges!'

'That's all very well,' remarked the first demon, 'but you shall have to wait until spring when the cobbles are less icy.' He grinned. 'Men and women have broken necks, arms and resolutions by hurrying. Until then, and even afterwards, you have us. Did not the dwarf tell you? The *Good News Grimoire* is only good for us; it is not just a key but a mirror. The old authors hid their knowledge in clever ways. They said the opposite of what they meant. It is not we who serve you, but you who serve us. The dwarf is free now; he managed to sell the book. We languish in Hell; we are most gratified when we are able to bind mortals to our purpose. We do not worship you, however.'

'Damask and brocaded velvet!' I roared. 'I have been stitched up!' Everything I knew about the black arts had been overturned. Grimoires enabled not sorcerers to invoke and harness demons (in exchange for their souls) but demons to harness sorcerers. Those who dabble in the forbidden secrets are, in truth, generally sad and ineffectual men. Now I was learning that some demons were equally frustrated; they too were willing to enter into a pact in return for love and comforts. It was both pathetic and awe inspiring. But I had no time to contemplate the issues any longer. I bade the monsters farewell and launched over the side. 'Chin chin!' I cried as I spiralled down. I landed with a crunch on something soft and greasy. It broke my fall.

Regaining my feet, I saw that it was Wynkyn de Rack-rent, my anæmic landlord. I had crushed him into a heap of leaking bones. Having left my own coat behind, I snatched up his, praised my good fortune and set off into the fogs. I fully expected the devils to make after me in hot pursuit. But as I passed the front door of the house, I heard soft laughter coming from the stairs. More curious than rational, I stole a glance through the keyhole. Monsieur le Purr had engaged the demons in conversation on the landing. They seemed to be enjoying his company immensely; they applauded his wit and cried, 'What a wag!' or *'Avoir la langue déliée!'* at each of his wry solecisms. At that moment, I was extremely grateful that my neighbour was a trifle odd.

I took refuge in the graveyard and weighed up my position. I sat on a tombstone until morning, dangling my legs and weeping. 'Harker,' I consoled myself, 'worse things happen at sea.' But I knew this was not true. I thought of Mina; this did not help. The demons would harass me forevermore, as they had Otho, unless I could follow his example and sell the cursed book. To comply with their requests was no solution; they would simply make greater demands on me. I would have to procure women, chocolates and rare liqueurs to feed their appe-tites. I would have to do the impossible to keep them satis-fied: turn them into animals for a day or knit them chin-warmers. And this would go on for twenty years. I would be reduced to the level of a housewife.

I had to return to my rooms for the grimoire. I stayed in the graveyard for a couple of days, forcing my way into a mausoleum and resting on the cold sepulchre, until I felt strong enough to make the attempt. All the time I was fear-

ful that the demons would seek me out. If only I had
summoned just one! Otho had plainly been even more
obtuse than myself; there had been a score pursuing him. I
pulled the collars of my landlord's filthy coat high about
my ears and slinked back up the hill. The front door was
open; the demons were nowhere to be seen. I crept up the
stairs and back to my chambers. They were all completely
bare. I gnashed my teeth and pounded my breast. Carnacki
had doubtless sent in bailiffs to appropriate my goods.
After a careful search of the rooms, I discovered a needle
and a length of thread wedged between two floorboards.
These had been overlooked. On the landing, as I left, I
heard a strange noise emanating from my neighbour's
room. I peeped through a crack in the door and saw
Monsieur le Purr himself crouching over a saucer of milk,
his tongue lapping the liquid.

I took the needle with me, but the grimoire was gone
and that was what really mattered. So now I was homeless,
penniless and in thrall to a number of silly men who were
not really men but cacodæmons. I needed to find a job.
Accordingly, I made my way back to Katzenellenbogen's
on the Rue Discord. Irving von Landshort, the proprietor,
was still under the delusion that I was a member of the
Secret Police. He offered me employment on the instant.
Thus I became a shop-assistant and general dogsbody to a
man who liked his piccolos to be polished with vigour but
his timpani to be treated with scorn.

In truth, I made a poor assistant. I was so nervous of
meeting one of the long chinned fiends that I rarely
answered the call of a customer but cowered behind the
counter. Once, indeed, one of the devils did come in; I
kept absolutely still and did not dare to breathe. He sniffed
the air, narrowed his eyes and gazed around the interior of
the shop. Then he shrugged, took a tuba from a rack,
played a few bumbling notes, shook his head and left. But
von Landshort had seen all. I was sacked and the furious

proprietor chased me off his premises with the aid of a hurled metronome and a barrage of musical oaths. '*Volti subito!*'

I wandered the city—my mistress now I had lost Mina (she would not care to marry a homeless man). I became a sort of busking tailor; with my single needle and length of thread, I mended the socks of drunks in parks, commuters on bridges, or audiences in queues outside theatres. This period of my life I wish to forget. I wept profusely and often. Whenever I passed a window from which wafted smells of cooking, I broke down completely. I could no longer seek out the recipe for Mina. But I was clever. I managed to evade the devils. Only once was I caught and forced to carry out a request; the freeing of the thin man I imprisoned in the wishing well years before. A jest at my expense. (He later went back to the well of his own accord, preferring the security of the wish to those wishbones of misery—the junctions of filthy streets.)

One evening, I was sewing socks outside the Theatre de l'Orotund when I happened to overhear two of the dilettantes in the queue. They were discussing the play they were about to see. It was the new comedy by Caspar Nefandous. 'But of course it is the music we are so looking forward to! A new score by Cobalt Hugh!' I bit my lip and returned to my darning. But after the performance, I waited outside the stage-door. He emerged at last; as blue as before but far more dapper. When he saw me, his jaw dropped open and his knees gave way.

'Cobalt Hugh now is it? A fresh start, eh?' I picked him up and shook him vigorously. Beads of perspiration stood out on his forehead. 'You knew exactly what you were letting me in for! I ought to twist off your scheming ears. But I am too weak: I have not eaten for days. You owe me an explanation and more; I will have my single silver florin back for a start. And to think I trusted you! Better by far the devil you know than the frilly shirt you know not! How can I pass this curse on? I have lost the book!'

He fixed me with a nonchalant eye. 'I rather like my nom de plume. But that's neither here nor there. I am successful now; I care nothing for you. Yet I will tell you something: I sought you out especially because I believed only a fool would buy the book. I was correct. Yet it is not the grimoire that needs to be passed on to free you from the devils, but the flask inside. A single drop on the tongue of each user; pass on the flask and when some other idiot tastes the fluid, you will be safe.' He paused. 'I had a standing ovation tonight!'

From the expression on my face, he saw that something was amiss. I blurted out that I had drunk all the liquid. 'Then you are doomed,' he told me. 'For twenty years, and not a day less, you must either serve or evade them. I was wrong. You are not a fool; you are an imbecile.' He stalked away and left me in a heap on the ground. But then under his breath he added: *'Glückliche reise!'*

The city was hazardous. I had a vague notion that I could flee to another land. Surely the countryside would be unsuited to demons? They liked urban facilities too much: trams, newspapers, gas-lighting. They would not enjoy the sticks. Their thin bodies would chatter; they would wrinkle up their saturnine faces in disgust. So I took to my worn heels and headed out. I was mistaken. The chinned menace came abroad; it kept to my footprints in snowy fields, it climbed glaciers in my wake, it wove between high passes where banditti stalked with Romansch tongue and smooth carbine. The pursuit across the Continent was a frenetic thing; again I sought the confusion of cities. They found me in Geneva, in Lausanne, in St Moritz, even in Marseilles. The life of a rat is less furtive than was mine.

I headed over the Pyrenees, to a small territory partly in the kingdom of Aragon and partly in Castile. I sold blood to a barber and earned enough to cross into Portugal and take ship from Lisbon to the remote Azores. But even on those storm-battered islands, far out in the Atlantic, the hellish chins caught up with me. I returned to France, rented an apartment in Calais (the most anonymous of towns) and called myself Otranto Van Helsing (the most unobtrusive of names). Still was I discovered. I crossed the Channel on a packet-steamer, roamed the streets of London and learned to cough green bile. No peace: in Soho they loomed out of a different flavoured fog, lopsided figures like harps, tongues lolling. I fled north; always north flee the desperate, the forlorn, the abominable. South is for travellers with donkeys, three men in a boat, gypsies and missionaries. The pole beckons to those who keep glaciers in their hearts. An arctic breeze played upon my cheeks that hinted of chills, brown ale and Yorkshire pudding: a foretaste of those icy regions to which I was advancing.

Finally, I found surcease of sorrow in the town of Whitby. Here, on the bleak northern coast, I was left in peace. I started up again as before (most definitely I did not become an estate-agent or solicitor) though eventually I grew affluent enough to give up parapsychology. The devils never harried me again, and I did not leave the environs of the town; for I knew they were out there waiting for me. It may seem strange to some that Whitby is so effective a sanctuary against the forces of darkness. What is it about the place that discourages evil fiends from entering? What is so awful about Whitby that even the lords of suffering shun it? There is no mystery. The answer is simple: a long-toothed gentleman with whom I became well acquainted.

I have resided here for nearly twenty years. My indenture is now rapidly drawing to a close. My tailoring business is doing well; I have replenished whole rooms with glass globes, rusty suits of armour and skeletons. I have written letters to Mina imploring her to come over and join me; I hear she is involved with a lycanthrope in Paris. I refuse to grow bitter, but I plan revenge on many. The one thing that troubles me is the thought that when the twenty years are over the devils will have to offer up their souls to me. And what will I do with them? I could imprison them in my glass globes but devils in bottles are *passé*. I have an idea. I shall lay the souls out like fine cloth and make waistcoats of them. These garments I shall send to my enemies in the post. Carnacki shall have one and Otho shall have another; I must not neglect von Landshort. And Mina? At the very least it will confirm what I always knew—these individuals have diabolical dress sense.

The Forest Chapel Bell

As Bishop of Debauchester, my duties included adding the final touches to our great cathedral. Twelve generations of labourers had toiled under angry skies to construct the most astonishing edifice in the whole land. Their bones, ground to dust, had been mixed with their blood to form the cement that held stone to stone.

And now all that remained was to cast a suitable bell for the belfry. I had a very definite idea as to what such a bell should sound like. Any note it might strike would have to take into account the character of the building. For me, the cathedral stood out as a beacon of hope in our ravaged city.

Naturally, the local forges were unable to produce such a bell. The craftsmen of Debauchester were no longer equal to the task. Their Guilds had grown surly and incompetent. A sign of the times, no doubt. It was obvious that I would have to seek elsewhere. I would have to take to the road.

Accordingly, on the first day of spring, I set off with an armed retinue and unlimited Church funds at my disposal. I was fairly confident my quest would not be futile. This land is large enough to accommodate all manner of fantastic and improbable things. All dreams and nightmares can take form here; we live in the dusk between ecstasy and terror.

Our first stop was the neighbouring city of Bismal. The wary inhabitants of this town had sought to avoid the plague by locking their gates to most visitors. Instead, they had shut it in. I bribed my way past the guards and towards

the famed smiths of Iron Street, a cobbled alleyway choking with fumes and resounding with the clang of hammer
on anvil.

Here we found many willing to help us but few capable
of keeping their promises. At the sign of the Black Orchid,
a sweaty smith claimed to have just the bell we were looking for. He led us into a room empty save for an enormous
mass of metal that hung suspended from a stout wooden
cage. He tapped his nose with a grimy finger and rolled his
bulging eyes.

'This is a very special bell,' he said. 'It is a bell that only
the most cultured and intelligent members of society can
hear. To fools it remains silent.' Wiping his palms on his
leather jerkin, he took hold of the bell-rope and pulled
with all his strength. The bell swung in a ponderous arc,
rattling its wooden frame and casting a monstrous shadow
over the wall in the flickering torchlight.

Nonchalantly the smith stepped back and leant against
the door-jamb. The soldiers in my company nodded at
each other and closed their eyes in rapture.

'Such a sweet tone!' they cried. 'Such a pure note! This
is the bell for us! Our quest is over. Let us take this one!'

'Very well,' I agreed, stepping towards the smith. 'I
have this for you in return.' As the fellow bowed in gratitude, my hand moved from my purse to my sword. With a
single blow I sent his head rolling into a dark corner.
Blood gouted purple on the walls. The body swayed and
toppled in a heap, hands clasping cold stone.

'Come.' I resheathed my sword while the bell hissed its
contempt overhead. 'Let us leave this pit to the rats. There
is work to be done.'

As we rode back out through the gates and left the city
behind, I explained myself to my companions. 'The bell
was unfinished,' I said. 'It had no clapper. It is an old, old
story.' I was generous enough not to laugh at their embar-
rassment, but I would not forgive their cowardice.

Thus began the first misadventure of many. We travelled the length of the land and listened to a great number of bells. Yet I was never satisfied. As I have already said, I had an exact idea of the note I desired. I removed the heads of all those who tried to cheat me and a few who did not. I pushed my companions to ever greater feats of endurance.

In the middle of the Aching Desert, we chanced upon the monastery of Soor. The plague had spread its wings even here. The Abbot listened gravely to my request and then arched an eyebrow. He was a thin hollow man, a scarecrow in which the crows had made their nests. His idols were Grunnt and Drigg and the one legged god, Hopp.

'You have come to the right place,' he croaked. 'We have suffered much lately. It is difficult to get the staff these days.' With an obscene chuckle, he gestured at his neck. The black boils of death were already swelling. 'But you are in luck. We have just such a bell.'

'Really? Then I demand to hear it!' I jangled the coins in my purse with one hand while I raised a perfumed handkerchief to my mouth with the other. My voice came as a muffled sob. 'Perhaps three hundred gold coins will help to ease your passage to the other world?'

'Oh, considerably!' He threw back his head and howled. 'Stand out there in the courtyard. It is almost time for matins. We have little to give us hope here. The bell will not be our salvation, but it might deceive some of us for long enough.'

We moved through a low arch into the courtyard. The fountains had dried up; sand drifted across the flagstones. As the sun rose above the horizon, the bell began to toll. The sound was a sensual hand that crept up the spine to massage the neck. From the inside. I shuddered under my ermine cloak. Tears burned the edge of my eyelids.

When the final echo had completely dissipated, I stalked back to the Abbot. Like my own men, he was writhing on the floor. His eyes were full of joy. Once again, I moved my hand to my purse and then, frowning, further across to my sword. I did not have the strength to hack at his sinewy neck, however. The bell had sapped all my anger.

Placing the point in the centre of his throat, in the centre of a pulsating boil, I leant with all my weight on the hilt. His blood was too thin to spurt, but as I wrenched my weapon free, it stained his saffron robe a pale, anaemic orange. I collapsed in delicious agony as the final echo of the bell returned on a sudden desert breeze to sing against my blade.

Afterwards, when we had all recovered, we slaughtered the rest of the heathen monks and set fire to that hive of corruption. 'The sound was far too pleasurable,' I explained, as we raced off into the Aching Desert. 'Not at all appropriate for our purposes. Our city may be a symbol of decadence, but our cathedral most certainly is not. It is our one redeeming feature.'

Such were the words I used to encourage my men to further acts of self-sacrifice. They were quite ignorant, of course, of the sort of bell I really wanted to hear. Before I could confess the truth, I had to be sure of their loyalty. No doubt, they saw the cathedral as an object of beauty and considered a beautiful bell ideal. But this is not what I meant when I said that the right sound would have to take into account the character of the building.

Onwards we journeyed, ever onwards, across a decimated landscape foul with the stench of rotting flesh. My ecclesiastical robes fell to tatters; my mitre crumpled on my head. Our mounts collapsed beneath us, rolling onto their backs and kicking legs in the air like dying locusts. Yet my confidence remained overwhelming. I am a hard man to discourage.

Slowly, as the months turned to years, and we grew more and more exhausted, this overwhelming confidence began to falter. My companions eventually deserted or, contracting the dread plague, had to be abandoned by the roadside. At long last, I too caught the illness, the boils spreading from my hand until my entire arm and chest was a mass of suppurating sores, bleeding yellow pus down my shrunken flapping stomach to my maggoty loins.

And then one evening, after I had wandered off the road into a dank tangled forest, I came into a clearing. In the centre of this clearing stood a small stone chapel whose windows had fallen out and shattered on the hard ground. Creeping plants and gaudy flowers now grew over the spaces, forming an adequate substitute for the stained glass, while on the grass verges, fragments of the originals wholly competed with the glow-worms.

Staggering to the heavy door, I pounded on the oak. Organ music piped from inside. A ghostly whispering rustled on the edge of harmony. After an age, bolts were drawn back and a shrivelled figure peered from the rosy gloom. Froth dribbled down its chin. Its eyes darted an amused and questioning glance.

'My name is Dorian Wormwood,' I said. 'Bishop of Debauchester. Plague has brought as unexpected an end to my revels as I have to yours. Yet I wish to complete my quest before I die. I require a bell whose note will do justice to my great cathedral and all it stands for.'

'Indeed?' The shrivelled figure rubbed its hands together, all four of them. 'But what exactly does your cathedral stand for? How am I to know that it stands for anything? You are far from home, stranger.'

I rotated a soft knuckle in a cloudy eye. 'I am very tired. I am too ill to argue. My city is a festering pit. My cathedral is a beacon of hope. What, then, is to be done? Is it not obvious? This cathedral is a blot on my soul, a stain that must be removed. I have heard that all things have a resonant frequency. I once saw a singer shatter a glass. I need a bell whose note will destroy the very cathedral it is housed in.'

The figure smiled. 'Have you noticed how the graves in my little cemetery are all open?' He pointed at the decaying headstones and weed-choked pits that ringed the chapel. 'Their inhabitants now form my parishioners. I do not have the bell you seek. But I have one even more remarkable. You will see it in good time. But now you must rest.' He led me into the nave, past rows of swaying ghouls, towards the altar, where a coffin lay waiting.

'We appreciate visitors,' he said, 'though not in the way you think. Sleep now and all will be revealed. Yes, sleep.' He threw the lid of the coffin back and pointed at the crushed velvet interior. I was grateful enough to lie down and let the dark thumbs of death press on my eyeballs. My mind soared into the vast reaches of space.

In the morning, I was dragged back into my reluctant body. Sinews and muscles screamed their protest. I knew at once what had summoned me. I fingered the mass of black boils on my chest and sat up. The flesh peeled away in one large sheet, revealing thorax and ribcage. High above, in the half-ruined belfry, my host was swinging from the bell.

He greeted me with a mock salute as I struggled out of my coffin. 'You have wandered into the borderland between your own world and Hell,' he hissed. 'And you have died. The plague, as you know, spares few. Yet you have seen my power over nature. This bell, needless to say, is one that can wake the dead. It has always been my favourite cliché.'

I fingered my chest again, reached into the gaping hole and felt that my heart was still. When he came down to join me, my hand reached for my sword, quivered, and then snatched the purse off my belt. I threw him the coins and began to laugh. My dead eyes were bright.

'This is exactly the bell I want!' I cried. 'Have it taken down. I wish also to hire some of your parishioners to help me convey it back to Debauchester.' I grimaced. The decaying corpses in question were shuffling in for the morning service.

The figure scratched its head. 'I thought you wanted a bell whose note would make your cathedral collapse. Not one that can wake the dead!'

'Is it not for sale?' I knitted my brows.

'Of course it is! Is not everything in this Universe?' He shrugged. 'I am a very minor demon. I will ask no more questions.'

'That is wise.' Slavering, I slapped him on the back and belched. The belch left my stomach through my wondrous hole. I was beginning to grow proud of my exposed organs. They were so diseased they were a delight to behold.

Later, sitting atop a covered wagon, flicking a whip over each gibbering corpse who wrestled to pull the load in its harness, I peered down at my prize. At last I would be able to fulfil my duties as Bishop. At last I would be able to add the finishing touches to our great cathedral. Here was the bell whose note would cause the entire mass to topple onto the heads of my fellow citizens.

After all, a bell that could wake the dead would surely have a startling effect on a building whose stones were held together by a cement made from . . .

Well, bones and blood, of course.

Flintlock Jaw

When Robin Darktree takes to the road, he carries two flintlock pistols, a blunderbuss, a rapier and a bag of ginger biscuits. It is best to present a formidable appearance when on the road. He also carries a spare tricorne hat. It takes only a single seagull to ruin a formidable appearance.

His mount is an elderly roan with the bumbreezes. He is too fond of her to consider a replacement. Thus he is given to wearing a black silk handkerchief even when not travelling incognito. His cloak is sailor's garb, filched from a Portsmouth market. His fine high boots were made by Alberto's of Sienna.

Darktree loves the mountains, the clear streams and wild flowers. When he goes into hiding it is usually here that he flees. He distrusts the forests—dank, horrid affairs—and positively loathes the marshes. He feels neutral about the sea, all but his wistful eye.

When the government sends a pack of hired hands on his trail, Darktree tries to enjoy the chase. On moonless nights he can thunder down the roads, hooves pounding, a wild laugh caught at the back of his throat.

At such times, full of gin and confidence, he often doubles back and trots past his pursuers with a polite nod. The true art of disguise, he maintains, is more a matter of poise than looks. He has never been caught.

Darktree at sunset: waiting behind a clump of bushes for the Holyhead mail. A solitary figure slightly bowed, but not devoid of dignity. Darktree during a mad gallop over the heath: foolishly romantic, arrogant, profoundly sad and almost comic. Darktree asleep: muffled.

Times are hard, he decides, as he puffs on his church-warden pipe. The coaches are becoming fewer with each passing day. He feels like a fisher who has over-exploited the resources of his bay.

Once he considered his smiling eyes to be hook and line enough for the ladies. Now even nets of flint, steel and smoke do not suffice. I am growing old, he thinks, and imagines himself as an ancient man, snug in the hearth of some old coaching house. Muffins and ale. White hair beneath crow-black hat. Nose aglow, gnarled as a bole. But no, who will really look after him in his dotage? His mother?

When Darktree's friend, Nick Cooke, was captured near Highgate, Darktree dressed himself as a woman in order to witness the execution. Although poise is the thing, there is also pleasure. Nick made a few jokes, sang a bawdy song, was fondly cheered by the crowd. Darktree shed a single tear.

And real women? Darktree can scarcely lay claim to a single meaningful relationship with a member of the oppo-site sex. He has tried, God knows, but it has all been so difficult. They never want to settle down with a highway-man: why should they? Always working nights, away for weeks on end, no guaranteed income. And all that oppor-tunity for philandering, never washing his socks. No.

There is a girl called Lucy who lives in Epsom. When-ever Darktree passes through the town he turns crimson. Lucy remains blissfully unaware of either his true identity or his infatuation. Darktree will often conduct long detours to avoid Epsom, or race through at high speed, eyes lowered.

Once, in a coaching house near Salisbury, Darktree dropped a tankard of porter. In the dark puddle that spread out on the stone floor, he caught his own reflection.

At first he thought the scar that crested his right eyebrow had jumped sides. Astonishment!

Another amusing incident: in Abergavenny, Darktree helped a lame beggar to a tavern and bought him a meal and a drink. Later, away from the town, passing beneath the purple scrub and blasted peak of Ysgyryd Fawr, he realised who the lame beggar was. Tom Jackstraw, his arch rival.

Yes, Darktree loves the mountains. Sitting atop Sugar Loaf at dawn, counting the clouds, dreaming about travelling to even more distant regions. He has heard that they are asking for settlers in the antipodes. Will he go? There are forms to be filled in, proof of identity, passage to be paid. And where will he find muffins among the men who walk upside-down? On the snowy slopes of the Southern Alps?

Occasionally, on the road, Darktree meets kindred spirits, bundled up tight like parcels, some of them with newfangled guns that require no flint. They will exchange news, opinions, snippets of philosophy and general laments concerning the weather and lack of traffic. Sometimes there is a mutual hold-up, a great joke.

'Good morning, sir! Whither bound?'

'To Halifax, for the fair. Pockets to be picked, stalls to be rifled.'

'Watch the gibbet, sir. Halifax is no place for the unwary.'

'I am Robin Darktree, no mere amateur!'

One day, Darktree reads about a new invention in a newspaper abandoned on the highway. The invention is a type of steam carriage that can carry passengers on rails. Darktree frowns. He cannot grasp this notion. The paper is several years out of date. What does this mean? That the roads are being forsaken? Impossible!

This story colours his idle thoughts for weeks to come. He tries to picture the diabolical machine, surely all clashing cymbals and roaring furnaces. And who will blow the post-horn at 18 m.p.h.? Absurd. He will not have it. He wrests the image from his mind. He regards the smoking bowl of his pipe with deep suspicion. The roads are the arteries of the country, the nation will bleed dry.

Another encounter, this time in the depths of the recently enclosed New Forest. A strange man without a periwig: Darktree more cautious than usual. A trifle sombre perhaps, impatient, a mixture of inappropriate emotions.

'Good day to you, sir! A fine day for travelling.'

'Indeed so. And I to Exeter before its end.'

'I see. And will you be taking the train, sir?'

Darktree scowls. 'Train? What is this train? I have no inkling of what you are talking about.'

But finally he can avoid the truth no longer. On the outskirts of Bath he comes across a pair of iron bars stretching into infinity in both directions. Stubborn as flint, he waits by their side. When the train eventually passes, what do the passengers see? An archaic figure mounted on a decrepit horse, a living ghost of sorts, an echo. And Darktree? A steam humbug.

When Darktree waits in the bushes for the Holyhead mail, he reaches into his pocket for his bag of ginger biscuits. But his fingers chance instead upon a locket. Lovingly, with a dirty fingernail, he flips open the lid of this locket. A lock of auburn hair, the hair of Lucy Reeves from Epsom, curled tight like the spring of a wheel-lock musket.

He wants to settle down, but how do you arrest the motion of a boulder rolling down a hillside? No, this is a pitiful metaphor. Darktree is less a boulder than a sack of gestures, hurled through the air by some gargantuan cata-pult. No woman will ever be able to catch him before he lands, or piece him together afterwards, not even Lucy. He will continue as he is, boiling soup on a fire struck from tinder, using saltpetre as seasoning, washing his feet in icy springs, collecting blackberries in his spare tricorne hat.

The laws of the land are changing. Men are no longer hung for poaching rabbits. Darktree is lost. He wanders the empty, rutted roads, leading his roan by the bridle, mud on his fine boots. Perhaps it is time for him to visit his mother again, up in Lancashire. Perhaps he will keep going. Do they have trains in Scotland? He doubts this. He prays.

Yes, times are hard. And when they hung Nick, he muses, they also hung me. After all this time perhaps they have realised this. Perhaps that is why they no longer send hired hands after me. A chilling speculation.

When Darktree is loading his pistols, cleaning his blunderbuss, sharpening his rapier, he whistles a favourite melody. But the notes sound more and more unconvincing, as if his lungs and throat have lost confidence. His flatulent roan salutes the rising moon. Should he hang up his black silk handkerchief on a nearby branch? Bury the adjuncts of his life in the soft loam? What memorials would they make to the spirit of a dying age? Is not the road itself his epitaph?

At a toll-booth in Rutland, Darktree tips his hat at the long-faced collector, paying his fare as would any honest fellow.

'See you again, when I return this way.'

'Not I, sir. The toll-booth is closing. Few use the roads these days. Locomotives are all the rage now.'

'Closing? But who will pay for the upkeep of the high-ways?'

There is no answer to this, and the long-faced collector merely shrugs. When Darktree returns that way, a fort-night later, the toll-booth has been dismantled. He considers desperate measures. Could he actually hold up an iron monstrosity? What words would he use?

Darktree firing his blunderbuss at a speeding train: by the time the flint has sparked and ignited the charge, the train has gone. The shot tumbles to the ground like dice. Darktree firing his blunderbuss at a swooping seagull: another miss. Darktree in the depths of winter, trudging through snow while the smoky black silhouettes cross the horizon, a frosty rime on his cloak: cold.

During the festive season he retires to a cave in the Malvern Hills. Here, for what it is worth, he keeps many of those stolen items that have caught his fancy. A bronze candelabrum, green with age; a miniature portrait of a beautiful, sullen child; an ormolu clock without hands. On Christmas Eve, he dances with himself in the middle of the cave, utterly silent, candles throwing his long shadow over the irregular walls. But it is not home.

He decides to visit his mother after all. So he covers over the mouth of his cave with parts of dead trees and turns towards the north. He is wearing the scarf she knitted him all those years ago, as a passport back into her heart.

At last, an hour after sunset, he encounters a coach.

'Stand and deliver! Hands up and valuables down!'

'Really, my good man, this is most old-fashioned. You are an anachronism, are you not?'

'Anachronism you say? And who might you be?'

'My name is Davies and I am a surveyor.'

'A surveyor? And what, pray, do you survey? Parrots? Plums? Boats that ply the Bristol Channel? Puddings, lanterns, old ropes? Walnuts? Come now, you must be more specific.'

'Very well. I am a surveyor for Great Western and I am travelling to Llandrindod Wells to map the area for a new railway line,'

'In that case you must come with me. The other passengers may proceed on their way.'

'This is ridiculous. You are already little more than a folk-memory. In ten years' time the question of your existence will be purely academic. The roads are dying, soon they will be gone forever. People will race back and forth, from one city to another, on rails alone. The future rides on wheels of iron!'

'No more! I can bear no more talk of the steam humbug!'

Darktree has never been a vicious highwayman, he has little taste for blood. But sometimes there is no avoiding it. Yes, he is a fisher who has over-exploited the resources of the bay. Now it is his turn to be a fish; the lines of the net that will catch him are being woven all around.

Darktree's favourite watering-hole is a small whitewashed tavern near the town of Flint. Here he can, for an hour at least, wipe clean his rusty blade and pretend that nothing has changed. He is still a man of the world, after all, and his actions must still have some bearing on events in general. This thought cheers him a little: he is easily cheered.

Darktree's favourite game, in the white-washed tavern near Flint, is solitaire. He lays the cards out on the table before him and frowns at them with sober intensity. It is wise to maintain a sober intensity when playing solitaire. Often, when no-one is looking, he cheats. At other times, to preclude a sense of false security, he deliberately loses. Either way, it is a game best played in the evenings, in a dark corner, with a single glass of sweet ale.

Velocity Oranges

The Cheating-Box

When Thomas was a bicycle, he used to talk to me from the depths of a dusty garage. Sucking on my pipe, I would grunt with primeval delicacy and attempt to match my facial expressions to the alarming profundity of his words. It was a cluttered garage, full of rusty garden tools and abandoned matchstick models. And Thomas was a cluttered bicycle, bristling with bells, water-flasks and unusable pumps. He could make me laugh with the ungainly honk of his decaying rubber horn. We were rather more than just good friends. Often I would try to mount him from behind.

But this romantic idyll was not to last. One wintry evening, as I groped my way through the garage with a broken hurricane-lamp, I saw that he had packed his basket and was preparing to leave. 'What is the meaning of this?' I cried. 'Is there someone else?' He blushed crimson, but his hasty denials fell at my feet like greasy pennies. At last he told me the truth. He had met a young bicycle mechanic who could work wonders with a spanner. He blew me a metallic kiss and explained that he was tired of being a bicycle. He wanted to be converted into a Tank-Engine.

I was distraught and collapsed in a pool of tears, but he ignored me and wobbled off into the night. Many hours later, when I had recovered my senses, I said to myself: 'What is a Tank-Engine?' I was confused. I assumed that it was merely an engine used to drive tanks. I had visions of

Thomas struggling to propel a caterpillar-tracked monstrosity over the dunes of a beach made dishonest with barbed wire. I saw him trailing loops of this mutant seaweed back to the cold ocean; I did not know the mundane truth.

I consoled myself by spending all my spare time inventing other unusual devices. Chief among these was the Cheating-Box, a cuboid that could not exist in our Universe. I donated most of my creations to Uncle Miasma, my next-door neighbour. Eventually we became firm friends and when my house burned down in a terrible conflagration caused by a mordant experiment with banana skins and cigarette papers, I moved in with him.

Incest and Morris-Dancing

Uncle Miasma was a pale, thin individual with a perpetual stoop and a diseased mouse-fur coat. His house was dominated by a lush and overgrown rainforest roof-garden whose immense weight had seriously weakened the building's foundations. Here, high above the city, he would fiddle with the controls of a radio-telescope whose dish revolved out of the artificial jungle like a coin at the end of its spin. I had designed the instrument for him as a birthday present; he was determined to be the very first person to receive the interstellar transmissions that any given alien civilisation might care to send.

Accordingly, he began spending more and more time in isolation, amid the squawkings of parrots and the hissings of tree-snakes. And before long, I grew lonely again. Desperate for company, I would often climb up the wrought-iron spiral staircase and peer at him through the quartz windows of his observatory. Whenever he left his monitors to urinate in the undergrowth, I would clasp his arm and try to engage him in conversation. 'What do you use for sexual relief up here?' I would demand, but he merely shook his head and stared at me with uncomprehending eyes.

One afternoon I received the answer to my question. I caught Uncle Miasma writhing on the cold floor of the observatory, stark naked, the Cheating-Box on his head. Enraged, I burst through the door and challenged him. My clothes were stained with the juices of huge dripping tropical ferns and monstrous orchids. He froze at once, but then offered me a wry smile. He held up the Cheating-Box thoughtfully. 'You should try everything once,' he explained. 'Except two things,' he added, after a little more thought.

Multifoiled Ether Orgones

So I decided to create another companion. I made a clockwork man who marched off into the night when my back was turned: very ugly, very wise. His name was Wilson. This did not seem to be the route to choose, so instead I arranged a huge furnace in the basement, heated by a large supply of coal taken from the prehistoric roof garden and prepared various retorts and crucibles. I resolved to attempt the True Great Work: the germination of a genuine androgynous figure. I was growing increasingly frustrated. Unlike Uncle Miasma, I derived little sexual pleasure from the Cheating-Box. Uncle Miasma now completely refused to come down from his observatory. He lived by eating wild fruits and the brains of green monkeys. In my imagination, I slowly shook my fists at the angry stars, the aerial that was their impotent lover and my own sweet smelling sexual organs. Weeks passed. I stoked the furnace. It was almost ready. Then there was a knock on the front door.

Jurassic Multi-Storey Car Park

An American traveller was standing on the threshold, asking if I could put him up in a polite Bostonian voice. I gazed at his firm body with greedy eyes, seeing an Ivy League Apollo aflame with a hot doughnut in each hand. I licked my lips and ushered him in. I took his coat and pressed him down into an uncomfortable chair, like a swollen cork into a swan necked bottle. The bulge in my trousers was more than a little noticeable: though not large, it protruded at right-angles to my pelvis. Heavy with clotted blood, it could not rise to a meaningful position.

The traveller explained that his name was Mark and that he was a dancer in a thoroughly modern, arty dance company. He had chosen to take a couple of weeks off work to visit those parts of the country he had always wanted to see. Unfortunately, he had lost his troupe and was now thoroughly miserable. I did not sympathise too much. I rubbed my warty face with my hairy palm. I told him that he was welcome but that I had some bad habits. I chew my toenails, for example, and scratch my behind with a toasting-fork. He answered that he did not mind, so I offered him a mug of phlegm and then sauntered into the kitchen.

When I returned, he was leafing through a coffee-table book of Escher's illustrations. I gave him the steaming mug and stood back to gain an overall view. He was very nervous. He admitted that he admired Escher's optical illusions very much. 'Ever since I was a lad I've tried to recreate his work for real,' I said. The American looked surprised. 'Really?' he asked. Unsure of whether or not I was joking he attempted a giggle. Snots ran down his chin. His dark eyelashes fluttered.

Approaching, I turned the page for him and rested an ivory finger on a picture entitled 'Belvedere'. The matrix of the woodcut was the same as that of the Cheating-Box: an impossible cuboid. 'Can you really build something like that?' he inquired, greatly disturbed. I nodded again, but he frowned and traced the edges of the drawing in disbelief. The whorls of the print defined the parameters of a new reality. 'And yet what would happen if a car crashed into such a structure?'

A Good Bicycle is just a Bicycle, but a Stilton is a Cheese

I resisted the temptation to molest the American and returned to my furious basement, where the flames of Hell were heating my due process. Alembics and Philosophical Eggs bubbled and hissed at me. I poked my tongue out in return and dreamed of fellatio and my old bicycle. Such things would be as nothing when the Great Work was complete: Hermes and Aphrodite joined as one, like a dividing amoeba in reverse, like the point of contact between hammer and anvil, time and motion, energy and despair. Both moulded from various mystic essences that I shall not divulge here. A true divine Androgyne that I could ride for hours, ringing as many bells as I desired on the way.

Anyway, my due process was rapidly becoming a growing concern. After much prodding and urging, my divine Hermaphrodite popped out like a tumour from an incised pus-sac. I danced a vast dance and clapped my hands, gurgling like a poisoned brook. Covered in pseudo-amniotic fluid, my star-begotten child writhed and howled a melodious sine-wave of a cry. I smacked its bottom and it winked at me, expanding into full maturity even as I watched. But the mix had not been perfect. Instead of a matchless blend, my Androgyne was a piebald, with a male upper lip, a female lower lip and a shadow that tasted of salt. I scratched my head.

'Let me see,' I said, as I consulted my arcane books and obscure manuscripts. I flicked through a tome compiled by Basil Valentine but soon discarded it in favour of a Paracelsus. 'Not enough tabasco!' I cried, beating my forehead in despair with the volume in an exotic and unusual rhythm. I braided my wax moustaches into whips. I coughed and belched. I grimaced and picked my nose. I knew that I could repair the mistake easily enough, by returning my creation to the furnace and adding the required deficit of Mexican flavouring. But I took the opportunity to vent an unfocused anger, breaking flasks and beakers and stamping my club-foot. Indeed, I was so angry that the mirrors in the basement closed their eyes and refused to show me that my Hermaphrodite had disappeared.

Strawberry Breast Milkshake

When I turned around, my mouth dropped open. I grimaced and chewed my tongue, a muscle already so drained of blood by constant biting that it resembled an ancient flatworm. I rushed up the stairs after my wayward masterpiece. By the time I reached the top, my ears were assailed by a curious cacophony of grunts, squeals, honks, groans and the snap of elastic followed by a yelp. Then there was a rapid series of heavy slaps and a deep moan of satisfaction. I lurched forward and discovered the American playing Eve to my flawed Adam. He was smoking a cigarette and trembling, while the object of his passion unpeeled slowly to fleshy shreds. I yelled and waved my arms and tried to scratch at his eyes with my nails. But I had long since bitten them to nothing.

Returning to the basement, I took hold of a flask of concentrated nitric acid, that precious liquid used in the distillation of toadstool wine, and I removed the glass stopper. I determined to hurl the contents of this flask into the face of the American as punishment for his desecration of my Great Work. By deflowering my Hermaphrodite, while it was still an imperfect model, he had destroyed the valency that held the etheric particles together. Massive waves of electromagnetic energy surged through the house. My beautiful creation was disintegrating at an exponential rate. I set my face in a snarl and bounded back up the stairs, three steps at a time, clutching the flask. But on the eighteenth step, I tripped and fell, breaking the flask under my body. Acid splashed my worthless face and torso. My melting mouth screamed.

The Further Cuticles of Kierkegaard

In great agony, I crawled the remainder of the stairs to where the American sat on the edge of his chair, eyes half-closed in portentous bliss. There was now no trace left of my Androgyne save for a dense cloud of sulphurous steam that rolled through the room. My charred skin was falling from my body in huge chunks and Mark, when he finally opened his eyes, did not recognise me. My face had run into itself like a chocolate statue in the desert sun. My club-foot had been reduced to normal size; my hair was falling out and my eyes were purple holes of ooze. I homed in on the American with bat-like squeaks.

'So what have you got to say for yourself?' I demanded, tapping my new foot impatiently. Enlightenment streaked in rays across his visage. He understood. My voice, at least, had not changed too much. 'Sorry?' he ventured, and I howled. 'That is not enough. Not by a long chalk!' I pouted. Something would have to be done. 'You have ruined the toil of many weeks. You will have to atone for your sins. It will be unpleasant.' Hastily, he buttoned his trousers. 'Downstairs,' I explained patiently, as if to a child, 'I have a mind-transference machine. It was one of my earliest inventions. It has never been used. I think that we should use it now. I think that we should exchange your healthy strong body for my disintegrating one.'

His nod of empathy became a vigorous shake of refusal. 'I think not,' he said simply. His lips curled in a sardonic leer. But I was not to be thwarted so easily. 'Either you help me or I'll have to torture you to death,' I replied. My tone was gentle, caressing, musical. I moved a step closer, clicking my tongue to determine his range more accurately. 'It's amazing what you can do with a few leaking batteries, a rusty razorblade and a bowl of vinegar.' I tried to smile, but my teeth fell out. The acid had corroded them into strange shapeless stumps. I scooped them up and put them in my pocket. Mark blanched. 'Look, I'll help you,' he croaked, 'but not in that way. Listen.' And bending closer, his words, and his greasy spittle, tickled my perforated eardrum. . . .

The Vindaloo Bottoms

Mark's idea was to stalk the streets, seize some innocent passer-by and drag them helpless down to my cellar where our bodies could be exchanged and then abused, or abused and then exchanged, depending on our particular desires at that moment in space-time. So we left the house and skulked, hugging shadows, kissing foliage and walls, touching up darker places, goosing alleyways, until we found a suitable place to wait for a suitable innocent. Soon a lone pedestrian did pass, and we dragged him into the shadows where I throttled him into a state of unconsciousness with an old fishnet stocking I keep in my pocket for a variety of absurd and sentimental reasons.

Between us we dragged, carried and tickled our hapless victim back to the house. In the cold air, the frost of our nostril breath solidified into ram's horns. Down in the cellar it was very damp. I strapped the victim into one seat of my mind-transference machine and took my place in the other. The circuits were closed, the current surged. Our bodies rippled. Our orgasms were intense and simultaneous, long and blue-green, grim and rather glib. It was over. I could see again. I stood up in my new body and carried my old over to the still roaring furnace, the hideous thing dripping congealed blood all the way. I hurled it in and listened to the satisfying snap, crackle and pop of bones.

Slipping on the aforementioned blood, I skated across to the sink and gazed into the cracked mirror. Here I gasped in extreme horror. I had just made the greatest mistake of my life. Fate had played the cruellest of tricks. The appalling realisation troubled my soul as much as the mirror itself troubled the depths of the Möbius-shaped basement. I covered my face and began to weep tears of oil. The concept was truly unbearable. I was now a walking timepiece!

The Onions of Ontology

A little research via the local radio station confirmed that Wilson, my old mechanical companion, had indeed returned to the city some hours earlier. He was due to play a benefit concert in the city centre that same evening. Since wandering away from my loving embrace, he had embarked on a successful career as a musician. Unwittingly, I had sandbagged and adopted the body of the stiffest biped ever to have been conceived in the entire history of human endeavour. I was inconsolable. But there was worse to come. I discovered that the mind-transference machine had blown vital circuits in operation and could not now be repaired. Thus there was no turning back. This meant that morally I was obliged to go ahead with the concert. I would have to ghost for the figure whose own ghost was a photocopy of the length of paper-tape unwinding in my chest at that very moment.

Together, racked by the needles of despair, the olives of anxiety, Mark and I made our way carefully towards the newly-built outdoor amphitheatre where the concert was to be held. On the way, we paused to pull the legs off an overgrown spider and to play a comical sort of game with a stray cat. With the strips of fur torn from its back and head, I made a hasty false moustache and beard. These enabled me to cross the entire city on foot without being recognised.

When we reached the stadium, I approached the doorman and tugged off my disguise. Yet he still insisted on blocking my path. I told him my name, but it only seemed to make matters worse. 'You bloody tin virgin!' he hissed. I realised that he saw me merely as the latest link in a chain whose grimy end reached back into a past of scrubbed bachelors and seasonal releases. Evidently I was hated as well as loved. So I had to rely on my travelling kit of blades, wires, shards of broken glass and an oblong sheet of sandpaper to gain admittance. With astonishing skill, and without soiling my hands, I managed to turn his cadaver completely inside-out. . . .

This seemed to have the desired effect and we pushed forwards unhindered. Soon I found myself waiting backstage while the stadium filled up. Peeping out into the crowd, I saw that there were other crusty celebrities present, modern stars of what used to be known, in the late twentieth century, as 'popular' music. There was Billy Tempest and the Skidmarks, The Inbreed Three, The Placebo Effect ('Hey this music is really terrible, but it works for me!' 'Yes, that must be The Placebo Effect') and the highly respected Dominic Dorian, who played modal music on Tuesdays only. The high note of expectancy turned into a loud hush. The first act was Wellington Smythe. When he went on stage and started singing, a justifiably outraged audience quickly dragged him down into their midst and forced an enormous aubergine up his nethermosts. When he struggled free, climbed back onto the stage and resumed his song, he sounded no different. Mark shook his head in disgust. 'They should have used a cabbage,' he said.

The Undivided Amoebae

Suddenly it was my turn. I girded my loins and walked out in front of my fans. 'I'm a virgin,' I squeaked. The crowd roared. 'I'm a virgin,' I squeaked again. The crowd roared. There seemed to be only one thing left to say to complete the introductions. I drew in my breath and steadied myself for the effort. 'I'm a virgin,' I squeaked. The crowd roared.

Why is There Only One Monopolies Commission?

I launched into my first number, gyrating my hips and reflecting camera flashes from my tasteless pearly trousers. I was quite pleased with my interpretation of the song, one of my most famed compositions, but the crowd were considerably less enthusiastic. So I attempted to slow the pace a little with an ironic blues. I sang: 'Woke up this morning / my colour vision was confused / Yeah babe, oh yeah / I've got those colour blind greens.' But still the audience were not satisfied. They began to mutter under their breath. I knew that root vegetables were on their collective minds. The situation was becoming more than a little desperate. Fortunately, I had planned for such an eventuality.

I held up an instrument they had never seen before. As I rotated it under the glare of the arc-lamps, a dignified gasp went up among the ranks of critical young things. It was, of course, the Cheating-Box, strung with nylon wires, as

sweet a lute as anything Orpheus dreamt up. A single pluck
and I had them in my grasp. Impossible cuboids sound
impossible chords. The music span out at them, like bats,
like gnats, like flying cats and drew them in, a web of my
own devising. Slowly, I forced them to their knees with the
stupendous beauty, wrung tears of remorse from their
smooth blue eyes, educated them, kissed their adolescent
bodies. What joy! What pain, despair, bliss and misery!
This was so utterly unique to them that they were lost for
words, thoughts, gestures. Finally they had felt something.
A sense of wonder?

The applause I received for this was absolutely gigantic,
so large indeed that I resolved somehow to experience the
flesh of the entire audience, in one way or another,
preferably another, before the two hands of the ebony
clock at the end of the stadium joined palms in supplica-
tion to mystic midnight. I bowed and bowed and idly
fingered my superbly boring genitals, licking the dirt off
the stage and picking black wax out of my inner ear. When
the lighting failed, someone poured a litre of high octane
over Billy Tempest, persuaded one of the Inbreed Three to
ignite it by rubbing his drumsticks together and forced
Dominic Dorian to reflect the glow with his diamond
rings. Wellington Smythe simply stood near with an inane
paedophiliac grin. The utter bastard.

Geiger Counter Revolutionary

I was exhausted. The concert was over. I had performed
eighty songs, twenty-seven in protracted encores, and
spilled my oily seed perhaps one thousand and seventeen
times. My best leg of three had committed adultery with
my left hand, so as a punishment I had plugged both into
the mains and frazzled them for good. Yet still I was
excited; I needed to return home, lock myself into my

inverted bedroom and seek the comforts of a flying helmet and a stick of celery. My lusts are stubborn bargees on a curry-sauce river: they pole their gondolas upstream, against variety's spicy currents.

So I hastened through the rear-exit, drawing my opera cloak about my shoulders. Mark followed me; my outstanding performance had turned him into an albino with moody crimson eyes. He talked incessantly about a vague doom and the forces of chaos, but I dismissed his prattlings with a casual wave. We clattered down the cobbled streets, through the Staré Mesto, over the statue-infested Charles Bridge and into the deeps of Malá Strana; I pretended to be a horse. I neighed and kept an eye out for grass, apples, a mare. The bulk of the castle above us crushed our lies.

Eventually, Mark resumed his talk of destiny and the Cosmic Balance. I was so infuriated by his pathetic affectations that I suddenly took hold of him and hurled him in front of an oncoming tram. The impact threw him against a wall, smashing his skull like a free-range egg. I walked up to him and attempted to communicate by sign-language, body odour, Esperanto, but he merely drooled. The accident had left him little more than a cabbage. As I pondered this latest development, I caught a movement from the corner of my eye. None other than Wellington Smythe was approaching. I looked down at Mark's twitching body and remembered his words of wisdom concerning cabbages. I laughed.

My Cheesy Armpits

I left both the American and the extremely ugly Wellington Smythe in a bloody mess at the bottom of the steps that led up to the Hrad. It had been difficult to fit all of Mark's solid frame into the constricted rectum of the asinine singer, but I had somehow managed it. I wiped my hands free of shreds of intestinal wall and green mucus. With a lightened step, I continued my homeward journey. As I crossed a railway-bridge, a bright light dazzled the evening. An alien spacecraft hissed overhead. I arched an eyebrow. Uncle Miasma had been successful after all. The craft was heading for our mansion.

'Who would have thought it?' I chuckled. I knew that the occupants of this interplanetary, most extraordinary craft were in for a surprise. Uncle Miasma had only one reason for attempting contact: he was a connoisseur of unnatural foods. He would be delighted. At the very least it would mean a change from moths on toast. I explored my face with my bachelor-boy fingers. There was much work to do. I could not possibly carry on looking like this. I would have to prise various bits of my anatomy off and replace them with more tasteful plastic or metal curios. A brass nose with flute-holes, for example, would be a vast improvement.

Also I would experiment a little with the structure of the house. Perhaps I would devise a system whereby any room could be converted into any other via the fifth dimension. Things were looking up. However, as I waited on the bridge, a train chuffed into view. I saw at once that it was Thomas, my old bicycle, and waved. But he merely stuck two fingers up at me and let loose an enormous fart, the stink of it lingering like gritty smoke in the ideal but darkling sky.

A Carpet Seldom Found

The street of shopkeepers lay between the bazaar and some nameless mosque with lantern minarets where dusty men came in an endless procession to wash their feet and sit away the sunset. Lawrence was growing stronger daily; three weeks had been more than enough for his body to adapt to the unknown smells, tastes, words and gestures that had so confused him at first. Now he could wander with genuine curiosity among the stalls and kiosks, his hand on his heart, his tongue ready to grapple with the guttural, yet surprisingly harmonious, sounds of a language as unique as a thumbprint on a polished globe.

Here, in Central Anatolia, far removed from the Greco-Roman attractions of the coast and their subsequent tour groups, he felt he had entered another plane of perception. Konya was a large, rotting hub of a city; there was no denying it. But at the same time it lured him into its depths with a subtle self-assurance, cast at his anticipations much as a fisher in autumnal Istanbul casts at the bluefish of the Bosphorus. And so he was entwined, entangled and hauled spluttering from the shallows of his own culture into the soul kitchens of another. He walked on and high above his fears and delights, on the shimmering air of evening, rode the boat of his invisible fisher: the fluted dome of the Mevlâna Müzesi, tomb of whirling Celâleddin Rumi, bright as dervish eyes, sea-green in a region where no sea glitters.

Lawrence, like many before and many who would come after, was searching for a carpet—that ubiquitous symbol of faded Ottoman glory. From the covered bazaar of old Istanbul (still Konstantinoúpoli to him, who had Greek blood and whose first experience of Turkish hawkers had been in Sámos) down along the Aegean coast and east to Antalya, he had inspected many examples of the art: kilims, embroidered silk squares hung from whitewashed walls or draped out on dirty floors, cicims, pile-less rugs of all descriptions, soft or stiff, old and new, pale and garish, carpet after carpet after carpet. Yet he had not found what he wanted. He had shared many tiny glasses of black tea, bargained long into jasmine-scented nights, smoked the nargile and perspired in the hamam. But all that he had seen so far had lacked feeling, that spark of emotion or inspiration which brought the colours into a real kind of life and made the patterns dance like abstract puppets before his critical gaze.

Here in Konya he expected, at last, to be satisfied. Few tourists spent any length of time in this area—merely passing through on their way to the stony pleasures of Cappadocia. Lawrence could understand why; the dust and fumes and conservative nature of the people was as unsettling as the cave dwellings of Göreme and rock churches of Zelve were secure. Yet prices were considerably lower in this Sufic capital; possibly the dealers would be more honest as well and more responsive to the genuine interest he would show. Down the street of shopkeepers he sauntered, the roar of traffic like a noxious river sweeping him further into the darker corners of the twisting thoroughfare.

Before long, he found himself investigating a narrow alley that led off the main street and lurched between houses that seemed as old as Selçuk dreams. At the very end of the alley stood a squat carpet shop, a single lamp doing nothing at all to illuminate the already gloomy exterior. Rugs completely obscured the front of the shop, hiding all windows, and the doorway of the establishment was covered by a tattered silk curtain, through which Lawrence could glimpse only a faint spiral of blue smoke and hear what sounded like a distant clashing of looms and the cracking of infinitely old knuckles; a sound as eerie and yet human as the *ney*, the plaintive dervish reed flute which calls always for its homeland in the Hatay.

Chewing a thumbnail in some vague anxiety, Lawrence brushed the curtain aside with his weathered hand and took a cautious step into the shop. The predominant colour was a rich blue; cool and dreamy in this bleached city, dark blues that shifted before his vision and melted away whenever he tried to pin them down with an outright stare. 'Anyone at home?' he said, more to himself than to any hidden occupant. The smoke that curled upwards without dissipating (like string; a miniature Indian rope trick) found its source in the end of a meerschaum pipe shaped like the head of a grand Ottoman. But the pipe protruded from a shapeless bundle of cloth and there seemed to be no owner at the end of it, lest he were an amorphous sort of creature; the very froth that would eventually solidify into the clay that held his apple-tinged tobacco.

Ears assailed by the clashings (which were surely coming from an adjacent room) Lawrence moved forward stealthily and prodded the bundle with his foot. Instantly it erupted, arms and feet appearing from unlikely holes, face beaming and nodding, the whole mass rising upwards to tower above Lawrence and then to bend forward to half his height as the strange figure scraped a deep bow, snorting smoke from its flared nostrils, blinking sly eyes and clapping delighted hands. 'Merhaba, my friend! Nasilsiniz? But of course you are well! Cheeks burned the colour of mountain rubies. What else can we expect? This is your first time in Turkey? Konya is very beautiful, very quiet. Not touristy place. You are from England? I have a brother in England.'

Instantly, Lawrence relaxed. Confronted with the usual patter of carpet sellers, he was able to slide into his role without having to worry about any ethics other than those of business. 'I may be interested in buying a carpet. Then again, maybe not. Shall I tell you what I am looking for, to save time and trouble? Many dark colours, much feeling, something from the heart.'

'But of course!' The figure swept Lawrence along to a seat arranged along one far wall of the tiny shop. There was always a certain ritual to be indulged when discussing business in a Turkish shop. Little glasses of black tea, cigarettes, all the adjuncts of the psychological game that so often disturbed callow visitors from Northern Europe. But Lawrence considered himself a hardened traveller, a haggler in the ranks of the best of them, not susceptible to the emotional blackmail and tricks of an experienced trader. He seated himself gracefully, while his host brewed tea and stretched his round face in false smiles that were far too large and lunar for credibility.

When tea and awkward small-talk had been safely deposited in the gutter of past time, the process of examining the carpets and kilims began. Lawrence's host—who had given his own name as Mehmet—laid out a selection in front of Lawrence and gleefully explained the meanings of the patterns and designs. 'I am not merely a shopkeeper. I am a textile designer. Seven years of study in Istanbul. Very dedicated team make my designs. Vegetable dyes only. Very best quality.' And with a flourish he cast a rug in front of Lawrence and pointed to the abstract shapes that floated across the wool and silk. 'Perdition design. One of my own. Very good price for you. Very good price. You are my special friend.'

Lawrence sighed. He had been the special friend of every dealer in every town he had even merely paused to visit. It was a situation that could be enjoyed, given the right attitude, but it could also be very tedious. He reached into his top pocket, removed his pair of reading glasses, held them close to his face, made a great show of scratching his chin and wrinkling his brow, bent forward for a closer look, replaced the glasses and shook his head. 'I just don't like this one,' he said. 'It doesn't move me.' It was, in fact, a very attractive carpet, but to admit as much would be tantamount to unbolting the locks of his mind and letting all and sundry filch ideas from his weary and bruised cranium. So he scowled: 'No.'

Mehmet instantly cast the rug into a corner and pulled out another from an enormous pile by his elbow. 'Very old one, this one. Thirty years old. Damnation design. One of my best. Good price. Konya not touristy place. In Bodrum or Ürgüp you would pay five times the price for quality such as this. Hayir? But this is my price!' And the wily dealer produced a pocket calculator from one of the many folds of his shapeless robe and held it up. 'In dollars, of course.' But when Lawrence shook his head again, he tapped out a new string of numbers. 'This is what I will do for you. Very special friend.'

Lawrence studied the new, lower price and gritted his teeth. 'I'm just not interested in that particular one. The price is fine, the design is good. It's just that there's no feeling. Do you understand what I'm saying? Show me something with darker colours, a darker purpose behind the creation. I want to see a carpet that was sweated over, a carpet threaded with the nerves of the very soul.'

Mehmet regarded him warily and a strange light came into his eyes. 'And you are a gâvur?' He appeared to be convulsed by some silent hilarity. He hopped from one foot to another. 'Then look at this one. Behold the hues, as dark as the tomb-cloaks of the Mevlevi. A dark soul knitted this one, like a Fate knitting doom. One of my most powerful designs. Eblis himself would tremble!' He threw out the carpet with a single undulating motion. The carpet seemed to sink into the floor as it landed, rather than resting on top of it. Lawrence blinked. The oleaginous surface of the rug was swimming with sickly sigils and geometric shapes that rose and fell like dying fish in an ocean of black scum.

Lawrence puffed out his cheeks. 'Very effective. But will it grow on me? It is not enough to be attracted to a piece of art. The art itself has to expand, warp, transmute into something new. So I say again: will it grow on me?'

'Ah!' Mehmet tapped his nose. 'Now I comprehend you. We are not so different after all, gâvur and devotee. One moment, lütfen. I have just the thing. But you must be warned: this is a special piece and it will require great devotion from you if all is to be well.' And so, with an expression caught somewhere between consternation and respect, the carpet seller seized him by the wrist and dragged him to one corner of the room. And now Lawrence saw a door with a tiny golden handle that Mehmet promptly opened and ushered him through. At once the clashings and clatterings were exposed for what they were. Lawrence attempted to cover his ears with his hands, but Mehmet did not relax his grip. Indeed, he forced the wrist into further submission with a savage pinch that made Lawrence adopt a shamed expression.

The door led into a low narrow room, inordinately long, that was crammed with looms and flying shuttles. Withered figures, completely devoid of colour, sat at the looms, their fingers moving with an almost mechanical grace. Lawrence regarded their dead eyes and precise jerks with considerable distaste. They had the haunted look of the autistic about them; as if motion were no more a negation of stasis than sleep itself. Lawrence noted that they did not look up; nor did they ever gaze at each other or make the slightest attempt at communication. Lawrence experimented with a nervous laugh, but in the cacophony it was as feeble as the scream of a mosquito ground to powder on any given evening (and how it disgusted him to see his own blood smeared from their bodies as he eased his nights with the heel or newspaper). But there was something more: something that threaded lines of unease between the weave of his curiosity and surprise.

'Good workers, eh?' he ventured. 'But what of village women? Is that not the traditional method? Low wages and ruined eyesight? A vast and massy chain of middlemen all the way from the East to the traveller's home? Is this some sort of co-operative?'

'Oh ho, a jest!' The carpet seller nodded in appreciation and finally released his hold on Lawrence. 'Co-operative, you say? This is true enough. Co-operate they must, to atone for that time when they did not! Bir dakika! Look at the quality of their work, observe with your own eyes their dedication. Here alone, my friend! They are wedded to their work. You too are married, hayir?'

'No,' Lawrence replied. How could he explain that his wife had left him, that she had denied planning permission for the extension he had intended to add to his ego? Camille was doubtless enjoying her own holiday from his selfishness. He felt no guilt, nor sadness, but a crushing realisation that it was all pointless, everything.

He eyed the workers more closely, as Mehmet encompassed the entire troupe with a single wave. Lawrence thought that some of the strange figures looked European, but they were all too shrunken to be certain. They worked in almost perfect synchronism, with nearly identical pauses and moments of incredible velocity. Even odder was the fact that they all seemed engaged in producing tiny squares of carpet that they promptly deposited in piles by their looms.

Mehmet began inspecting these individual pagodas of colour and Lawrence was free to crumple up his face against the appalling noise. In an effort to seek relief, he made his way to one end of the strange room. Here, to his considerable discomfiture, he discovered another door, bolted and chained this time, but worn through with so many holes that it was a relatively easy matter to determine what was happening on the other side. Pressing his bulging orbit up to one generous crack, he squinted and gasped. This other room was an ill-lit chamber (a single ray of sunlight filtered down from a large rent in the ceiling) containing yet more colourless mordant figures. These figures, however, were invariably malformed. Most lacked hands or feet or limbs entire. Others had no nose to speak of, or were missing eyes, ears and scalps. They moved in slow fitful circles, as isolated within some private universe as the poor creatures on the machines. And those detached limbs bundled up in corners? Did lepers still exist in Turkey?

Choking back his questions, Lawrence turned towards Mehmet, who was rummaging through one of the absurd piles of textiles, finally emerging with a tiny piece of cloth, no bigger than a pocket handkerchief. Clutching this prize, he led Lawrence back the way they had come and closed the door. 'I think that we can guess at each other's motives. You have made a pilgrimage of sorts, even if you are not yet aware of this fact. A golden cord has led you from your own country to mine, and all the trinket-scimitars sold in antique shops throughout the land have failed to sever it. Here, in Konya, the end of the cord lies knotted to my very tongue. I cannot lie.' And he thrust out the said organ, as if to add emphasis to his rather sullen metaphor.

Lawrence measured his words carefully. 'This is a joke?' The lines that creased his brow were longer than the threads of the rug that Mehmet was holding up before him. And yet there was no denying that this was an exceptionally beautiful piece of work. 'If this is a sample then show me the real thing and have done with it.'

Mehmet seemed offended. He eyed Lawrence soberly and replaced the pipe between his thin lips. When he spoke again, from the corner of his mouth, his words were augmented by a faint whistle: some of the syllables were entering the stem of the pipe and emerging from the Ottoman bowl as subtle notes. It was an effect as unnerving and yet human as any *ney* cut by the light of a sinister moon. 'Now you play games with me, hayir? First you claim to be a special visitor, one of the select few. And now you feign ignorance.'

It slowly dawned on Lawrence that he had unwittingly stumbled into a peculiar, and not entirely unwelcome, situation. This dealer obviously assumed he knew more than he did. Perhaps he had, while making innocent conversation, said something that Mehmet had mistaken for a deliberate attempt to mould some arcane contact. Lawrence decided to forge ahead, to see where bluff would take him; to what heights of novel experience the magic carpet of pretence could carry him, smug smile and all.

'Forgive me. But I had to be cautious. You are right, of course. It is a magnificent piece, and just the thing I have been searching for. Possibly my quest is now at an end. I would like to hear your thoughts on the matter.'

'Ha!' The carpet seller resumed his earlier vivacity. 'How can you persist with your false doubts now? Look at the way the pattern writhes! From what subterranean abyss was this form and matter glimpsed, you ask? How far along the ladder of the milky way, that dips down below our imaginations? Uzak! It is best not to know, hayir? And all this for a pittance. See!' And once again he took out his pocket calculator and tapped a series of numbers, holding the result up to Lawrence.

Lawrence felt a sudden, burning need to be free of this Mehmet and his disconcerting shop. Almost unbidden, his hand reached for his wallet, took hold of the notes and pressed them into the carpet seller's palm. He could think of nothing to say, so merely repeated his earlier inanity: 'Will it grow on me?'

'You can be sure of that.' Mehmet scraped his lowest bow yet and dusted the floor with the crown of his head. He handed the small square to Lawrence who, embarrassed, folded it into his pocket. 'A foot for a foot! It has been a pleasure doing business with you. Tesekkür ederim. There are too few of us left, you understand. Now perhaps I can interest you in a selection of fine pots from my very own workshop? And then brass and copper ornaments? I have chambers where the best crystals are cut into designs that will caress your soul. . . .' He made his way to the middle of the room and now Lawrence saw a trapdoor set into the floor. Indeed, as he looked around, Lawrence became aware that the room, which he had assumed was a singular entity, was replete with dozens of little doors, entrances and exits, set into the walls, floor and ceiling. There scarcely seemed to be an area that was not a means of access to somewhere else.

Mehmet grappled with the trapdoor, heaving it up with a jocular curse. 'Just through here lies my pottery and its workers. Very best quality. Good price for my special friend.' He had turned his rippling back on Lawrence. Gripped in the warp of fear's own loom, Lawrence forgot all about magic carpets of bluff, gaped for a moment in abject terror and then, legs spinning ludicrously, ears still filled with the demonic noise of the eldritch workers, took himself and his more modest purchase out into the oily mists of the wider city.

◈

The flight back had been a smooth legato, following the sun as it set over a blanket of clouds as large as a celestial carpet; a carpet rolled out for a visiting deity to recline on, puffing on the nargile of some distant volcano. Lawrence had found it all so much more pleasant than he had anticipated. There had been no turbulence and few crying babies.

And he had sat next to a charming girl, eyes bright with the honey of her adventures and amorous trysts. He had even fulfilled a childhood ambition: asking and receiving permission to visit the flight-deck for a brief chat with the moustachioed Captain and a wonderful view of the landscapes below, the passing jets flashing their lights at them in merry recognition.

The coach ride from Gatwick had been depressing in comparison. Weak tea and poorly-made sandwiches, a truculent driver and an endless stream of traffic that was like a scream had combined to make him feel decidedly petulant. He was relieved to leave the motorway and to pass through the outskirts of his home town. He took a taxi to his house and did not tip the driver. The house seemed reluctant to admit him back, almost as if it had forgotten who he was. Through the grimy back window, he saw how the sad little garden had withered and died, the enormous sunflower drooping like a hanged man.

On his doormat he had found his waiting mail, a selection of bills and unsolicited insurance propositions. There had also been a single personal letter; a message from Camille to the effect that she was coming back in the near future for a single visit, before leaving again forever. She wanted to take something away with her, a personal item of his to remember him by. This was not because she still loved him, or indeed ever had, but because life with him had only been extremely annoying ninety-seven percent of the time. She wanted to remember that other three percent: the boating trip to the Isle of Wight.

Lawrence felt neutral about this prospect. He quickly put it out of his mind and settled back into work, his colleagues welcoming his return and descending on him like the blade of a paper guillotine on fingertips. This was a week spent reviewing his recent holiday. Not a great success, he decided; no love affairs himself and too much time wasted in carpet shops rather than in the Taurus mountains. He recalled Konya with a shudder; nasty, grimy sort of place, full of shoeshine boys and rusty samovars. Possibly Antalya had been the highlight of his trip. The saffron he had bought had turned out to be turmeric, but the raki was good stuff. He sunk his doubts, like misty islands, into the milky sea of intoxication.

Searching through his pockets, perhaps rummaging for the more prosaic detritus of his trip, he came across the little square of carpet. He snorted a laugh and took it to his spacious lounge, a room rosy with the glow of an open fire and the polished bare boards that creaked with homely delight to the lightest of footfalls. He laid the absurd miniature rug in the centre of the room and regarded it with a critical eye. It looked incredibly pathetic among the oak bookcases and enormous stone hearth; a lost toy. He practised sitting on it; his generous rump totally obscured all signs of the thing. This was a great joke, he decided; but one at his expense. He grew miserable, and then angry and considered the option of hurling it onto the fire.

That night he was troubled by strange dreams. Mehmet came to him down an enormous corridor bristling with tiny doors that opened out onto varied and abstract dreamworlds. The carpet seller held up his pocket calculator to Lawrence and nodded a head swollen to pumpkin size, teeth the same hue as his oil-black hair. Somewhere beyond, a camel bell tinkled like a frosty planet struck by a comet. Lawrence tried to shield his face, in his dream, but Mehmet's sombre chuckle still came through to him. When next he dared to look, he saw a myriad of strange figures peering at him from the many doorways: vast faces, infinitely sad countenances, blue eyes like distant stars.

Lawrence awoke, sweating profusely from every pore. The bedsheets and pillow were sodden with his fear. He sat up, still shaking, partly relieved and partly bemused. He made his way to the bathroom, where lashings of cold water reassured him of the permanence of reality. When he returned to the bedroom and adjusted the crumpled pillow, he discovered a piece of folded paper beneath. He furrowed his brow and held it up. It was an invoice, marked simply with a single sum: $100. It was as if some malignant tooth fairy had turned entrepreneur, for what purpose he could not imagine. He dressed hurriedly and set his short-term destination as the kitchen and the coffee-pot.

Passing through the lounge on his way to the cordless kettle, he stopped and blinked thrice. The tiny carpet had disappeared and been replaced with another identical in every way save size; this carpet was exactly twice as big. It was a metamorphosis so startling, and yet so mundane, that Lawrence decided merely to ignore it and continue on his way. He stepped over the enigma, reached the kitchen and switched the kettle on. As he was waiting for it to boil, he realised that he was still clutching the mysterious invoice in his hand. He studied it again and then everything came clear.

He threw back his head and let loose a laugh; the first genuine laugh that had escaped his lips since Camille had left him. The mystery was an entertainment, as alluring as any tale told in the weave of Scheherazade's nights. There was magic after all, or at least the illusion of it. Lawrence had to admire Mehmet for his skill and restraint. No flying carpets in his presence, no bottled genii uncorked under his nose like a vintage wine; merely a carefully planned splinter of wonder that would lodge in his guest's eye long after he had returned home. How Mehmet had arranged for the carpet to double in size was an astounding trick, but Lawrence did not care to delve into its mechanics too deeply. He was satisfied with the result, and that was enough.

Of course, magic never came cheaply, and Mehmet had already stated his price. Lawrence was prepared to pay it for two reasons: he was amused (a rare enough occasion in itself) and also he was less embarrassed by the carpet's new dimensions. He brewed coffee, retired to his study with the invoice, wrote out a cheque for the required amount, folded it inside an envelope addressed to Mehmet and wrote his own address on the back. He would take it to the post-office on his way to town and dispatch it with an echo of the pleasure he had once taken in dropping his early love-letters to Camille through the hungry mouth of the pillar-box. So long ago now. Not that the bundled Turk had redeemed himself in his eyes any more than Camille could, but there had been a genuine talent behind the prank. A talent that deserved some mark of appreciation.

He pulled on his coat, stepped out into the street, the envelope flapping before him in an outstretched hand. The weather turned moody in his presence; now it wept over some long-forgotten slight. The tears spattered on Lawrence, his scowls and hunched frame, the loose paving slabs that rocked under his feet. He duly reached the post-office, sent his reply to Mehmet's wonderful joke, lingered over a long lunch in some gloomy wine-bar, considered how happy he felt himself to be. There was already, in one corner of his five-sided mind, some inkling that momentous events had not ended just yet; he toyed with the notion of extending recent developments. Supposing that the carpet doubled in size every day? What would happen if he refused to pay the new bill? Would the carpet cease expanding? Was he supposed to keep paying only until the dimensions he desired were reached?

He submerged such ideas in the mayonnaise of a limp ploughman's and drank up his oxidised Retsina. His jaw ached. While he rubbed it with a greasy palm, a stool scraped close by his side. He turned to regard a work colleague, Tom (or Tim?) Morris from Marketing. Lawrence had played squash with him once; Camille had possibly been friendly with him a long time before, in some abstract college life totally at variance with all his own experience.

116

Tom was a thin figure, nearly always enclosed in a tasteless suit with zany tie that supposedly indicated an individualism not at odds with company loyalty. It was all nonsense, Lawrence knew: his mother bought his clothes. Tom could scarcely even tie his own shoelaces. He nodded curt acknowledgement.

'Hard times, eh?' Tom took the stool, which happened to be higher than Lawrence's own chair, and beamed down. 'Drowning your sorrows? Join the club. Some of us are going to be let go, you know that. The Recession has really bitten deep this time. So are you going to take voluntary redundancy? I'm in two minds about it all.'

'What are you talking about?' Lawrence decided to be cruel. It would amuse him a little. 'Our Department has no problems. It's Marketing that is overstaffed. Jefferies realises this at last. No, my job is safe. I'm celebrating.' He raised his glass. 'To the future!' And noticing Tom's dour visage, added in a hearty tone: 'Oh come now! What about taking each day as it comes, each little nibble at the great cracker called happiness, creamy and rich with the cheese-spread of ambition? Positive thinking man! Didn't they teach you anything on that self-encounter course? Anything is possible, you make your own joy. What was it now? We are all strolling players, jesters who alight and perform in the global village?'

Tom shook his head. 'I'll see you around.' He sauntered off in the direction of the bar and Lawrence returned to the more serious business of his wine. He could imagine his envelope, with his cheque, already being loaded on some plane for the journey to Turkey. But how to spend the rest of the day, the weekend for that matter? Lawrence had never liked weekends. Without Camille, they were hardly any better. He was free of certain duties, but not a whit more immune to the unspeakable drabness of long rainy Saturdays and mock-righteous Sundays. To blot them out at the bottom of a glass was no longer appropriate; not without a wife to disapprove.

He drank up, abandoned the wine-bar, walked into town and purchased a small bag of groceries, just enough for a modest risotto. The walk back, through fallen leaves, despicably beautiful in Lawrence's eyes, was one in which each step seemed to be accompanied by some unseen presence weighing him down with woes as heavy as cauldrons. He opened his garden gate, tramped solemnly up the steps to his back door, entered the house, deposited his provisions on his kitchen work-surface and set to work. He wondered about the conversation with Tom. It was, in fact, the first he had heard about prospective cuts in the workforce, but his blasé approach was more than justified. He was one of the best workers in his Department, he knew Jefferies socially. If anything was afoot, he would know about it. Indeed his relationship with Jefferies was so secure that he had managed to take his four week holiday without giving any sort of notice. Jefferies would have tolerated this behaviour from no other employee.

Other thoughts, as he chopped vegetables with savage delight, included the imminent return of Camille. How should he react to this prospect? There was not enough time to train a guard dog and mantraps were difficult to come by these days. To change the locks would be far too prosaic a solution; he would studiously avoid that course. Obviously the best thing to do would be to simply let her take whatever she chose and to ignore her. This would disconcert her more than any frantic defence with elaborate snares or court injunctions.

The risotto was a poor example of the form: Lawrence decided that it suited his present self-image. He enjoyed the tasteless meal with another bottle of Greek wine in front of the television. Then he sat in the chair for long hours until the sky turned dark and the screen bade him a good night. He yawned once, cast a sly glance at the carpet and made his slow, painful way up to bed. He fell asleep quickly; this was most unusual. And the dreams came again: Mehmet waving and bowing at him, only this time the Turk had the face of Tom (or was it Jefferies? Curse the fluidity of dreams!) and the pipe he smoked had its own words for him, the Ottoman head reciting some verse or other while the doors in Mehmet's abysmal room opened and closed like the portals of the soul. Lawrence shook his fist at Mehmet, but the Turk merely looked at him and opened his mouth, green ink dribbling down his chin.

The next morning, Lawrence woke up without a leg. 'I don't much care for this!' he cried as he surveyed his stump. There was no pain or phantom sensation. The leg was quite simply gone. But where? Leaning over the edge of the bed, Lawrence looked underneath. His leg was not there. It was beyond absurdity. 'How?' Lawrence struggled not for understanding, which he knew would be a mistake, nor for recompense, but for the point of the joke, which doubtless had disappeared along with his leg. 'Why?' he asked. But he knew the answer to this. The blame lay in the clouds, their grief. Under the pillow, another invoice awaited his nervous fingers.

He hopped out of bed, clutching furniture for support, dressed somewhat in the manner of a sartorial stork, and made his way painfully down the stairs. At the bottom, under the letterbox, lay the confirmation of his answer. The cheque he had posted to Mehmet had been returned. Scooping it up, he surveyed with bland annoyance the smudge of green that covered the front of the envelope like a mossy sigil. In the rain, the ink had run into an abstract no more pleasing than any to be found in the average art gallery or handkerchief. The thoughtful post-office had returned it to the still legible address written on the back. In the lounge, Lawrence was forced to raise an eyebrow, although he had already anticipated the sight. The carpet had doubled in size yet again. It now covered an area nearly equivalent to that of an honest rug. Mixed emotions assailed him once more; pleasure at the carpet's new-found confidence and consternation about his leg.

Lawrence studied the envelope again. There was nothing for it now but a second attempt at sending the thing. He rummaged in the little room under the stairs and emerged with an old wooden crutch (abandoned there since that day when he had broken his leg launching himself off the wardrobe onto the bed in a vain attempt to spice up his and Camille's flagging sex life) which though wormeaten and uncomfortably short was in reasonable working order. He rewrote Mehmet's address and swung himself back out into the world. Fortunately, the weather was more clement this morning. As the wooden end of his crutch tapped the paving slabs, Lawrence seemed to detect in the rhythm a curious echo of the looms in Mehmet's shop. He shuddered and shook his head.

As he slipped the envelope through the slit of the pillar-box, he remembered Mehmet's arcane reply to one of his questions. 'A foot for a foot,' the wily Turk had said. Lawrence was contemptuous. He had always loathed literal-mindedness; in this case it was a sad betrayal of the subtlety he had attributed to the carpet seller. Perhaps he had meant a foot of flesh for a foot of rug? This was marginally more acceptable. Whatever the answer, Lawrence decided that he would take yet another day off work. It is not every morning that a man wakes up to find that his leg has vanished, walked off on its own as it were, left him out on a limb. He was completely stumped.

The day passed. Lawrence shut himself away in his study and consulted a selection of medical textbooks. He had not expected to find any explanation of his particular problem, but surprisingly there was limited documentation of similar cases. Legs, arms and even heads had disappeared overnight in at least a dozen other cases. There was even a name for it: Spontaneous Deconstruction. The phenomenon was exceedingly rare, utterly inexplicable and probably had little to do with diet or lack of exercise. As he studied the individual cases, the telephone rang no less than four times, but he ignored it. Probably Jefferies wanting to know where he was. Well he was too busy to worry about that. He would return to work tomorrow, he decided. The loss of his leg would not be a disadvantage to his career: he worked with his head.

That night, the dreams were more mocking than ever. Mehmet floated before him with his leg tucked under one arm, wagging a finger in some weary disapproval. Lawrence railed and shouted his defiance, but Mehmet merely raised the leg to his hideous lips and began to smoke it like a pipe, ill-smelling vapours steaming from the tips of the hollow toes. Lawrence reached out to snatch the leg back, but Mehmet suddenly seemed a long distance away, down some infinitely long corridor exposed by the opening of one of his infernal secret doors. So Lawrence was reduced to pleading. 'Please return my leg,' he said simply. Mehmet shrugged at this and this shrug was a negation that admitted of no compromise. The figure and the room faded and Lawrence awoke.

His left arm had disappeared. There was no arguing with the truth of this. Lawrence realised it as soon as he tried to prop himself up on his elbow. The elbow had vanished with the rest of his arm. Beneath the pillow, as always, the latest invoice crackled as he drew it out and crumpled it into a tight sphere. He lay on his side and wept. It had been a terrible week all in all, and this did not help. Slithering out of bed (and taking most of the tangled bedclothes with him) he reached out for his crutch, raised himself unsteadily and greeted his reflection in the wardrobe mirror. He looked like a broken man, a cloven executive, half gone or half there, depending on how you looked at it. Lawrence decided that he would rather not look at it at all. He dressed and, shirt sleeve and trouser leg flapping ludicrously, made his way down to the lounge and around the rapidly expanding carpet to the comforts of the coffee-pot. He certainly felt lighter in body, if not in spirit.

In the kitchen, he learnt the reason why his second cheque had not been posted successfully. A local station on his portable radio informed him that a postman had been knocked over by a hit and run driver while in the process of collecting the day's catch from the pillar-pox Lawrence had used. The impact had split his sack and sent the letters flying across the road, over neighbouring walls and into private gardens. Not all had been recovered. The postman had been seriously injured in the incident. The Police were eager to contact an employee of a local company who had been made redundant that very morning and who apparently had greeted the news by speeding off in his car.

Lawrence guessed instantly that his letter had been one of those not recovered. It was an irony reminiscent of some contrived fiction. He felt almost as if he were the unlucky character in a macabre and rather affected short story. He hastily scrawled another cheque (finding the utmost difficulty in holding the paper down as he wrote) and folded it inside yet another envelope. Bad luck three times in a row he would not accept. Holding the letter between his teeth and his coffee in his hand, he somehow managed to propel himself back through the lounge. As he did so, the telephone started to ring. He ignored it and puffed out his cheeks. When he returned to work—not today, of course —he would have to leave instructions with Jefferies that he was not to be disturbed at home even if the matter was urgent.

He did not even bother to glance at the carpet—which now covered most of the floor—until he tripped over a crease on one side, spilling his coffee over his remaining foot. He dropped to his knee and shook with mirth. A crease? Mehmet was slipping up. He smoothed the crease out and tried to stand. The rotten crutch splintered as soon as he placed his weight on it, sending him back down to his subservient position. He flailed around on the floor, his giggles of despair turning into tears of hatred. It was odd to admit it but the carpet seemed to be holding him down, like a viscous sea. Entrapped, he struggled against the swirling patterns, hierograms whose meaning was beyond his ken, symbols of an alien consciousness.

As he flapped ineffectually, his rage turned to blind panic. He was indeed caught in the netting of this mystic web. It was as if the square of carpet was a cutting from another universe, a patch stitched over the fabric of his more familiar cosmos. His awareness of his own world receded, sliding against his identity like pebbles drawn along a beach. He could still hear the telephone, but now it was as distant as the cry of a whale. The hands of the clock above the mantelpiece seemed to be spinning far too rapidly. The wan light and cold shadows outside the window wavered and shifted direction. Unbelievably, he saw that morning had already spun into afternoon; his carpet was a raft on a sea of hyperactive time. As he attempted to focus his will, he knew that he would be swallowed whole, like Jonah, in the matrix of the design.

He summoned up all his reserves of courage and crawled towards the edge of his shimmering isle. It was something akin to scaling a sheer wall, his nails tearing at the fabric, his single leg scraping against the smooth weave. At last, gasping and wheezing, he gained the edge and threw himself back into a more homely reality. He recovered his breath and glanced at the clock. The hands had slowed to a normal speed, but a dart of urgency pierced his forehead and made him wince. The telephone was still ringing, but he could no longer comprehend its nagging persistence. All he knew was that if he did not hurry, spittle flecking his lips, he would miss the last collection of the day from the pillar-box. And if he missed the last collection, he would have to forfeit another bodily part.

From the utility cupboard at the back of the house, he took a broom in lieu of a crutch and jerked himself out of his front door and into the windswept street. Bristles tickled his armpit as he hobbled towards his destination. The envelope was clenched tightly between his teeth; nostrils flared he wove through startled pedestrians like an injured jackdaw, squeezing between strolling couples and groups of chatting students (one of whom—a girl with a magnificent blaze of red hair and a bunch of battered roses— offered him a look of such subtle power that he was momentarily reminded of Camille). In the distance, he could see the postman opening the little door on the side of the pillar-box, reaching inside with sack and gloved hand. 'Wait!' cried Lawrence, but the postman ignored him. Gritting his teeth, he forced himself to increase his pace.

His way was blocked by a grizzled figure who reached out and gripped him by the shoulder. Lawrence regarded his wild gaze with the resignation of utter despair. He recoiled as the harsh odour of alcohol stung him in the eyes. 'Well, well! What do we have here?' the figure said, slurring its words. 'My old friend Lawrence! It was me, you know. Yes, it was me. The man in the car. I ran him over. They're after me now. Letters everywhere, like thistledown, like feathers from the wing of some ill-omened bird. But don't think you're so lucky. Jefferies wants to see you. I won't be alone.'

Lawrence tried to escape. 'Tom, you fool! Let me go!' He hopped in anguish as the postman closed the little door, locked it and hoisted the sack over his shoulder. 'I've got to post this letter!' He twisted around and bit Tom's wrist, drawing blood. But Tom merely shook him into submission, glowered once and snatched away the envelope. 'Please give it back!' Lawrence pleaded, but he knew that such an appeal would have the opposite effect. He burst into tears again. Tom laughed, his own tears mingling with his victim's on his creased shirt, and savagely kicked Lawrence's brush away. Lawrence crumpled to the ground and appeared, for one astonishing instant, to be a man embedded in the pavement. Tom's eyes grew very wide. Clutching the letter, he made off at high speed, overtaking the postman who had already climbed into his van and was starting up the engine. 'Come back!' Lawrence moaned.

His dreams that night were particularly horrific, not least because he had been anticipating them all evening. After the incident with Tom and the letter, he had crawled back to his house, raided his wine-cellar and proceeded to try to drink himself into oblivion. But for once the wine had little or no effect. It was almost as if Mehmet was determined that he should remain sober for what was to follow. In the dream, he saw that Mehmet was playing a vast drum with his arm and leg as sticks, a pounding rhythm that throbbed like blood. What disturbed Lawrence the most was the fact that his arm seemed to be aiding the carpet seller, curling its fingers into different positions to alter the pitch of each blow. It was hideously enjoyable music. Lawrence found himself pleading with the Turk: 'Please do not take my head. I work with my head.'

When he awoke, he discovered that he was unable to even sit upright. But his head was still on his shoulders. For that he was grateful. Yet he would not be needing a crutch anymore. He sighed and rolled his eyes. An idea came to him, an idea of such simplicity and beauty that he would have congratulated himself by shaking his own hand had he possessed more than one. He reached out for the little bedside table and the notepad and pen that he always kept there. In careful letters, he made out his Last Will and Testament. He left the carpet to Camille. This was a superlative jest. Then he threw the notepad back onto the table and smiled. She had wanted to take something of his to remember him by. But it was all academic, of course. He was not going to die. He was not even going to lose his one remaining limb. From now on, he would post his cheques without any problems.

After all, he earned enough money to keep paying the instalments on the expanding carpet indefinitely. The only difficulties that might arise would be if he ever lost his job. But this was an unlikely prospect. Tom had tried to worry him the previous day, but his words were probably no more than the ravings of a drunken lunatic. No, Jefferies would never sack him. True, his performance would be somewhat impaired by the loss of two legs and an arm, but the important thing remained his head. As long as he kept this everything would be fine.

There was a knock on the front door. Lawrence frowned. Who could this be? Not Camille surely; she had her own key. Wriggling to the window and pulling back the curtain with his good hand, he saw none other than Jefferies himself standing in his driveway, looking up at the house. Lawrence tapped on the glass and waved. Probably come round to reassure me, Lawrence thought. He wondered if he should ask him to post his latest cheque. A simple request. He could not understand why Jefferies looked so stern.

❧

Mehmet awoke from an alarming dream of his own, which was unusual—he rarely dreamed scenes that he had not already chosen. In his dream, a strange woman of extraordinary grace and dark power entered the house of one of his clients with her own key. The carpet had all but taken over the whole building, crashing like the waves of an impossible ocean against the walls of every room. But the woman trod as lightly on the swirling patterns as on any earthly rug. Up the stairs she glided, unerringly making for the bedroom. There, lying on the pillow, she found what she was looking for. Picking it up by the hair and thrusting it deep into her voluminous handbag, she departed as soundlessly as she had entered.

Mehmet scowled. He hated the idea of the dream as augur or warning, save when it was his to control. But he had to admit that in this case, he had come up against something it was better not to oppose. It did not matter. He was growing stronger by degrees and that was enough for him. One day, there would be no confusion in his world. He would create his own; indeed it was being woven at this very moment, in a hundred different cities. The dream still lit up his eyes. The carpets would expand, join with each other, cover the entire globe. And finally he would feel at home on this planet, a reality whose symbols were his, whose workings were based on his own designs, whose flaws had been deliberately engineered in advance. There would be nothing to fear then: no misunderstandings, no Western values beyond his comprehension, no wine or unfathomable music. In his mind's eye he could see the carpets bursting out of their confines, spreading like a plague.

Sighing, he swung himself out of bed, raised the hatch in the floor of his little bedroom and lowered the ladder. He had anticipated this minor problem and had made arrangements. He descended down into the first of a warren of linked chambers and made his way to his glass and crystal workshops. So his client would remain without a head? It was of little consequence. He did not require his workers to think. Besides he had prepared a suitable alternative. Reaching the room he sought, he picked up the finished item and held it critically up to the light. The bowl of an enormous water-pipe smoked in his hands. But the smoke did not come from burning tobacco. The nargile fumed and hissed with the sentient vapours trapped inside. A captive genii.

Bearing this gift through the interminable corridors, Mehmet climbed down a flight of stone steps and reached the room of the looms. His workers were as busy as ever, weaving the tiny pieces of silk and wool that would eventually make his dream a reality. He regarded them with fond affection. Despite what others might think, he was no devil. Merely a man who had sought understanding in a deaf and dumb cosmos, had received no answers and so had sought to impose his own patterns and conformity. It would be a softer world at the very end, he mused. A world akin to a hearth rug in front of the fire of the sun. A world where his subjects could recline and break bread together; a world whose physics were known ultimately only to himself.

Patting some of his favourite workers on the head, he placed the steaming crystal bowl under one arm and unbolted the door at the furthest end of the room. Here, the new workers were growing daily. In the dim light that seeped through a crack in the ceiling, he checked the progress of each. Once they failed to make one instalment they were generally his. He motioned to one figure seated against the wall and it stood up and came towards him, arms outstretched, groping blindly for a more fundamental reason than the pervasive gloom. Mehmet chuckled. This one was as ready as it would ever be. He could give up waiting for the head. That woman was welcome to it.

The figure stopped before him and carefully, lovingly, Mehmet screwed the crystal bowl in place. Then he led the new recruit back out into the room of looms and towards an empty machine. Unsteadily at first, but with growing confidence, the figure threaded a length of wool into the loom and began weaving. The shuttle sounded like the cracking of infinitely old knuckles as he swept it from side to side. With precise jerks, the new worker wove the doom of others under his master's benign gaze. Mehmet took out his pipe, stared at it for a moment, shook his head and replaced it in one of his many pockets.

Reaching for the tube that trailed from the crystal bowl, he raised it to his lips and puffed gingerly on the end. Strange smokes curled like tusks from his nostrils. It seemed to him then that he was growing larger with each breath, that he was expanding like one of his own carpets, becoming more and more intangible as he spread upwards and outwards, filling the room and then passing like a ghost through the walls to tower high above the shop, to waver and dissipate and finally merge with the shadow of the Mevlâna Müzesi itself, tomb of whirling Celâleddin Rumi, bright as dervish eyes, sea-green in a region where no sea glitters.

The Chimney

I am a sad man. I have never known a woman. Actually that is not quite true: I knew a woman once, but it was in a mirror. I caught her reflection in the attic of an old dark house. Possibly she was my mother. I do not know. Perhaps the house was mine; again I cannot say for certain. I was ignored as a child by my parents and did not learn to speak until a late age. Thus my early memories are hazy and vague and undefined by the geometry of language.

Once, I nearly kissed a woman. It was on a train. The lights had failed and we hurtled through a tunnel. Everything was suddenly as dark and heavy as oil. I stumbled out into the corridor and lurched against a girl who had also sought the freedom of the connecting passage. Her lips came within a mere three feet of my own. I was in ecstasy. I could not speak for a whole month. I did not wash for a whole year.

Every morning, I go down to the park to feed the ducks. This park is a meeting place for all the other sad men in this city. There are many of us. We cast torn shreds of sliced white bread at mallards who do not want them and withhold our crumbs from seagulls who do. Sometimes we talk to each other. Thus it was that I met a companion in bathos who suggested that I take a holiday in Jersey. There were many available women there, he insisted; he himself had been wildly successful on his last trip. He had almost been hugged no less than three times.

His words seemed to offer a balm for my despairing soul. I resolved at once to make arrangements to spend a couple of weeks on that blessed isle and to see for myself whether his extravagant claims were true. I could not imagine what it could feel like to be almost hugged by a real woman. I suspected that I might succumb to some sort of haemorrhage out of sheer unbearable joy. But such a demise would be infinitely preferable to my present condition. I decided that I would welcome such a fate with open arms.

Accordingly, I took ship to Jersey in the year of our Lord 19— and landed on the wharf of St Helier during the whole of a dull, dark, and soundless teatime. I was at once impressed by the quality of the females who were moving through the streets of the town. Many of them seemed capable of returning my gaze, but this was mere conjecture. Probably my intense excitement was encouraging this belief without any true justification. Yet I had a positive feeling in my bones, most of which were still inside my body despite the exceptionally rough crossing and the jarring that had been occasioned by the unfailingly regular, though wholly unnecessary, use of the fog horn.

I booked into a cheap but clean hotel and spent some time planning my next course of action. Should I infiltrate the afternoon immediately and attempt to actually talk to a woman? Or should I stay in my hotel and ring for room-service and hope that it would be answered by a maid? I was in such a state of anticipation that I could do little more than hurl myself onto the bed and bite the pillow with my horse-like teeth. I remained in this position for the better part of the day and did not stir until the sun had gone down and darkness folded itself over everything like an opera-cloak.

I instantly regretted my indecision, but resolved to make the best of what time I had not wasted. So I left my room and made my way to the beach for a midnight walk. My feet were full of an unknown vitality and I kept up a brisk pace for an hour or so, away from the town and down the deserted coast. Before long, all signs of civilisation had vanished. The sea pounded the shore and slid pebbles and plastic bottles against each other. It was very romantic. I knew then that I needed a woman more than ever. My life was slipping past quickly and I had never been smiled at. Tears sprang to my eyes as I realised that I was not only sad but bald as well, and there is no more pathetic combination. I vowed that if I did not find a woman this very night, I would walk out into the sea and drown both my worthless identity and my over-shiny pate in the briny deeps.

Whether the sheer dynamism of this thought had any bearing on my perception, I still do not know. All I can relate is that when I rounded the next rocky headland and gazed out across another enormous and deserted expanse of sand, I saw the figure of a tall svelte woman standing in the middle of the beach. I clapped my hands for joy. I capered and leaped. She appeared to be looking in my direction. This was beyond all rational hope. With a sudden and unexpected cry of triumph, I launched myself towards the figure, arms outstretched, lips puckered, heart beating an irregular tattoo on the stave of my ribcage.

That short run across those moonwashed sands now appears to me like a half-remembered opium dream. I know that I reached the woman in a trice, flung my arms about her, planted a long, lingering kiss on her mouth and then recoiled in shock. I know that I rubbed my eyes, blew my gargantuan nose in my sleeve and tangled my wrinkled fingers in my one remaining strand of oily hair. Slowly the truth dawned. It was not a woman after all—it was a chimney! I had hugged and kissed and whispered passionate words of love not to a feminine example of flesh and blood but to a brick structure designed to emit smoke into the atmosphere.

'Ha!' said I, 'and yet you are a very gorgeous chimney, if truth be known.' I was determined to cut my losses, so I

planted another kiss on the chimney's smooth body and
stood back to regard it more critically. It was not an unat-
tractive chimney; to be honest, it looked like the sort of
chimney I would want to marry, if a time ever came when I
would want to marry one. But it was not a woman. Chimneys can be hugged and kissed but cannot return such
gestures of affection. In this respect they are only marginally preferable as amorous partners to hatstands, bread-
baskets and vacuum cleaners. A woman was what I really
wanted, and I did not think that anything less would ever
really suffice.

Of course, I had to wonder what a chimney was doing
in the middle of a deserted beach in the early hours of the
morning. But no doubt it would have asked similar things
of me, had it been sentient. Besides, the answer seemed
obvious with a little ratiocination: the chimney belonged to
some house or factory that had been completely buried by
the shifting sands. Somewhere far below, the building must
be bristling under tons and tons of ochre grains. I scratched
my cold brow and my lunar chin and took the liberty of
patting the chimney on the flank while I debated what to
do next.

'Perhaps I will find a woman down here?' I cried,
climbing onto the top of the chimney and peering into the
opening. It was darker than a nightmare's armpit but there
was the faintest hint of a spiral of warm air. I guessed that
this would be as good a place as any to seek a female and
so, with little more ado, I clambered down into the flue,
bracing myself by means of legs on one side and my back
on the other. The inner walls were quite slippery, but I was
careful to maintain a steady pressure with my feet. In this
manner, I began the descent, marvelling at the contracting
circle of starlight high above me.

After what seemed an age, I started to catch wisps of
sound from far below. The mortar that held the bricks
together was crumbling badly and at one point I dislodged

a large piece of masonry. It tumbled away, striking the walls repeatedly as it fell. But I did not hear it strike the bottom. Much later, the most dissipated of yelps floated up to me. I frowned. An unthinkable notion had entered my brain. I trembled. I clutched tightly onto the mossy stone. I chewed my scabrous lower lip. But then I mocked myself for my superstition and resumed my heroic climb into the very bowels of the earth.

Slowly, by almost imperceptible degrees, the wisps of sound grew louder and clearer. They seemed to be chiefly composed of moans and groans and sighs. There was still no light from below, but the air had become considerably warmer. The moans and groans were modulated by this rising air and warbled past me like the attenuated cries of ghosts. Again I shivered and it was only with the greatest determination that I could force myself to continue. I knew in the bottom of my heart that this was a mistake, but I prided myself on showing the power of will over flesh. The very antithesis of my previous condition.

Eventually, the glow came, as I knew it must. A point of light very remote: as pale as a dying star in another galaxy. The air by now was so warm that the roof of my mouth had started to dry up. The perspiration on my limbs evaporated almost as soon as it had sprung out on my quivering hairs. The moans and groans were now much more obvious and I could no longer pretend that they were tricks of my mind. It sounded as if they emanated from millions upon millions of throats; an inconceivably vast unholy choir, prodded into the high notes by tridents and pikes. It also seemed that this ungainly crowd was running about, for the combined pounding of feet produced a vibration that carried along the chimney and made my fingertips ache and throb unbearably.

At last, after another hour of descent, I could no longer hide the truth from myself. The howls and screams were mixed with outpourings of diabolical laughter. 'Damn!' I cursed, as I nearly slipped on the greasy masonry, and then everything came clear. I knew, with a clarity of vision that I had never experienced before, that I had to retreat; that I had to scramble back the way I had come, my weak heart gripped in the vice of an ineffable terror.

There would be little chance of finding a woman down here, after all; at least not the sort of woman who would be willing to pay me much attention. Any women down here would be more likely to be preoccupied with other things. Things such as being roasted on a griddle, dragged through a forest of metal spikes by grinning demons, forced into blue-green bottles made of burning ice and all that other Dantesque sort of stuff. For I was heading towards no less a place than perdition itself: Tartarus, Hades, Gehenna, the underworld, the boiling lake, the endless drop, Limbo's cesspit, the other place, the eternal dentist's-chair, the rather long day out in Cleethorpes. In short: HELL!!!

With a brief, incomprehensible prayer to Providence, which in my haste I somehow confused with Provence and subsequently delivered in the langue d'oc, I attempted to reverse the motion of my limbs. But my muscles would not cease their blithe and terrible descent; my brain did not send the urgent signals of *brake* and *return*. I even—in that grotesque instant—almost forgot about women and their peachy lures.

I was as frozen by my own inertia as a wax apple falling towards the sun. The light grew brighter as I stared; the sounds of screaming and moaning assailed my poor eardrums; my mouth began to throb with the heat, as if I had but lately partaken of a subterranean vindaloo. In short, I was in a pickle—nay, a chutney—and there was no way that I could see of climbing out of the jar. I was also forced to review my own beliefs concerning the brimstone pit. I had been raised as a Catholic and thus had early learnt much of what there was to know about the punishment of the damned. But there had always been a nagging doubt in the corners of my judgment. Would a benevolent God ever really allow souls to burn forever? Was Hellfire really far hotter than the heart of a fission reactor? How could such energy be harnessed?

There was one discrepancy that disturbed me mightily, even as I raced onwards down towards my eternal doom. The discrepancy was this: the flames of Hell themselves were supposed to give off no light, and yet there was a definite glow beneath me—brighter now by far than the headlamp of a girl's bicycle. I could only speculate that whichever Church Father had first reported on Hell (Origen probably, or Joyce) he must have worn a blindfold when shown through the massy wrought gates into the Stygian Realm. This is the sort of thing that a smart God would do; it would be bad form to let mortals know the exact route into these regions. They might try to retrace their steps with a bunch of their friends, a couple of bottles of Jacob's Creek and a badly tuned guitar. People will do anything to attend a free barbecue these days.

The waves of heat from below now lapped over me like the hot steamy breath of a thousand women from Camden. Can you possibly imagine what it feels like to have your tears evaporated the instant they start their crawl down your cheeks? It is like the dry retch of a whole body; like having your tongue pinned to the roof of your mouth with a silver brooch; like sunstroke on the inside of your nose; like licking a cheese grater or attempting an oral assignation with a paper shredder. And yet, again, my thoughts returned to amour. How could they fail to do so? Women had been the very warp and woof of my existence. I had investigated recommended substitutes: watermelon, soft cheese, jars of worms. But nothing would ever be able to replace a real living female, preferably a redhead with nipples like Chianti wine-corks.

So I commended myself to whatever ontological being really sat around on a cloud creating perfect islands and golden mountains and waited. As I waited, I discovered that my windmilling arms and legs were beginning to slow down. Had fear reduced my reactions to Saurian efficiency? By now, the groans from beneath were a form of physical pain in themselves, an unimaginable counterpoint of microtonal expressions of suffering. There was a certain mad grandeur in their sheer strident volume, but nothing that would ever pass as music beyond the first few nights of the Proms. The men were all singing soprano and the women all singing baritone. I knew that the courts of Hell were courts of misrule, where the natural order of all things was reversed, but I had never expected to encounter such an ear-numbing inversion outside Brighton.

It then dawned upon my reluctant consciousness that the real reason I was slowing down was because the chimney was beginning to narrow. I was forced to contemplate all that I knew concerning the layout and mechanics of chimneys. This was a not inconsiderable collection of tubular facts and smoky figures, garnered from various textbooks and technical journals devoted to the topic. As a sad man, I am a great devotee of the public library, and a great consumer of obscure texts. In *Fuming Vents*, the quarterly of the Chimney Spotter's Society, I had once picked up the following information, which I had committed to memory in case I ever needed to impress any female chimney engineers I might happen to meet in casual society:

'The most aesthetically pleasing, and thus inherently desirable, chimneys are those whose proportions are a perfect match for the intent, purpose and appearances of the inglenooks that serve them. A typical chimney is an identity and its hearth is its heart; sickness in the one will be shown plainly enough in the character of the other. Shallow indeed are those who claim that a fireplace and its chimney do not have to be mutually compatible in a psychological way or that the relationship between grate and vent is not a spiritual one. For like any worthwhile predication it is a two way process, a question of give and take, of push and shovel. An holistic approach must needs be taken when considering which chimneys are worth spotting and which are mere cylinders jutting into the sky, above and beyond whether that aforementioned sky is beautifully grey or despicably clean.

'Generally, the taller the chimney, the wider should be the fireplace, save in those chimneys whose tallness is more a question of utilitarianism than pride. As stated in the Chimney Spotter's Manifesto, compiled by Grimes and Twist, the internal topography of the flue is even more crucial to the colouring scheme of any mantelpiece that might be used to enhance the portals of the domestic furnace proper. Murgatroyd's own interpretation of the Tarnished Mean would suggest that any chimney of vast and unlikely dimensions, which nonetheless tried to hide itself by artful means, would be possessed of an inglenook more baroque than rococo, and that although said mantelpiece might conceivably be of an ultramarine hue, each assorted oddment and shell arranged on top would be both of a concentric tendency and yet also of a dimension no less or greater than 1/3 of the democratically elected volume of its fellows. . . .'

To be perfectly candid, I did not find this information particularly helpful, although reviewing it in my mind did have the pleasant effect of blocking out thoughts of a more serious nature. I vowed to myself that, should I ever escape my predicament, I would join the Chimney Spotter's Society myself and conduct lecture-tours based on my experiences. This would surely be a useful source of second income, even if not a radically promising way of meeting women.

Before long, my motions were reduced to a crawl and then, finally, I found that I had completely stopped. Wedged tight, my position was a curious one. Knees thrust up behind my ears, nethermosts dangling free over the abyssal drop, head thrust between my legs, I was thus able to contemplate the entirety of what was occurring below. There was little of note to add: the bright light and the blast of hot air still dominated the general prospect. But now the very nature of the sounds had altered. The groans and moans petered off into an acutely troubling silence and then a concerned muttering. I had that peculiar sensation that I was being watched, as if faces were straining upwards from below, trying to gauge the reason for what must have been for them an inexplicable blockage.

Long hours I hung there. At first I struggled to free myself; I strained and pushed against the baked stone and mortar. It soon became obvious that I was wasting my time, that my attempts at escape were even more futile than my attempts at finding a partner through the Lonely Heart's column of my local paper. I could only resign myself to what seemed an exceptionally rigid fate and entertain myself with thoughts of a cold ocean and old Julie Andrews songs. This was scant comfort, but at least it provided an agreeable experiment in holding two separate images simultaneously in the mind without combining them. I had no wish to visualise the immersion of the world's greatest interpreter of Mary Poppins. Metaphorical depth to a role was one thing . . .

It was during my fourteenth rendition of 'My Favourite Things' that I caught the first hint of another presence in the near vicinity. On the line, 'brown paper packages tied up with string', I saw that the light from below was being blocked out by a vague silhouette. A tiny dot appeared in the centre of the light, and this then gradually expanded until a tenuous rim was all that was left of what had been hitherto a scouring and overbright illumination. And shortly afterwards, I caught the sound of the thing, the hideous rustling and scraping of what I suddenly realised were its legs.

It was an enormous spider that was racing up to greet me! A spider as black as the juice squeezed from Bibles; Deuteronomy black. As black as the eyes of a shrunken head pickled in vinegar. And here are my own eyes: popping and rolling like pearls sprung from their oysters with a green rusty knife. Oh, for blades on my boots to kick away the rising horror! Oh, for a corrosive spit to dribble from between my trembling lips onto its chitinous hide! But I was helpless, as weak as a fly in a web; as utterly doomed as a snowflake in a female undergraduate's first toaster. And my nethermosts would be the first to feel the bite of the fangs! Such an ignominious demise! At long last, it appeared, the riddle of the sphincters was about to be solved. . . .

Riddled or not, a loosening of those dire regions was certainly in the offing, for I had reached the very threshold of my fear; that doorstep over which fear becomes fertiliser. I clenched my teeth, and sundry other extremities, and crossed my fingers. This was a gesture I had not resorted to for many years. Closer and yet closer rushed the hideous arachnid and then, in the those final few seconds, I closed my eyes and an ineffable sadness overcame me; the appalling truth dawned that I was about to die without ever nestling into the jasmine scented cleavage of any given female.

Imagine my inordinate relief, and disbelief, when instead of fangs piercing my flesh, I felt nothing more savage than a firm push and the itch of wiry fibres. Suddenly I had popped free and was travelling upwards again, through no power of my own. I dared to open my eyes and discovered, with some feelings of bemusement, that what I had at first taken for a spider was in fact no more than a chimney-brush. All mysteries then became clear; to the devils and demons down below, I was no more than a blockage to be disposed of in the traditional manner. At the same time, the mumbling and chattering ceased, and the screams and moans resumed apace.

So I had interrupted, for a brief instant in eternity, the smooth workings of Hell! This thought was in the vanguard of all sorts of confusing and original emotions, which I stored in the back pocket of my mind for later reference. I contented myself with sitting—now that I was in the wider section of the chimney and free to move once more—in an adapted lotus position on top of my quaint mode of transport and studying the scenery. This scenery, though, was dreary in the extreme, and soon I was unable to repress a yawn and a sooty rub of bleary eyes. It was perfectly possible to make a clean sweep of all the sights in any one-minute period.

As I rose, faster and faster, the Plutonian sounds from below grew fainter, until I began to feel decidedly more confident. My one remaining worry concerned the velocity at which I was now travelling. The chimney-brush, with myself atop, seemed to be accelerating steadily. The walls rushed past at frightful speed and I was reluctant to touch them lest they tear the flesh from my bones. I reached inside my jacket for my pipe, stuffed it with mouldy tobacco and thrust it between my overlong teeth. As I puffed defiantly and sullenly, I folded my arms across my chest. Slowly but surely, as we ascended, the temperature began to drop.

I have already mentioned that I had resorted to the use of Julie Andrews songs to keep myself amused. By this time, I had so thoroughly exhausted my repertoire that I was forced to consider alternative pastimes. I gave myself over to nostalgia and the poppy-seeds of reminiscence. I recalled my early life, with its undefined memories; my confusing time in a rather unfriendly school, that later turned out to be not a school at all but a warehouse for shop window mannequins; my very first job, as a table in a Chinese restaurant, where I was required to spin on my bony knees and where curvature of the spine was a sacking offence; my very first pint of beer, on the salty Isle of Man, served to me in a limpet shell with a hole in it. Ah memories!

I also recalled my very last confession. My priest had but lately converted to Buddhism and was forever trying out doctrines of his new faith on members of his woolly-headed flock. In the confessional, I blurted out that I no longer believed in Hell. The priest nodded and folded the edges of his cassock. He then proceeded to tell me this fable, which may or may not be of Japanese origin: a man who was neither good nor evil died and was allowed to make his own choice about whether he went to Heaven or Hell. He mulled this over and finally responded that he wanted to take a look at both before choosing. So he was shown first to Hell, where there was a large banqueting table, piled high with rich food. The only problem was that the chopsticks were all seven foot long. None of the guests seated at the table could eat anything. So the man asked to be shown Heaven instead. In Heaven the situation was identical, except that the guests, instead of trying to fill their own mouths, were feeding the faces of those who sat opposite.

I suppose that this fable was meant to illustrate some cheesy point or other about how virtue is its own reward and how assisting your neighbour will eventually benefit yourself. But for me, the story had different connotations. It suggested to me that even fundamentally intractable oppositions were merely questions of interpretation. Heaven and Hell were really not that different. Supposing I had been mistaken all along? Supposing it had not been Hell I had just been delivered from? Supposing that the moans and groans and screams had not been the products of torture and pain but of ecstasy and abandonment? This was a thought that threatened to swamp my senses.

What if I had just missed out on not the eternal terrors of Beelzebub's buffet, but the delights of a divine debauch? It was more than possible. The high notes of the wailing souls might have been prompted not by tridents and pikes, as I had earlier suspected, but by the aids and adjuncts of some celestial bacchanalia; the wine, the song, the riding-crop studded with whole stars. I gnashed my molars in rage and frustration and tore out my last strand of oily hair. I fought against the brush that was sweeping me up and away from my desire and howled to be let down again. But the brush pushed harder than before and my speed merely increased until the force of my motion crushed me flat against the spiky bristles.

Looking up in despair, I saw a rapidly expanding circle of pale blue light, and I knew that I was close to the surface of the world again. Many hours had obviously passed since my first sighting of the chimney and it was now morning. But I had no wish to see daylight. I bellowed at the top of my voice down the flue: 'Please let me back!' But I knew that this was a redundant gesture, as futile as all my actions. There was nothing more I could do but sob and dribble and feel profoundly sorry for myself, a poor bruised creature forever doomed to a pending tray in the office of fulfilments; the saddest man in a universe of sad men.

Finally, the brush deposited me back into real life, propelling me out of the top of the chimney like a spring-heeled Jack from the mouth of a cannon. The top of that infinitely long brush lingered awhile, like the unkempt head of a curious sweep, before being drawn down. I soared in a graceful arc; so high that I had a pleasing view of all the other Channel Islands. When I began to fall, I thumbed my nose at them. But there are some happy endings after all: I landed in the arms of a woman who was out walking the beach with a book of poetry and a suitably knitted brow. 'My very own soot fairy!' she cried, planting a kiss on my smoky cheeks. Throwing me over her shoulder, she hurried back to her house and set me up in her garden next to a small pond. And that is where I am still registered and where, though my floppy hat itches terribly on Fridays, I sometimes catch fish.

One Man's Meat

For Raymond it had been one of those abstract evenings; formless desires, a quick splash of reckless paint on what had been a blank canvas, and then out into the city. He could hardly colour the town red; a blue-green fugue was clanking its counterpoint on his aching ribs. Too much tobacco, too little sleep, and Clarisse gone barely a week. So he hunched deeper into his overcoat while rain warm as curdled milk lashed his face and hands. A city, and a life, without straight lines.

He found the brothel down a cobbled backstreet, a low building with heavy curtains. At the entrance, he was greeted by a doorman who politely inquired whether he had made a reservation. Raymond shook his head. Was he supposed to feel inferior to those patrons who had previously arranged to displace a volume of the establishment's air? He was unsure. Nothing in the doorman's demeanour provided a clue. He allowed himself to be ushered into a waiting area, where he took a comfortable seat and accepted a drink. Filthy muzak whispered from concealed speakers.

'Sir?' Almost immediately, a waiter came to take his order. Raymond relaxed. They were not going to punish him for his minor transgression of etiquette. He adjusted his tie and smoothed back his damp hair.

'I'm a vegetarian,' he said. He pulled down his lower lip to expose gums as healthy as the release of tension. The waiter nodded and led him past rows of rooms, the air bristling with soft moans and the strains of sweet melodies, or else harsh screams and atonal cacophony. His pulse began to race, his nostrils flared. He caught the mingled odour of myriad scents, exotic flavours on the tip of his tongue. A thousand combinations to sample, innumerable moods.

'Rhona is a root vegetable,' the waiter remarked casually, as he stopped in front of a narrow door. Raymond proffered a small tip, acknowledged the resulting wink with a curt nod and stepped into the room. His eyes adjusted slowly to the light, he blinked the sweat from tired lashes and regarded his new surroundings. She stood lovely and demure in an earthen pot in the centre of the room. Her tendrils beckoned to him, impossibly alluring in the steamy atmosphere.

Yet he lingered awhile near the threshold. 'Why don't you take your coat off?' she asked seductively and he obliged, hanging it up on a hook on the back of the door. 'Now don't be shy. Take your time. Real nice and slow. You look a little nervous. First time, eh? Well nothing to be worried about. Come a little closer. That's it, darling, I don't bite. Just talk to me, tell me what you like.'

'My name is Raymond.' Raymond felt an absurd shame at being here, bedraggled, unsure of himself or his real intentions. He dripped over the short-pile carpet and wrung his hands. 'I'm a vegetarian,' he repeated. He managed a nervous grin.

'I hope so! One man's meat . . .' Rhona winked and reached out to stroke his cheek. He winced but did not pull away. 'Why don't you choose some music? It may help you to relax.'

Raymond nodded and moved over to the wall, his knuckles rapping quickly on the oak veneer. Instantly one of the panels slid back, exposing a beaming violinist who struck up a jaunty air. Raymond shook his head and the panel slid shut. He rapped at further points along the wall, exposing musicians of varying calibre. Eventually he settled for a combination of flute, guitar and cello.

'That's better!' Rhona giggled coquettishly and reached out to touch him again. 'Why don't you loosen some of your clothing? You must be steaming under all those layers. Why don't I help you?'

Conscious of the grins on the faces of the musicians, Raymond scowled. 'I'm not some pink cheeked virgin! I do have a wife, you know. She's gone away for a while. That's all. A man gets hungry, his tongue rolls around inside his mouth. I'm just not used to places like this!'

'Of course not.' Rhona's eyes flashed with a secret mirth. 'But I can be your wife tonight. I can be anything you want. I can love you heart and soil. I'll be your slave, your mother, your mistress. A real turnip for the books!'

Raymond swallowed the bile that had been building up in his throat and pulled off his tie with savage jerks. As he undressed, he wondered about Clarisse, alone in a big city for the first time. How would she be filling her own form-less evenings? Perhaps she was betraying him at this very moment, glutting her own maw with forbidden delights. He shuddered. She had always accused him of being uncouth; this despicable thought proved the truth of her words.

Raymond's impulsiveness had meant that he had not checked the condition of his underwear before leaving the house. Acutely embarrassed, he huddled in his stained underpants while Rhona offered him an amused glance. He looked up at the musicians in despair, but although they were grinning broadly they were intent on their instru-ments. The music was now a gentle lullabye, an ironic murmur of sound that washed over him but could not clean his shame.

'I've seen worse, darling.' Rhona licked her lips and Raymond cursed her mocking nonchalance. 'Well big boy, let's have a look at your tool. You have got one, haven't you?'

Raymond exploded. He leapt forward, brandishing the potato peeler. 'Here!' he cried, throwing back his head. 'Take it bitch!' He thrust the point deep into her face and removed one of her eyes with a savage twist. Then he drew the blade down along her body, shedding the skin in a single flapping sheet. He was vaguely aware that the musicians had changed tempo, improvising a ragtime no less sardonic than their earlier number.

Rhona groaned with pleasure, but Raymond realised that this was merely an act for his sake. Senses dulled by numerous other such encounters, she could scarcely muster any genuine enthusiasm at all. Raymond felt his blood boil: he would be the lens of what little she could still feel, magnifying it beyond anything she could have anticipated. 'Taste this, you jaded hors d'oeuvre!' he screamed as he drew the blade back up, removing the flesh that lay under her skin. A single tear of surprise popped from her remaining eye.

Over and over again, he raised and lowered the blade, his vision a red mist, Rhona's cries of pain and delight pounding in his ears. Never had he felt so lost to the world, so abandoned by reality, so originally and refreshingly alive. Specks of peel and warm flesh spattered his face. Pale juice trickled between his fingers, the odour of damp earth plugged his nostrils. He screamed aloud as he approached orgasm and gave himself wholly up to the nirvana of ultimate release.

Finally it was over. He dropped the blade and, trembling, reached for his clothes. They were lying in a pool of viscous ichor. The musicians had stopped playing. They stared sombrely at their feet. Raymond shook his head and the sliding panels shut away their gloomy countenances.

There was a knock on the door. Raymond opened it and regarded the bowing waiter who stood there. 'Every-

148

thing to your satisfaction sir?' In the waiter's smile was a subtle contempt whose depths Raymond could not fathom. He jerked a thumb over his shoulder at the mess that lay behind.

'You can lead a horticulture but you can't make her think!' he joked. The waiter merely returned the slightest of smiles. Raymond pulled on his coat, reached inside his pocket for his wallet and paid the fellow. As he did so, another waiter with a wheelbarrow entered the room and carted away Rhona's remains to a door at the rear of the establishment. As the door swung open, Raymond caught a glimpse of a huge vat of bubbling oil.

The waiter noted his surprise. 'Crisp weather this time of year,' he said. He showed Raymond to the front of the building and the doorman waved him out into the night. 'Very good, sir. Call again soon, sir.' But Raymond did not look back. He hid in the comforting darkness.

An ineffable bleakness enveloped his soul. He knew that he had made a fool of himself. No doubt the waiters were all laughing at him now, sharing the joke with each other as they sat around in that back room, frying the remnants of his inadequacy. Clarisse was right; he was too much of a boor to visit such places. They were for people of breeding and taste, not for riff-raff such as himself.

Suddenly he felt a great hatred for Clarisse and with this hatred came an overwhelming urge to betray her, to teach her a lesson. He altered his direction and made his way down to the docks, the red light district where he would find ample opportunity for revenge. As he walked, he kept an eye out for the police.

At last, he came across what he sought. They stood there in a line, wearing the seductive garments of their trade: the apron and tall white hat. As he peeped at them from the shadows, he felt a rumbling in his stomach. There were a dozen choices available. French, Italian, Indian and Turkish, they lounged on the corners, swinging their cleavers and ladles. A burly Swede with a bristling beard noticed him and gestured with his chin. 'Smörgåsbord?' he hissed.

As Raymond moved closer, his attention was distracted by a suave Chinese spinning a wok on the end of a chop-stick. Raymond paused. He had always fancied a bit of Oriental. He drew in a deep breath and summoned up all the last reserves of his courage. If he was going to pay for it he might as well ask for something really dirty. 'You do stir-fry?' he whispered. The chef eyed him suspiciously for a moment and then nodded. Raymond followed him down an alley and into a dark doorway, where a small portable stove stood waiting. The chef cooked the meal with brisk efficiency and Raymond, startling himself with his own seediness, had it up against the wall.

The Man Who Mistook his Wife's Hat for the Mad Hatter's Wife

They live in a house shaped like a hat. Music is in their blood, but they have different groups. In the evenings, they play backgammon by the light of a single candle. It is difficult to determine, with any degree of accuracy, whether they are inspired romantics or simply trying to save money. The dice crack on the baize like knuckles. They play with chocolate-covered mints, plain and milk, and eat them as they bear off.

One day, the house blows away in a strong gale and lands on a hill. The view is terrific. The man, frilly shirt open at the collar, carries a saxophone out onto the veranda and takes revenge on the storm. The clouds pour hail down the mouth of his instrument and then part. He serenades the ideal stars.

A frosty rime glitters on his lips. His wife comes out to join him and they embrace. Her hair is a hundred shades of the darkest red.

The Mad Hatter is writing out invitations with a pen made from the leg of a spider. He is much happier now. He has bought a new suit and shaved his whiskers. Alice has finally consented to marry him. She is very young, but he is confident.

He pokes out his tongue as he forms the words. He wants only eccentrics to attend his wedding reception. He has heard about a couple who live in a house shaped like a hat. The notion tickles him. He is thoroughly tickled. When he has finished, he drops the invitation into the mouth of a winged cat that flaps up the chimney and soars away over the rooftops.

My invitation has already arrived. I am the last existentialist. This is eccentric enough for the Mad Hatter. As a writer with no imagination, I look forward to the party. I will meet many characters there whom I shall be able to use. I pack my notebook, a piece of cheese, an apple and set off on my way.

Desire is not difficult to maintain. The couple in the hat on the hill are kissing. They are making love in front of a fire piled high with green wood. The wood spits as they suck and smokes as they blow. Each freckle between her breasts needs to be kissed. A constellation of incomparable delight.

Afterwards, they help each other to the bed and fall asleep under the heavy duvet. The clouds have returned and it starts to snow. As the snow settles, the preternatural landscape grows brighter. The snow dusts my coat and I turn up the collar. I pass the hill and gaze up at the house. Something small and dark has just landed on the brim. It scratches at a window and forces entry. I am reconciled.

As I walk, the unknown creature disappears inside. When the sun comes up, I sit on a hedge and chew at my apple. The couple awake and find a cat curled up between them.

Alice is playing the harpsichord, to calm her nerves. Her fingers fly over the keys, building up a dress of notes which cling to her naked body. These notes will shimmer and tinkle when she moves. These notes, semi-quavers and minims, glisten like ice. The piece she has chosen is old and cold and firm to the touch on the stave of her belly. As her arms are encrusted and grow heavy, her tempo decreases.

The Man Who Mistook his Wife's Hat
for the Mad Hatter's Wife

I have arrived at the designated spot. In a clearing in a wildwood stands the shell of a church. I am the first. I explore the crumbs of rock with a dispassionate eye. The spiral staircase to the belfry has collapsed.

Alice is ready and is on her way. The coda was the veil. Her bare feet make blue impressions on the mossy carpet of the forest floor.

The couple are also dressing for the occasion. The man has selected a frilly shirt of a different hue and a saxophone of black wood trimmed with silver. The woman has selected a hat in the shape of a young girl. The cat will guide them, like a kite on a string as long as a river.

Ribbons rustle, silk and crinoline folds and unfolds into a meaningless tangram. And you and I? We know how to cling to ourselves, but not yet to each other. It is not true that no man is an island. We are all islands, misty islands, connected only by an irregular ferry service.

While they prepare themselves, I am joined by the caterers, the Husher, Father Phigga, a few guests. Tables and chairs are laid out. Prebendary Garlic has written a speech as creamy and corpulent as his own aspirations.

The Mad Hatter arrives and fills his mouth with his fists.

The cat lands in the belfry and the couple emerge into the clearing. There is a great deal of aimless chatter. More guests appear. Hands are shaken; large knotty hands, thin reedy ones. Father Phigga takes his place at the ruined altar of the abandoned church. When Alice breaks through the dense foliage, the musicians strike up on their bone xylophones. The long and the short of it is that there is a wedding, the wrists of Alice and the Mad Hatter symbolically bound with a braided cord.

And then it is time for the guests to kiss the bride. The man who lives in a hat takes rather longer over this than his wife would like. While she watches her husband with a frown, I watch her with a pounding heart. Prebendary Garlic is watching me. Observing the observer of the observer.

Soon, very soon, the guests sit down to the banquet. The cat wanders off into the forest and falls asleep in the hollow of an oak-tree, snuggled up tight with a large owl. There are three tables arranged in parallel lines, each table with only one side in this dimension, and the guests are seated as follows:

Humpty Dumpty	A White Rabbit	Edgar Allan Poe
A Glass of Water	Bram Stoker	Dante Alighieri
Baruch Spinoza	Tweedledee	A Velocity Orange
The Hat Couple	Boris Vian	Achilles' Tortoise
A Sea Horse	Guy de Maupassant	D.F. Lewis
Tweedledum	The Holy Grail	Grace Under Pressure
The 600th Orgasm	A Volcano	A Traitor's Gate
Caliban	Leopoldo Alas	A Bloody Mary
A Wild Goose Chase	Søren Kierkegaard	The Narrator

The caterers mill and cough over the cutlery, wiping it clean with dirty handkerchiefs, while the Husher, Father Phigga and Prebendary Garlic stand at the head of each table declaiming avant-garde poetry. They are not guests and therefore not entitled to food.

We drink celery wine and toast the bride and groom. The caterers serve the meal. There are olives and mango slices for harlots d'oeuvre; toenail soup for starters; red onion bunions with pillow rice as the main course. For dessert we gorge ourselves on strawberry fool and raspberry idiot. The man who lives in a hat is staring at Alice.

Anticipating disaster, I take out my notebook.

The Man Who Mistook his Wife's Hat
for the Mad Hatter's Wife

There will never be a past as remote as the one which is now the present. Everything seems asleep and vague, outlines of events thrown onto a paper screen in a magic-lantern show. Even as they happen I feel nostalgia for such events. As the remnants of the meal are cleared away, I am already regretting a lost chance I have not yet had. Fires have been lit and dancing is in stately progress. I boost my courage with more celery wine and approach the woman who lives in a hat.

Suddenly, my nerve unravels and I merely nod at her and walk past. I continue through the fence of trees that rings the clearing. She is far too beautiful to make any attempt at contact. As I gaze up at the highest elms, I stumble over the supine bodies of Alice and the man who lives in a hat.

It is obvious that they have slipped away during the dance to consummate an illicit passion. They are entwined together, crumpled, oblivious of all else. I race back to the clearing, my teeth shining brightly. I fall at the feet of the wife and babble everything. In the same static moment I see that the real Alice is dancing with a White Rabbit. . . .

Relationships sometimes end for good reasons as well as bad. I should have been pleased that the hat was in the shape of a girl. I should have blessed the fate that directed the wife to leave her hat on the table and the man to mistakenly carry it off into the forest. But it avails me little. I have the story and nothing more.

The Mad Hatter and Alice fly off on a magic carpet, tins clinking on lengths of old string behind them. I am ignored. The couple who live in a hat become separated forever. She leaves him dumbfounded and when he returns to the hill he discovers that he is now homeless.

Hats, it appears, have gone out of fashion.

Cello I Love You

Opinions as old as green hams, that's what she has. Not that her own hams are green; far from it. She scrapes her living with supple fingers, a furrowed brow; the wanton hussy, sitting there, teasing the notes up from between her spread legs! How I despise her; and yet I am forced to admire her restraint, her subtlety. She knows how to make you sing. But I would be kinder, I would be gentle. Yes, I will help you escape from this brutal regime, this exhausting circuit of concert-halls, hotel rooms and morbid rehearsals. Just you wait.

Cello, I love you. Won't you tell me your name?

I have followed you around the country since I first saw you in her arms. It was a gala concert, the opening of some new public building. Fireworks sputtered in the air, the fountains played and the streets were full of people in cars, motorists with pedestrian tastes. You were one among many, clasped tight on the podium together with your cousins and sisters. But I guessed you were unlike them, that you were at once more sensitive and charming. I could not tear my gaze from your gracious curves, your lustre. I was enchanted.

With the magic came anger. I saw the way she treated you, the disdain with which she forced the sadness from your strings. There were no tears in her eyes that night, you can be sure of that. You were merely a tool to be exploited, a possession to be used in any way she saw fit. She knew how to play, but she did not know how to feel. I felt for you then; I resolved to find out more about you both. I listened to your profound songs and knew your despair, your tragedy.

She was an itinerant and therefore hard to track down. You were an unwilling slave, snatched from the trees of an Italian forest, sawn and shaped by the rough fingers of a moustachioed Signor in Cremona. She was upstart cynicism, fresh weariness. You were sighing strength, endurance through the centuries. After the concert I followed you both home. She was staying with friends. I waited outside the window and amused myself by imagining your name, your wondrous name.

When I knew it, I would be able to crystallise my fantasies, focus the lens of my desire. Until then, I would be grasping at a void. Names are all we can ever really have of a life, an object. Without them we are lost; we can expand few truths, generate few ideas. Lacking eyes, feet, hands, you were already more content than form; I could not allow this to be my sole impression of your existence. I required a name as smart as a green olive; a name that spoke of your seasoned expressions, your pickled ambitions. Where would I find such a name?

Possible names for cellos: Dolores, Celestine, Twinkle, Mervyn, Panjandrum, Thomas, Dionysus, Jemima, Sooty, Oswald, Remorse, Lucy, Paraquat, Edna, Gambol, Jonah, Garam Masala, Gillian, Sheridan, Gabriel, Harriet, Juliette, Erasmus, Mercy, Acheron.

I am not a thrifty man by nature, but I have saved enough in my long life to make possible the indulgence of my whims. I took to the road in your wake, booking rooms in the same hotel as you, eating in the same restaurants as your owner, sitting in the audience night after night as she caressed your body. I was not blind to her skill, but neither was I deaf to her arrogance. I would weep over the former and punish the latter.

I sent you a bunch of red roses once; this was a mistake. She assumed they were for her. It was in a guest-house in Croydon. I had booked the room directly below you and I could hear her pacing the floor. Balancing on a stool and pressing my ear to the low ceiling I could even make out her words. 'I have an admirer,' she was muttering to herself. The blood boiled in my head and I wanted to strike on the ceiling with my fist and cry back: 'Not for you, not for you!'

Had she known they came from me, her ardour would have cooled quickly enough. I have never been attractive to women, which is possibly why I mostly form relationships with inanimate objects. I have a single arm and a single leg and my stale green eyes are so close together that I am able to peep through a keyhole with both of them at once. Nor does my beauty lie beneath my skin; I have no skin.

Before you there were others; I will not try to hide this from you. There was a hat-stand in Reading; an antimacassar in Norwich. But these were youthful affectations. They fluttered away on the wind of my desire like the pages of some half-finished novel in the passing of a train. It is you that I love now, a feisty sort of cello that has spoken to me across the gulf of a crowd. I will not be satisfied with any other.

A plan hatched in my head over the months. I would have to kill your owner. She alone was keeping us apart. How I would effect the murder I knew not, but I would scheme until I found a way. For the nonce, I would content myself with keeping close to her heels. We travelled up and down the land. I kept discreetly to the shadows; continuing to attend every concert you played. With only one hand, I could not applaud you in the normal style; my efforts at clapping were more like the solution to a metaphysical enigma than a gesture of appreciation, but my cheeks burned with tears and my clockwork heart wedged in my inverted mouth.

Many ingenious methods of ending her tawdry life suggested themselves to me. Most of these, however, contained some fatal flaw that became apparent with a little more thought. The idea of sending more roses to her room, thorns coated with poison, was abandoned after I realised they would cause momentary pleasure before death. Similarly, my notion of surprising her down an alley—bounding out of the night on a spring loaded shoe and lunging with sharpened umbrella—seemed less promising when I recalled that eyes as close-set as mine are incapable of judging distance.

Eventually, I could restrain myself no longer. I picked a definite date for her demise and resolved to keep to it, no matter what. As the date drew near, I wrote you a passionate love-letter, an epistle declaring the way I felt about you, but I was too shy to post it and I kept it in an inner pocket of my frock-coat. In this letter I rhapsodised about your elegant gooseneck, your inviting f-holes, your coquettish keys, your sensuous G-string, the way you bowed out with such good grace.

I took my umbrella apart and replaced the struts with special rods of my own, so thin that they were scarce visible to the naked eye. I grew a sort of beard to disguise my features; I dyed my frilly shirt purple. I turned my waistcoat inside-out and practised uncharacteristic expressions in front of the mirror. When I had perfected these, I merely had to wait for the fateful day. It came round soon enough and I made sure that I had a seat in the front row of the concert hall.

We were in the garrison town of Aldershot and so the audience was packed with jeering soldiers who shook fists and brayed for more Beethoven. I knew that their riotous behaviour would provide useful cover for my own actions. During the Schoenberg—played to appease the mob—I began to dismantle my adapted umbrella. I removed the rods I had placed there and screwed them to each other, feeding them out across the empty space betwixt auditorium and orchestra. The improvised lance started to reach closer to your owner.

Within minutes, the point of my weapon was poised over her very heart. Thinner than a human hair, the rods remained unseen by all. A little push and happiness would finally be mine. I looked at you then; I blew a subtle kiss with my absurd lips. In my mind's eye, I saw you in a bridal veil—lace and petals. Yet I could not pierce her heart, I did not transfix her callous bosom. Instead, my hand trembled; the rods broke loose and shattered upon the floor. I gnawed my knuckles in anguish. Why? Why had I spared her ignominious soul?

The answer, let me tell you, has haunted my dreams ever since. Had I impaled her there, she would have relaxed her grip on you. Her hands would have flown to her breast and you could have slipped out of her grasp and injured yourself in a fall. Worse still, it is conceivable that her colleagues—in rushing to her aid—would have trampled you underfoot. It was a risk I was not prepared to take. So she escaped to live another day and you remained her prisoner. Forgive me, my darling.

It was obvious I would have to kill her at a time when she was parted from you. Such moments were rare. She was extremely possessive and did her best to keep you close at all times. Or else she entrusted you to the care of her fearsome lackeys. There were many of these: rogues and monkeys, lazy diamond-studded flunkeys. I despaired of ever finding a chance to spill her blood without exposing you to the horror. It was essential that I shield you not only from danger, but also from any sights that might disturb your impressionable spirit.

As the orchestra became better known, it seemed only a matter of time before they were invited to play abroad.

Although they had performed once in Scotland, they had never sailed across any sea to reach a foreign audience, much less one that slept in the day and applauded in a different language. But now they were off to Spain, the lush and verdant lands of Galicia. Your owner could hardly refrain from smiling and making tiny jumps for joy. She had been chosen to mark the event with a grandiose gesture. On disembarkation, she would plant you in the ground and the entire company would kneel and offer up thanks. In sooth, they were all excited.

I withdrew the last of my savings from my account and purchased a berth on the same ship. I need scarcely mention my fear of water. Yet I was willing to conquer my terrors for love. We set sail from Portsmouth in a storm; the ship shuddered and lurched across the perilous Solent. In the bar, I overheard her whispering to you. 'You are a sweet darling. I enjoy your caresses best in the morning.' She was drinking heavily. I could do little but gasp. Had I misjudged her feelings?

I was so intrigued by this possibility that I actually approached and tapped her on the shoulder. I offered to buy her a drink. To my utter astonishment she did not seem repelled. 'I recognise you,' she said. 'I attend every concert you play,' I replied. A frown creased her brow. 'Was it you who sent the roses?' she asked. I shook my head and she heaved a sigh of relief. 'You are very ugly,' she pointed out. 'But I don't really mind. Unless you try to kiss me.'

If this was a short story or other work of fiction— rather than a factual account—something unlikely would occur at this point. I would continue to buy her drinks. I would wait for her to lurch drunkenly back to her cabin. I would follow and seize her. Perhaps I would kill her by driving your own spike through her throat. Almost certainly I would cut off her head and conceal it within your body. When it was my turn to play, the head would augment the strings with ghastly singing. The story would end with it rolling its eyes to the coda.

But I did nothing of the kind. Choked with sorrow and sea-sickness, I left her alone. I hopped my way from the bar out onto the deck. I felt my whole life had become a retch. I steadied myself against one of the rails. Suddenly, a freak wave swept me over the side. I swallowed brine and coughed. When I looked up, the dark mass of the ship already seemed out of reach. A face was peering down from the departing vessel. It was she! The next thing I knew was that an object was floating in the water near my head. An object of gracious curves.

It was you. I reached out and hauled myself up and we began to drift away. Your owner had cast you to me in lieu of a life-jacket. She called down to me, but I could not make out her words. To this day, I do not know whether her actions were born of a fundamental contempt for you or a desire to make the ultimate sacrifice for what she thought was her one admirer. I both suspect and fear the latter. At any rate, I clung on fast and three days later we were washed up on the exotic shores of the Isle of Wight.

We lay exhausted on the multicoloured sands. I kept you warm with my frock-coat and reassured you with my oily words. At the same time I confessed my long-standing love. You were sceptical at first, but then I showed you the love-letter I kept in my innermost pocket. The ink had run, the letter was illegible, but you had faith; I like that in a cello. Eventually, help arrived and we were given mugs of coffee and ginger biscuits, as is the custom amongst those islanders.

Life is strange, my darling. We made our way back to the mainland and I set you up in my house. We heard no scrap of news from Spain; we had no idea how the orchestra had performed without you. Indeed, we never again received any word about them. I do not know where your old owner is now, or even if she still plays. Whatever the case, I am certain her opinions have not changed; they remain as old as green hams. She believes the world is flat, for one thing. And that there is a man in the moon.

If this was a story, I would have fallen in love with her instead of you. I would have forsaken a mere cello for a real woman. But it is not a story. My love for you is as strong as ever. In the twilight in my garret, I play you myself. It is not easy playing with a single arm, but somehow I manage. I no longer dream about keeping her head imprisoned within your body; instead I keep my own head there. And when we sing together, the tears from my eyes merging into a single bright stream on my cheeks, I no longer even care to know your name.

What To Do When The Devil Comes Round For Tea

What to do when the Devil comes round for tea? First you must attempt to establish his intentions. The concept of tea is an indefinite one. Does he mean a cup of tea, or a full-blown meal? If the former, then what blend? If the latter, then how many courses?

No-one can answer these questions; the Devil is ever a subtle guest. His tastes are varied and even obscure. There is a smörgåsbord of suppositions; a veritable goulash of guesses. To play safe is often to be lost. Conversely, to gamble with exotic spices and strange herbs can provoke the Devil to shuddering rage.

I live in a castle deep in the midst of a forest. Few travellers ever grace my home. The twirling branches of the oaks and elms are hands that squeeze the breath from the throats of all who venture beneath the dark canopy. I hold an empty court in my gloomy manse; there is a table decked out with cutlery and jugs waiting to be filled. There is a fire in the grate waiting to be lit. I am ready to entertain guests at a moment's notice. But no guests are ever to be found seated at this table; no wanderers to tell tales or sing songs.

One morning, I find a note fixed to the door with a blood-red nail. It is from the Devil. He has invited himself round for tea. He will appear at sunset and expects to be thoroughly satisfied by the time the new sun has risen. What should I do? I am at once both fearful and relieved;

fearful because I have heard what happened to those hosts who displeased the Prince of Darkness with stale bread and sour wine, relieved because I have at last a justification for my existence. I fret and pace the flagstones of my castle; at times I raise my head and utter a laugh of cautious joy. I rattle the pots and pans in my draughty kitchen.

There is, however, no time to be lost. I must saddle my horse and be off, through the forest, to the nearest village. Mandragora, my steed, snorts as I lead him out of the stables. With an empty sack tied to my pommel, flapping in my callow face, we fly over brooks and streams, between the trunks of towering trees. We reach the village by noon; the village whose markets are crowded with those who bring produce from the five corners of the land. The heady aromas of saffron, caraway and oregano mingle with those more homely odours by which we identify cheese, fruits and seaweed. But this is not the market I seek.

I fill my sack with that I have chosen, paid for with gold and tin coins, and race back the way I came. Mandragora resents the exercise; foam flecks his mouth and trails off behind him, like a hippogriff nosing through a cloud. By the time we reach the castle, the sun slants low in the west. I make for my kitchens and my hands become wonders to behold, dancing lovers with a purpose beyond desire. I chop, I stir, I taste; I reduce and simmer and strain and urge. Finally there is a knock at the door and I wipe my greasy hands on my apron, cast off my tall chef's hat and compose myself to welcome my guest.

The Devil lingers on the threshold awhile, toying with the hem of his cloak. He is much shorter than I had been led to believe; a tiny man really, with a long beard and eyes of different colours. I invite him in formally, seat him at the head of the table and retire back to the kitchen. One by one I bring in the courses I have prepared, filling up his jug with mead and standing dutifully behind him, waiting to push aside the remains of each dish and replace it with another.

The whole meal can be outlined as follows: for Gustatio (Hors d'oeuvres) there is Honeyed Whine and Red Being Salad. For Fercula (Prepared dishes) there is Vampire Stake, well done; Lemon Soul in Tartarus Sauce; Pale Pulses and Veins; the whole washed down with Wandering Spirits that—*tu facies bonum bibendo*—by your drinking will make you good. And then for Mensae Secundae (Dessert) we have Blacker Olives, Seedless Gripes and Heretic-Roasted Chestnuts. I hover uncertainly while the Devil samples each delicacy, his throat swelling like a misplaced echo.

At the end, he wipes his lips with a satin napkin and knits his brows together and winks his ill-set eyes. He nods his head and stands up, pushing back his chair with an arrogant heel. His voice is at once musical and jarring and specious; like the avalanche on a deserted mountain, or the fall of a tree on an uninhabited island. He is pleased; he is extremely pleased. He picks crumbs out of his absurd beard and splinters from between his black teeth. The food, he insists, was diabolical. With a smile and a bow, I indicate the collection of empty plates that form a row beside him.

He lets loose a guffaw. Wrapping his cloak tightly about his hunched frame, he departs into the night. The heavy door slams behind him of its own accord, but I hear his footsteps in the cosmic silence. I return to the Banqueting Hall and hold up the plates to the fiery tongues of the hearth. They shine brightly in the orange light and, when I slant them at different angles, scatter this light up the walls and across the musty tapestries.

I have mentioned that I was always ready to entertain guests at a moment's notice. And yet, the Devil's note had me scurrying to the village for supplies. It was not food that I sought but the hardware market, where I purchased half-a-dozen mirrors. For only by eating off his own image could the Devil be satisfied, yet not wish to employ me as his permanent cook; only by feasting off his own preservation could I hope to be preserved in turn. For any judgement would have to be turned against himself. The mirrors were the aspic of his own tolerance.

Reflect seriously upon this advice, friend; for it is only in reflection that you can be assured of a favourable result when the Devil comes round for tea.

Arquebus For Harlequin

Harlequin shot me in the twilit garden. He used a primitive handgun, barrel stuffed with dead leaves and hailstones. My wounds glittered; I sat down in the arbour, under the darkling sky.

My wife found me next morning, still in the arbour. I said: 'A harlequin shot me with an arquebus.' She considered this carefully. 'What sort of harlequin?' she asked. 'Yellow and black,' I said. 'And what pattern of arquebus?' 'French, I think.' She nodded wisely. 'Well I'm sure you had it coming. Perhaps he was your conscience.'

My wife is not a sympathetic woman.

But why should she be? I neither require nor desire her comforting words, her smooth hands. That night I dreamed about the harlequin, a middle-aged figure too plump for the role. He was playing a pantaleon in pantaloons; the slumbering brain is fond of allusions. He shot me again, in my sleep. I awoke to a lightning storm. 'Pisht!'

My wife told me the storm was God's way of taking a photograph. I liked that. 'Are you saying I made the wrong choices in life? Are you implying that the world is no longer my bivalve shellfish?' We fought with pillows for the truth; the truth would not out but the stuffing flew loose. I liked that less.

My wife's name, by the way, is Cora. Once, when we were young, we ate multi-layered chocolate cake in arcade cafés. Cacao bliss; our knees knocked under the table. Cake was not all. Cappuccino to first sear, and then drape in milky shrouds, our tongues. We had a full relationship,

based on calorific value. Cora was a divorcee; her husband
had been a cheesecake photographer, strawberry and
ginger mostly. We did not dance through the park. There
are limits.

I said to my wife: 'Did you hire a harlequin to assassi-
nate me? Did you think to settle my hash with the aid of a
precursive archetype in mask and motley?' She rigorously
denied these allegations. But in the waste-paper bin the
following morning, I found two discarded notes. One said:
'Will 'arlequin be requiring another harquebus, milady?'
The other: 'No Parker, thank you kindly.'

My wife distrusts me because I have forsaken engineering for the pen. I was on the verge of improving the
linear motor, twisting it into a Möbius strip and creating
perpetual motion, when I suddenly abandoned it all and
began writing short stories instead.

This was a terrible mistake, I know; the world requires
no more fiction. Motion, the breath of engines, is more
important than emotion, the mist of maturity. I have
entered wordy swamps crowded with fools, I have raised a
callus on my middle finger for nothing. The dynamos of
reason are waiting for me. Why have I forsaken them?

My first story was about a talking chair. Whenever
people sat on it, a voice would compliment them on the
contours of their buttocks. Because of this, the chair was
locked in an attic during dinner parties. One evening it
escaped and wreaked havoc. The moral of the story was
that it is foolish to criticise a chair for such behaviour.
Chairs know guests only by the lower part of their
anatomy.

This story did not sell.

My wife wants to kill me because she believes it will
teach me a lesson. I wish her luck. I see Parker smiling
ambiguously at me over the breakfast table. He is her
willing slave, he will obey her orders to the letter. I despise
his bulging eyes and thinning hair, the fact that his coat has

tails. He distrusts my ignorance of pâté and dressage. After my demise, Cora will take his creaking frame into her bed, press his dribbling lips to her ample bosom, guide his servile hands between her thighs. This is unfair. He is not even her gardener.

I know what I need to do to win her back. I need to pleasure her long into a humid night. I need to return to engineering. The first of these I cannot attempt; I plead my wounds. The second is even more tricky. It would be an admission of defeat.

This writing business has cost me many friends. I used to drink and laugh in honest surroundings. Now I attend literary lunches and frequent wine bars. I have slowly substituted naturally balding companions in check shirts for grimier fellows who wear felt and paisley and whose baldness owes more to the razor than the gene.

Exactly a week after the harlequin incident, my wife said to me: 'He'll be back, you know. He won't give up that easily. It is essential you placate him by burning your manuscripts. Take them out to the bottom of the garden. Offer them up to him as a sort of sacrifice. Your life has become a sad joke; let the particoloured jester weld shut the ducts of your tears, leaving you dry as wit.'

I knew she was right. But I can be stubborn. 'I want to reclaim a sense of purpose,' I told her, 'but I can also succeed here. I need some more time. I need to complete my latest piece. Let harlequin lunge with the slapstick; I'll be ready for it. Fuel for the fires of my fancies!' She scowled. 'Then you shall die,' she replied. When my wife is feeling exceptionally vicious, she uses my name: 'Diggory!'

My fancies are my stories. I despise realism, I admire and wish to emulate the fabulists. There is more truth in delicate webs of fantasy than in the gutter or bottle. I would rather read about a talking cake than the struggles of an unemployed miner. The truths of the former are sweeter by far; tongue meeting tongue not in language but in taste. I denounce the Drawcansirs of fiction, thugs devoid of imagination and beauty. May they rot in Hull: may they not earn release until they learn how to scatter adjectives like stars, to stretch similes to the snapping point and nod in time to the music so plucked.

I keep a thesaurus in my hip pocket. I am very particular about my pockets. Thesaurus in hip; dictionary in breast. Reference books are the weights of comfort, the bricks of form. Do not assume I am ever without them. My fountain pen shares not this security. Sharp as the bolt of a crossbow, it has gone missing. I cannot remember the correct term for a crossbow bolt; neither can Cora. Over this we quarrel.

My latest story concerns a talking harp. There is an old man, an instrument-maker, who lives alone in a shop full of violins, trombones and tubular bells. The harp is his masterpiece. It is a small harp. Each string has been designed to sound not a note, but a phoneme of language. Thus the harp is able to relate stories at night. After a week of tales, the old man tells the harp that he believes nothing of what it has said. 'Why not?' cries the harp. The old man points an accusing finger at the inanimate raconteur and answers: 'Because you are a lyre!'

This is good. I have the beginning and the end; I lack merely the middle. What stories exactly did the harp tell the old man? One story a night for a week means seven originals. Am I capable of such invention? Will the stories be sufficiently different from each other or will I be harping on the same theme? An interesting question.

I have six so far. The first is about a talking cheese. The second is about how February, the shortest month, takes umbrage and becomes the Napoleon of months, conquering the whole year. It is a talking month, this February. The third concerns a talking kiosk. Fourth, fifth and sixth: belfry, printing-press and legume respectively, all blessed with the gift of speech. Is this not variety?

Harlequin shot at me again in the twilit garden. The same motley, the same arquebus. This time the shot was seedless grapes, young wine exploding against my chest as each purple torpedo struck its target. I fell backwards with a good nose, sticky fingers. I saw Parker staring at me from the highest oriel. These damned American butlers, they are far too traditional. Cora has his loyalty entire; I could never hope to buy it off him. While he gloated, I fermented. 'Tush!'

I said to my wife: 'Is that harlequin really my conscience?' She nodded. 'Oh yes, I stole your conscience from your head one night while you were asleep. You felt nothing; it was a very small conscience. But I planted it in a window-box. I nurtured it and spoke to it. Strong it grew and archetypal. It has you in its sights.' I trembled all over, I bit my fingers. 'How can I evade it?' I cried. 'Return to engineering,' my wife replied. 'One more story!' I implored. 'One more!'

I set up a mantrap in the garden. It will snap harlequin in two. It will teach him never to descend from the stage again. Wooden characters are best left as puppets. The mantrap I chose had big yellow teeth; I wondered if it would kill Cora or Parker. But Cora loathes grass; she takes her morning constitutional on stilts. And Parker is an indoors creature. To him the Hydrangea is fear of water.

The harp's seventh tale must concern Cora and myself. But I detest tales about relationships. How can I possibly hope to convey even a fraction of our misery, the shallow-fried taste of our present? I would have to mention that I was an engineer who had become a writer and that Cora wanted to kill me. I would have to begin with the incident in the twilit garden, the first incident. I would have to depict Parker as the sinister figure he is. I might forget to mention that the thesaurus in my hip pocket saved my groin during the second incident.

I am not skilful enough to write about such things. And yet the harp must have a seventh tale. Can I think of no more clever ideas with which to regale the hypothetical reader? At last I have it: a talking windmill. I am astounded by my own originality.

I need my pen, my lethal dart, but it is missing. I instruct Parker to look for it. He nods with malice; he will not search far, he will merely look in biscuit-barrels and suchlike. I have his measure, it is less than a quart. That night, I hear the jaws of the mantrap clash together. I race out into the frost; Harlequin is dead. I tell my wife: 'I have slain my conscience and now care naught for you.' She smiles a sly smile, more secret than any garden. 'You have killed yours, but mine is abroad still. They grew side by side.' I scoff at this. 'Yours will never be strong enough to wield a Gallic arquebus,' I say.

What was it about that yellow-and-black wight that makes me almost hope to glimpse his ill-mannered form again? Were the colours of his motley significant? Did they reflect my cowardice and heart of darkness in shameful lozenges? And the arquebus? An ironic symbol of progress, no doubt; a sardonic comment on those who forsake the true poetry of calculus for the lesser doggerel of language. I once sought the holy integral; I have broken my vows and must suffer.

Columbine shot me in the twilit garden. She used an arbalest. I frowned. Arbalest? I reached for the dictionary I keep in my breast pocket. It was no use: the pen had fixed it to my heart.

Éclair de Lune

The girl who lives above Udolpho's pâtisserie has earned her name many times over. For one thing, she lives entirely on cream cakes provided from below—devouring them solely by the light of a gibbous moon. For another, she keeps a piano in the corner of her dusty room on which she is forever composing melancholy nocturnes, sometimes with quite eldritch harmonies. Thirdly, she is quite mad.

Signor Udolpho himself tolerates this strange denizen of his upper floors partly because of her compelling music and partly because of the bohemian credence it lends his establishment. His pâtisserie is really no different from a myriad other such places scattered around the city. But the fitful light of the demi-monde, his patrons, and the paler yet far more alluring light of his singular lodger combine to throw the shadow of his name in a grotesquely enlarged fashion over the fevered lips and undulating throats of the cake cognoscenti.

Nobody knows her real name—even Beerbohm Soames, who once claimed to be her lover, is vague on this point. There are rumours, of course. According to one story, she was a Carmelite nun expelled from the order after conducting a torrid affair with a mysterious man often seen climbing over the rooftops of the abbey. Others would have it that she was once the leader of a group of roving banditti who lived the high life in the mountain passes. Both these tales are less popular than they were, though they still have their adherents. I happen to know that both are equally, shamefully false—I invented them.

In those days, I still harboured ambitions to be a writer. I was a profound romantic at heart. 'Joris-Karl,' Signor Udolpho would say to me in a fatherly fashion, as he served scones and coffee, 'one of these days you will end up shooting yourself for love, as did poor Herr von Kleist. Ah, but I remember him as if it was only yesterday! He had a watch that did not work and a cough. Also he never paid me for his last custard slice. I put it on credit for him and he blew his brains out in a park overlooking the river the following morning.'

I soon grew out of that nonsense. Now if I kill myself for love it will be because I am loved, rather than because I am not (this is not quite true; as you shall see). And yet it was not Signor Udolpho's wise words that prompted me to see sense. Rather it was a blow on the head I received from a meteorite as I was walking down the Rue Discord. As my chin struck the cobbles, I remembered how I loved life too much to sacrifice it on the altar of an artistic movement. At once I picked myself up and became stoutly pragmatic— burning my poems and finding profitable employment selling life insurance to the employees of the Kingdom Noisette Engineering Co.

We will discuss them in detail later. For the moment, suffice it to say that I have met Kingdom Noisette—and his charming wife, Morag—in the flesh. The first time was at a garden party thrown to celebrate the opening of the underground railway link between Hauser Park and the Town Square. A string quartet, more rococo than baroque, played us the charming melodies of Telemann and Lodovico da Viadana. A bit of nostalgia always goes a long way at such events. Morag even asked me to dance, though I was too nervous to do anything other than flap up and down like a shirt on a washing line. I will never forget the look on the old man's face and his exclamation (in what I believe must be a northern British accent) when a waiter

offered him some Beluga caviar: 'Is there nae black puddin'
to be had here, lad?'

But though I had successfully repressed my yearning for
the gothic, the sublime, the fantastic, yet was I still curious
about the girl who lived above Udolpho's pâtisserie. The
syllables of her name endlessly reverberated in the confines
of my bruised cranium: Éclair de Lune. Why did she refuse
to budge when all the other adjuncts of Romanticism—
wild scenery, gravestones, poverty—had long since fled my
mind? I had even torn into strips my frilly shirts. But that
girl haunted me beyond the boundaries of reason and self
control.

It was not that she was especially beautiful or even
elegant—her ankles were remarkable enough, it is true.
Although she rarely descended from her lofty seclusion, I
had witnessed her more than once standing at her window
in the moonlight. Hidden in the shadows on the other side
of the street, I had watched with a sort of horrible fascina-
tion as she had raised the cream cakes one by one to her
small mouth, consuming them with restrained, yet
curiously merciless, bites. The delicate probing of her
tongue for rogue crumbs was visible as she swallowed,
sensuous as the writhings of a snake. It was all strange,
unhealthy and perfectly morbid and yet, at the same time,
a little too obvious.

She was up to something, of that I had no doubt. Below
her window, a flue from Signor Udolpho's ovens
discharged hot scents into the hungry night. As the rising
air passed her figure, it refracted and warped her form into
a towering mirage. Ensconced in the protection of a doorway, I licked my lips twice: her body, the smell of maca-
roons. Fired by these twin lusts, I was almost engulfed by a
purer form of rage. I had nothing that could possibly interest her; she would mock my attentions, ignore my over-
tures. Invariably, as I sweated in my febrile desire, she
would turn away from the window and make for her

piano. And then her music, more innovative than ginger-bread devils (Signor Udolpho's latest and most successful invention), would vibrate among the eaves, each chilly note like a drop of water falling forever upwards. Imagine, if you will, a combination of Satie, the latest jazz melodies and something yet more primeval and mysterious, the rhythms of cell division.

I was not alone in my infatuation. Beerbohm Soames, whom I often met in the City Library, claimed to be of similar disposition, though with him it might have been mere affectation. He was still a poet—sense had not yet penetrated his wrinkled brow. A dapper fellow, it must not be denied, with a penchant for working cats and clouds into his lyrics. He was desperate to publish a slim volume between yellow covers before his printer discovered how to mix other inks. 'I was her paramour for almost a year,' he would say. 'I know her body but not her mind.' He was always describing the texture of her skin. Most women naked are two colours; he insisted she was only one, magnolia. I did not approve of the way he handled my fantasy, with the grubby fingers of a man who reads too many newspapers. 'A pretty little cake,' was his main comment.

I more than half-suspected he was lying. But in those days, truth had gone largely out of fashion. The guiding spirit of the age, amongst artists at least, was insouciance and style. I was in that grey-green area between the studied wit of the writer and the smelly honesty of the engineer. I had forged links with both camps; I was a bridge of sorts, but one as yet untrampled by the felt slippers of the former or the hobnailed boots of the latter. A cantilever bridge over which failed poets threw themselves to their doom. In what other way has science and art merged with such verve and creativity?

My evenings were thus spent at the Library, among the cafés of the Passage de l'Pretence, talking with dreamers,

Nietzschean philosophers and print-makers in Udolpho's pâtisserie, or lurking outside that creamy establishment, hoping for a glimpse of Éclair de Lune. My days, however, were spent deep underground with the employees of the Kingdom Noisette Engineering Co., as they extended the network of tunnels across the city. I had to remind them that theirs was a dangerous task, that buying life insurance might not be a bad idea in their circumstances. I would walk the line of workers, chatting to them about the probability of a roof-fall in the not too distant future. It was often a painful death, I would tell them; slow suffocation under tons of rubble. I was aided by the fact that the first attempt to dig under the river had resulted in the drowning of a score of men.

They were a stoic breed, no more nor less worthy of attention than the pampered rhymesters of my former life. I was somewhat repelled by their feeding habits: anchovy and egg sandwiches for lunch. But I was also impressed by their courage. A second tunnel was being driven under the river, parallel to the first. It was hazardous work; most of the surveyors believed they had not dug deep enough. This was a concern shared by Kingdom Noisette himself. When the tunnel was half completed, he descended to the bed of the river in a bathysphere and managed to drive a metal rod through the mud into the tunnel. When he resurfaced, he claimed to have heard the voices of the men, ringing faintly against the iron hull of his vessel like the despairing cries of aquatic ghosts. This information had little impact —I sold one or two more policies that day. They were either very brave or very miserly.

The problems I suffered when I began to scheme a suitable way of wooing Éclair de Lune cannot be glossed over. To snare a woman who is all ethereal sensation and little corporality, it is necessary to fall back on the more abstract symbols of courtship. No use pacing outside her window, rustling a sheaf of my policies and discussing my improving finances with my bank-manager in stage whispers. My feathers would have to be preened by more aesthetic means. How I detested the conventions of the mating-game! I knew it would come down to poetry again—I guessed I might have to revert to the ode, the sonnet, the glossolalia of love. No spanner would turn her nut; no reliable feet would crunch the glass of her disdain. The feet would have to be shod in soft words, the armpits would have to sweat with sentiment.

If I, Joris-Karl Jekyll, was ever to achieve my head's desire, I would have to disguise it as my heart's, fool her into believing I was still what I once was. If ever I was to make her my very own Bakewell, covering her lithe body with whipped cream and balancing cherries on her nipples, I would have to borrow a ladder and a morceau. There was no help for it. Loathsome creature that would result! I shuddered at the changes I would have to make—allowing hair to brush collar again, drinking coffee black, quoting Rimbaud in public urinals. No more greeting friends with savage blows on the back, no more dark beer or pickled onions. Back to the tender embrace, the unbuttoned cuffs, the roll of the chocolate liqueur on the glib tongue, washing teeth as rotten as amorality. The decadent poise.

I did not know if I was capable of effecting the metamorphosis. I was rusty as a rain-swept tram—my cheeks had forgotten how to swell with rhythmic words. I spent a whole week in preparation, taking time off work and shutting myself away in my attic. I did not stir abroad during this time; I lived on thin gruel, neglected to wash and took opium. I forced myself to write poetry—I filled notebooks with the repellent stanzas. My progress was slow; I had largely lost the talent of younger days. The spark had died, but I persisted. I stood in front of the mirror for long hours, holding the back of my hand against my brow. I composed with a quill and green ink.

At last I was ready. I borrowed the ladder from work and also a length of india-rubber insulating cable used for conducting telegraphy between the tunnels. I waited until nightfall. It would have been far simpler to simply stand under her window and shout the poems up at her. But then I would be giving myself away. Signor Udolpho would come out to see what the fuss was about; my former friends would learn of the escapade and take it as a public recantation and amusing attempt to seek re-admittance to the fold. Besides, I was not at all confident of the quality of these new poems.

Accordingly, I acted with extreme stealth. I placed the ladder gently against her balcony and scaled up it with careful steps. Over my shoulder swung the amplifying horn of my phonograph, and I trailed the hollow cable behind me. When I reached the window, I placed the horn on the balcony, facing inwards and just touching the glass. Next I affixed the cable to the horn and secured it to the wrought-iron projections of the balcony railings. I should then have immediately descended, but I was distracted by an alluring noise, a song fainter than the sigh of pleasure of a toad swallowing a moth. I climbed onto the balcony, placed my face against the glass and peered inside.

What I saw startled me more than anything since a film maker from Berlin had screened an unusual reel about a contortionist named Thalia and a pair of Siamese twins the previous summer. It was Éclair de Lune—my desire—lying in a bath in one corner of the room. A single candle illuminated the gloom, but I could plainly see her naked form. She was crooning to herself as she wiped her arms and legs with a sponge (I could not discern the filling). As I blinked, and grew increasingly excited, she stood up and faced me with a sly sort of smile. Three things crucified my reason at the same instant: the raised tattoos that covered her thighs, skeletal figures, writhing orchids, coupling devils, stylised and interlocking cakes of every description, all completely colourless and visible only as a still paler white on her marble flesh; the size and lustre of her sex, swollen and hungry as a hothouse carnivore; the fact that her skin was as dry as my mouth. No water sparkled on her limbs: her bath had been a sham.

My cheeks burned. I could not stay, I could not linger on such a threshold of exquisite pleasure without gnawing my knuckles to pieces. I limped back down the ladder as rapidly as I dared, thrust it under my arm and unwound the other end of the hollow cable deep into the shadows of a nearby backstreet. With thumping heart I raised the tube to my lips and began to recite what I had been a week composing. The lyrics would travel the length of the cable, expand in the mouth of the horn and then explode like a lover's tongue on her window, bending the thin glass as a diaphragm, filling her chamber with my metrical lusts.

It was impossible for me to remove the image of her finely sculpted features and slightly menacing smile as I breathed down the mouthpiece. I stumbled over my words—they were pitiful enough, it is true, poor echoes of my earlier productions (once collected in manuscript form as *Twilight of the Anti-Idols*). But I forged ahead. I would do anything now to possess that deathly maiden, even publicly decry the Universal Joint. I ranted my passions with more desperation than tact—I grew feverish, my fingers were aching to entangle themselves in her hair, play ghost xylophone on her ribcage, trace her tattoos to their logical and moist conclusion. I called: 'When on your breast there weighs the scone / And your oven bakes with ravishment / When you impale my soul-cake on your sweetest fang / And aromas sickly invest an iced-bun air / Then shall I be your slave-meringue.' It was adequate.

Just at that moment, I was startled by the point of an umbrella in the small of my back. I dropped the cable and turned around. It was none other than Beerbohm Soames, a sardonic smile creasing his face, dressed in his customary yellow. '*Car le tombeau toujours comprenda le poëte,*' he muttered cryptically. And then: 'I am reminded of the famous atheist philosopher, Salammbô de Balzac, who was caught attending Mass in a church on the other side of town. Your crime, however, is far worse. Wait till the others hear of this! What a jest! No more the poet who ventured into Engineering via Insurance. Now the hypocrite who came back! What joy we shall express as we sip our Grand Marnier.' Though his tone was standard ironic, he knitted his brows furiously.

I held up my arms to protest my innocence. 'Éclair de Lune!' I cried. 'I did it all for her!' He regarded this with mocking contempt. I stooped to retrieve the cable as evidence, but it was vanishing around the corner. I stumbled after it, hands outstretched to snatch it back; it slithered out of my grasp and I fell. I heard a clattering on the cobbles behind me—Beerbohm Soames was also in pursuit. I regained my feet and together we flew down the twisting alleyways, the end of the cable retreating before us. I pulled ahead but the cable always eluded me. Finally I emerged in front of Udolpho's pâtisserie to see it being wound up through Éclair de Lune's window. I held my head in my hands and whimpered. Beerbohm Soames came puffing up behind; he mopped his brow with an ochre handkerchief and leaned heavily on his yellow umbrella. He had not seen enough to be convinced.

'Anecdotes shall be born from this,' he gasped. He made a gesture with his hand that dismissed my unspoken plea for mercy. I turned away sadly—I had been condemned to new depths. I would become a symbol for every poetaster who frequented a café and scratched rhymes on napkins. Beerbohm Soames would waste no time in embellishing events with his own florid conceits, seeing in my actions a justification for his belief that art was superior to science. I had betrayed myself and had gained nothing from the treachery. I could picture their faces and hear their laughter—Edwin Saltus Abbott, the defrocked priest and photographer, who wrote of little girls, rusty cymbals and talking cubes; Villiers le Gallienne, who composed vignettes on the labels of absinthe bottles; Novalis MacDonald, whose night-sweats formed the basis of his latest work in progress, *The Freshman Faustus*.

I reached Hauser Park and sat on a bench overlooking the blackly rushing river. If I kept my head down, grew a moustache and started to wear a hat, I might avoid them for a certain length of time. A genuine effort on my behalf to sell as many life-insurance policies as possible and I might save enough money to flee this accursed city. I would have to work hard; I would have to vary my route home each day. Furthermore I would have to abandon any thought of taking Éclair de Lune with me—the expense would prove prohibitive. Or would it? Something had fallen into place in my mind that would, if true, explain a great many things about her. I would soon have the opportunity to ascertain the validity of this revelatory notion—I had no choice now but to try to gain access to her room. I had to retrieve the insulating cable or else lose my job. And if I lost my job, I would be stuck in this City for the rest of my life, easy prey for Beerbohm Soames' moribund witticisms.

With not a little trepidation, I made my way back the way I had come. My mind was so occupied with my forth-coming ordeal that I did not realise for some time that I had taken the wrong turning at the end of Machen Street. I found myself wandering over crumbling Werther Bridge and then suddenly thrust into the midst of the Rue Discord. This was something I had not anticipated— though the avenue was quite deserted, I felt buffeted as by waves of savage pedestrians. I clung onto a nearby lamp-post for support. I choked back my nausea (I know a politico called Jean-Paul who cannot do the same) and reached inside my jacket pocket for my wallet. The satisfying thickness of the leather pouch, stuffed with paper francs and share-certificates, had a soothing effect on my nerves. I took an indefinite number of deep breaths and managed to keep my balance as I retraced my steps back into the security of streets both less significant and more harmonious to ear and soul.

The Rue Discord—so named because the wind whips down it at absurd speed and plays astonishingly creepy, atonal music on the cast-iron awnings of the shops (I know a composer called Karlheinz who bases all his work on this frightful phenomenon)—has been a thoroughfare I have scrupulously avoided since my accident. The dent in the road where my chin, borrowing the eagerness of the meteorite, came to respect both cobbles and gravity, is still visible. The impact loosened all my teeth; I had to have them re-sealed in my gums with a foul glue made from capers and debtors' limbs. I had tried to think about the incident as little as possible—this chance meeting once more propelled it to the top of the agenda in my consciousness' list of worries. It is true that everything had seemed subtly different after the accident. Strangers had ignored me; my friends were courteous but somehow remote, squinting at me whenever they spoke and tugging at their ears as if I were a distant figure obscured by swirling mists.

I was also much concerned with the question of why Éclair de Lune had stolen my insulating-cable. I could not imagine that anyone else was responsible for drawing it up into her room; she lived alone. There were a number of options, none particularly comforting. It was possible she had been so appalled by the quality of my poetry that she had removed the means of its transmission, hoping thereby to preclude recitation of more. This was a depressing idea—it was equally possible, however, she required the cable for some mysterious purpose of her own. Knowing what I did of her tastes and habits, this would almost

184

certainly involve either cakes or music, though I could not see in what capacity a simple India-rubber tube might serve such pursuits. The mind boggled with the ensuing speculations. An apparatus for inserting clotted cream at high pressure into the heart of an hermetically sealed profiterole? A method of relaying tone-colours into the pâtisserie below?

As I crossed back over Werther Bridge, whose jagged stones were an unhealthy metaphor for my teeth—resembling them in colour, condition and means by which they were fixed—I pushed aside these two concerns (the meteorite, the insulating cable) and re-entertained the startling notion that had pricked me in Hauser Park. Éclair de Lune was both coy and obtrusive; though rarely venturing down from her attic, her profile was high. Everything she did— her exclusive diet, her waterless baths—seemed calculated to create a single impression in the minds of those who came across her. In the Park it occurred to me what this impression was supposed to be: the fact that she lived at all.

Let me explain. Her actions were not those of a woman who wished to lead a full and useful existence; this much was obvious. They were, indeed, those of an entity that merely had pretensions to life. They were the bare minimum anyone (or anything!) could rely upon to preserve the deceit. What I am trying to say is this: I no longer believed in Éclair de Lune's humanity. I was prepared to accept her earthly origin, but not the present vitality of her soul. The flask of her outer form, I suspected, was not brimming with *anima mundi*. (Yet I still desired to place my lips to that vessel and imbibe whatever stood in its stead.) In other words, I deemed her a ghost.

What else but a spirit would live on undunked madeleines, tease odd tone-poems from a strangely-tuned piano, bathe without water? What else but a phantom would eat confectionary by the steady illumination of an unequally convex moon, standing by a window as it did so, image hugely magnified by rising air (for the benefit of witnesses)? What else but an apparition would add a syncopated beat to the left hand accompaniment of a modal Gymnopédie? And surely only a shade would pretend to regular ablutions in a chilly and cobwebbed iron bath? In my mind the matter was settled: my love was dead. This did not quite affect my lust, nor did it explain the mystery of the insulating-cable, but it did lend a certain colour (funereal violet?) to anticipated events.

I had little experience of phantasms. A patron of Udolpho's whom I knew slightly, a grumpy scholar by the name of Mark Xeethra Samuels, had once shared his theories of spooks with me. He believed there were a great many dimensions parallel to our own, each slightly different from the other. All probable, possible and inconceivable things were true in at least one of them. For example, in one dimension, elm trees tasted of strawberries; in another, words left people's mouths on feathery wings; in a third, ghosts were perfectly natural phenomena. He justified this last on grounds that genuine supernatural events rarely seemed strange to those who experienced them. There was a sort of acceptance that was not questioned until afterwards. Did this not indicate (he ventured) the likelihood that those who witnessed spirits had accidentally crossed over, for a brief instant, into that dimension?

I remember how he leaned towards me and lowered his voice. 'In yet another,' he whispered, 'our city might be a fictional locale for the posturings of absurd characters. Chaud-Mellé itself may be nothing more than a sewer of gothic influences, and our own lives burlesque parodies constructed with the sole aim of entertaining the jaded reader!' As the evening wore on, he continued to babble such nonsense into his cups. He jabbed a sharp finger at my chest. 'You, my dear Joris-Karl, are being exploited at this very moment by a foolish postmodern humorist—you serve no purpose other than as a fulcrum on which to hang an orgiastic tale of cake-crossed lovers, set in a nightmare pâtisserie!'

At the time I paid little heed to his words; I assumed him at least as affected as the rest. Now I craved his wisdom, but in vain—he had recently left the city for the wilds of Highgate, where he hoped to find and unearth the remains of Thomas Caliban Ariel, whom he claimed as an ancestor, and upon whose brass bones were supposedly engraved, in ogham and other silly scripts, all the secrets of analytic philosophy. There was no-one else I could turn to for help. But it did not really matter; I had little choice but to confront Éclair de Lune in order to retrieve the cable.

As I made my cautious way back towards Udolpho's establishment, I beheld a curious sight. A man I recognised as a local couturier rushed past with rolling eyes and foaming mouth. He wore a filthy coat and was being pursued by a small band of long-chinned fellows who wore extremely tall top hats. Even as I watched, one of these hats blew off in the wind of motion and exposed a ridiculous helical hairstyle. As they clattered into the distance, I shrugged my shoulders. It was none of my business and I saw no reason why I should intervene (though I did feel a little sympathy for the harried tailor—quite evidently I was not alone in having to avoid certain social groups).

I returned to the exact spot where I had left the ladder and again manoeuvred it back into position against Éclair de Lune's balcony. I ascended as silently as was feasible—I tried not to exclaim with delight as I passed through the emissions of the flue. I reached the balcony, pulled myself over the railings and felt along the window for a method of ingress. To my amazement, the window was unlocked; I pushed and it yielded. With heart pounding like one of Kingdom Noisette's patent toffee-breakers, I swung myself through the casement. Halfway, I became stuck; I wriggled the way of the worm and landed with a crash on the warped floorboards of the interior.

There was a grating and suddenly I found myself caught in the beam of a dark-lantern. She stood there with the ambiguous smile of a pastry merchant who confuses contango with backwardation on a stock of lemon curd tartlets. 'Joris-Karl Jekyll,' she said. It was not a question— neither was it an accusation. I shuddered, but took the opportunity of eyeing her up. This was definitely the girl I wanted, whether spectre, reanimated corpse or what-have-you. 'You look a trifle pale,' she added. She opened fully the dark-lantern and indicated a chair. Numbly, I did what was expected: I sat and waited to see what would happen next. She was evidently amused by my expression—burning lust co-meddled with extreme terror. 'Yes, trifle,' she repeated.

I held up my hands in resignation. 'It is true that I love you and know you are a ghost, but at the moment I am only interested in the insulating-cable. May I have it back?' Her eyes twinkled merrily as she set the lantern down and offered me a plate of croissants. In her lithe movements, she resembled a bed sheet that has been called into life by a runic whistle—she billowed and flowed. She took a seat opposite mine and forced a whole cake into her mouth; her cheeks were still pallid and beautiful, even when so grotesquely enlarged. She chewed with an air of superiority and danger and then grinned at my discomposure. 'It is very important that I get it back!' I persisted.

'Of course. I knew that all along. It is why I took it in the first place.' She spluttered crumbs. 'Oh, Joris-Karl, why did it have to come to this? Why were you so slow to pick up on my clues? Now it may be too late to do anything: Beerbohm Soames has not been idle.' She reached out to smooth my frown with a cool hand. I began to tremble in my chair. I sat bolt upright and clutched my knees. But she continued massaging my brow, her fingers like chocolate flakes. What did she mean? What clues was she talking about? I was at a complete loss. I elaborated on my earlier assertions that I loved her and yet knew she was not a living being. 'Hush now!' she replied, raising a finger to her lips. She patted my hand and told me to prepare myself for a shock.

I shook my head. 'No, it is you who must prepare, *mon petite chou*.' I threw myself at her feet and confessed that I had loved her for a long time, weeks at the very least, and wished to elope with her. However, at this present moment in time, my first priority was to return the cable to the place from whence it had come: without it, the team of engineers digging a tunnel under Rubellastrasse would not be able to communicate with the surface. They would have to tunnel without any directions and might veer off course. 'And then they could end up in Liechtenstein!' I cried. On their wages this would be a disaster. And they would hold me responsible. It was too much to bear. 'Please give me the cable,' I whimpered. 'Pretty please!'

She sighed and moved to a large globe near the piano in the corner of the room. It was one of those hinged models; she opened it to reveal an impressive array of alcoholic confections. She fixed me a stiff gin syllabub and came to sit on the arm of my chair. Draping an arm around my shoulders, she told me, in a calm voice, that she had been awaiting this moment even longer than had I. 'I tried to excite your curiosity by acting the part of a ghost that in turn was acting the part of a living woman. Thus I hoped to gain your attention. But I overestimated your intelligence. You ignored all the hints.'

'So you are not a real ghost?' I struggled to make sense of this deception. 'But why did you want me to seek you out?' I hoped that she would cite love as a reason. I was to be disappointed. With a sudden quick movement, she pinched me savagely on the arm. It seemed to me then that I had been rudely awakened into knowledge. Tears filled my eyes. I had been such a blind fool! What I knew now I had known all along in the back of my mind—but my consciousness had rejected the truth. 'So the meteorite killed me!' I whimpered. 'It is I who am the ghost!' I bent over and thrust my face into her bosom, my tears running like globules of mercury down her exceptional cleavage.

She dried my eyes for me with a petit four and patted me on the head. 'That is correct. However, it was not a meteorite that brained you on the Rue Discord. It was a well-aimed piece of masonry dropped from the roof of a private house by Beerbohm Soames. He knew that you walked down that street every morning at the same time—he rented out the building for the sole purpose of killing you.' She then went on to relate a tale of treachery and intrigue which was so complex and vicious that I could scarce credit my ears. I was obliged to spoon the gin syllabub at high speed into my gaping maw to preserve enough composure to refrain from swooning. I asked for seconds.

It seems that Beerbohm Soames had been jealous of my talent right from the beginning. He had read my work, *Twilight of the Anti-Idols*, in manuscript form and had seen in my petulant pentameters a serious rival to his own planned masterpiece, *Gods of Dusk and Mourning*. At that time, Éclair de Lune really was his mistress—he kept their affair secret for a very good reason (more of which later). He was always sharing his thoughts and schemes with her—thus she came to learn of his plan to kill me. He was not alone in his nefarious designs; most of the patrons of Udolpho's pâtisserie hated me as well. I had been blissfully unaware of all this, of course. I had not even realised my verse was rated so highly by them. (Now I understood why Signor Udolpho had tried to talk me into giving up Romanticism—he was also a member of this murderous brood.) What I had taken for a meteorite was really a bust of Xelucha Dowson Laocoön, the noxious sage, donated by sculptor, Rodin Guignol, and personally dropped by

Beerbohm Soames. It had been designed to shatter into a myriad unrecognisable fragments on impact.

'Wait a moment!' I cried, interrupting her astonishing tale. 'This surely cannot be true. A meteorite did strike the city that morning. It was reported in the Chaud-Mellé Chronicle.' She acknowledged the truth of this, but explained that the object had struck the river. I had read the headline on a news-stand the following day and assumed it applied to me. I had not bought the paper and checked the story because my head was throbbing too much. She then claimed the blow had killed me instantly but my ghost, bold as a bagel, simply stood up and carried on walking. Beerbohm Soames and the other plotters were apparently much put out by this—they continued to treat me as if I were alive (this accounted for their difficulty in seeing and hearing me) and were enormously relieved when I turned away from poetry of my own accord.

The deception had continued ever since. They were delighted when I set fire to *Twilight of the Anti-Idols* without any prompting. But she, beautiful and honest Éclair de Lune, had been disturbed by the whole sequence of events. She had tried to approach me with a letter revealing all, but her intentions had been discovered by Beerbohm Soames. With the aid of Signor Udolpho, he had imprisoned her in this attic. That was when she had decided to attract my attention by acting in a suspicious way: living just on cream cakes (for which she possessed a genuine love) and wallowing in dry baths. It had never occurred to her that I might fall in love with her—she merely wanted me to think she was a sort of phantom. My own real ghostly nature would thus be attracted to a kindred spirit ('elective-magnetism' she termed it), and I would stop at nothing to gain access to her room. Then she would be able to finally let me know the true state of affairs.

'But your ghostly nature was not attracted. It seems I appealed more to your carnal desires than your ethereal soul. Though I ate dozens of éclairs by the light of the gibbous moon, though I composed several extended pieces for piano solo (that have been subsequently performed at the Lycée d'Gottschalk) and washed without water until I began to smell like an over-ripe cheesecake, you did not come. So when I heard your new poetry reverberating throughout my chamber, I seized the chance to snare you in a more practical way. I drew up the cable, compelling you to enter this very night. You are in great danger: if Beerbohm Soames finds out you have resumed rhyming, he will arrange for an exorcist to banish you instantly to Sussex!'

Glumly, I confessed that I had been so caught by the yellow peril. Yet I was still not entirely happy with her version of events. I had wisely planned for my death, stating in my Will that my body must be left to the scientists of Ingolstadt University. They were doing wonders with their re-animation process these days. Beerbohm Soames would not have been able to contest it—my body would have duly been carted to that hallowed Institute and resurrected. I had little doubt of that. Had I really been killed that day, whether by meteorite or murderous bust, I would soon have been up and about again, not in spirit form, but as an honest walking cadaver, flesh and congealed blood. This seemed to be a flaw in Éclair de Lune's story. I told her as much.

'But Soames volunteered himself as your executor,' she replied. 'He made sure your body was left to science as instructed. Unfortunately, you did not state which science. He arranged it to be delivered to the Social Sciences Department. At first the economists there did not know what to do with you. They hid you in a cupboard and hoped you would go away on your own. Later, when they thought about it more carefully, they hoped you would not. In any event, you soon went off in a different way and your limbs were boiled to make glue for the teeth of debtors. A curious irony, to be sure—but Soames is a sly one!'

'Evidently!' I was startled by a crash from outside. It sounded as if a carbine had been discharged at the balcony, the shot ricocheting off the railings. It was not Harpy-shooting season for another three weeks; until then guns were not allowed to be fired in the city. I jumped to my feet and rushed over to the window. Signor Udolpho was standing at the foot of the ladder, hastily reloading his firearm. He saw me—his second shot shattered the glass of the window. I shook crystal shards loose from my hair. Éclair de Lune beckoned me back into the depths of the room. 'Silver bullets, eh?' I called down. 'You have mixed your folklores, Signor Udolpho! I am no bloodsucker.'

He calmly proceeded to pour more gunpowder down the smooth-bored barrel, reaching into a pouch at his belt for the shot. 'Not silver, Monsieur Jekyll. Chrome! All supernatural beings have an aversion to one metal or another. One of these pellets lodged in your insubstantial hide will slow you down!' He raised the gun to his shoulders and let loose a third volley. He was a poor shot; the result of this one was a number of loose tiles that slid off the roof and smashed at his feet. 'Ah, but I have already summoned Monsieur Soames and the others. They are on their way at this moment with an orthodox priest!'

I turned back to Éclair de Lune. A long look passed between us; I was asking her to come with me, to forsake her life of piano and pastry for one of greater hardship—the girlfriend (and then perhaps wife?) of a phantasmagorical insurance-salesman. She nodded assent with an almost imperceptible motion of her fine head. 'Come then!' I wailed. 'Let us be gone from this frightful place.' I spotted the insulating-cable lying in a corner and coiled it around my shoulder. Then I clasped her hand tightly. She shrugged. The door that led from her room was not locked, but there was no way down. Beerbohm Soames had removed the staircase. I flung open the door and teetered on the brink of the musty abyss. I wrapped the cable around the leg of her piano and lowered the doubled length into the depths. Éclair de Lune was less fearful than was I; she grasped the cable and slid its entire length with the grace of an angel cake. I followed in trepidation. When I reached the bottom I tugged the cable after us. It dropped at my feet like liquorice.

We groped our way through the gloomy stairwell into the pâtisserie proper. I cursed myself for not drawing the ladder up after me when I had entered Éclair de Lune's room. Signor Udolpho's insomnia was well documented; he had probably ventured out for a walk and collided with the ladder as he stepped out of his front door. 'Hurry! Soames will be here soon!' I hissed. We entered the pâtisserie; it was as dark as black-cherry gâteaux. We would have to leave by the back way. All at once there was a spark, as of flint striking steel. Then there was another, and yet another. Phosphorous matches were being struck all around us—some flared into life, others merely scraped their heads away on invisible sandpaper. It was like a chorus of cicadas, accompanied by sardonic laughter. One by one, candles were lit—the room wavered, the colours ascended an octave and then all was plainly visible.

It was a trap. They were all there; they had doubtless been waiting for us the whole time. Signor Udolpho's shot-gun antics had served the purpose of driving us into their clutches. Beerbohm Soames, in yellow silk pyjamas; Edwin Saltus Abbott, wearing a hat with an outsized price-tag stapled to the brim; Villiers le Gallienne, absinthe bottle raised to green lips; Novalis MacDonald, in kilt and Tyrolean hat, a reference to the ancestor who had helped found the city (originally named Umber-Scone and changed to Chaud-Mellé, at the turn of the last century, when duelling was finally legalised and the city seceded from the Federation, becoming, in Mark Xeethra Samuels's phrase, the first 'Cantonesque take-away'). But there were some present who I thought too successful to be envious of my work: Rosemary Gibbet-Pardoe and her lover, Dennistoun Homunculus; the renowned minor composer Cobalt Hugh; the evil Sumerian pervert, Cuneiform de Sade.

And among the familiar faces, I saw one I did not know. A furious gentleman with an oily chin, dressed in black robes and almost crushed by the mass of ornate necklaces that rested on his bloated stomach. Beerbohm Soames noted my confusion. 'Allow me to make introductions. This is Canon Alberic, an unconventional orthodox priest. He has come to banish you to East Grinstead.' I studied the figure more closely. His jowls shook with rage. Obviously Canon Alberic had a short fuse. I moved in front of Éclair de Lune, to shield her from any designs they might entertain upon her person. But Soames shook his head; he was genuinely affronted. 'We shall not touch her. It is you we want; we will simply return her to the attic.'

I exploded with self-righteous fury. I noticed a chocolate éclair resting on a plate on the counter. Without thinking, I snatched it up and advanced towards Beerbohm Soames. 'Come then, you swine! Face me like a man, poet to poet.' This had an astounding effect. The greater mass of those gathered seemed mentally to draw back from Soames, though they did not physically move. If he refused my challenge, he would lose all authority in their eyes. He scowled and seized an unsheathed éclair of his own. This was a highly symbolic choice of weaponry. We were, in effect, fighting over Éclair de Lune with the emblems of her identity. I lunged at him, but he jumped back, knocking over his chair and spitting oaths at me. Then he counter-attacked, grazing my elbow; I clutched my arm and felt the cream oozing between my fingers.

The pâtisserie was now utterly silent, save for our puffings and pantings, and the squishy clash of cake on cake. Fortunately for me, he was not an expert fencer; to my disadvantage, neither was I. We parried and thrust clumsily from one end of the pâtisserie to the other. Beer-bohm Soames bawled to his compatriots for assistance, but though despicable rogues, they knew the rules of the duello could not be broken. I leapt onto a table; it collapsed beneath my weight. Soames knocked candles over as he swung, setting tablecloths alight. Signor Udolpho chewed his knuckles as several small fires merged into one larger one, exposing the sweat and grime on his face. And then I tripped over an abandoned scone, falling forward with outstretched éclair. By some fluke, it caught Soames with his guard down. The point poked his eye; cream spurted. He moaned and collapsed to the floor. I did not hesitate. Anyone who has lived more than four-and-twenty summers will always choose mercy over justice; I offered Soames the latter. Taking a gingerbread devil from the counter, I administered the coup de grâce. I was in half a mind to saw his head off with the implement, impale it on a baguette and parade it in front of his friends. But I could not find a baguette.

I looked over my shoulder for Éclair de Lune. I had expected, in a typical male sort of way, that she would be meekly waiting while the two rivals for her attention fought it out. In fact she was engaged in a duel herself, taking on Edwin Saltus Abbott, Villiers le Gallienne and Novalis MacDonald simultaneously. More to the point, she was handling her weapon with a good deal more panache than I ever could; her stricken antagonists fell rapidly to her superior technique. Soon they lay in a heap together, their hearts riven, a pool of strawberry jam spreading from under their prone bodies. 'Hurrah!' I cried. 'Salut!' I continued with other similar phrases, in a dozen languages, much in the manner of a pretentious short story writer who wants to sound like an educated European, but in fact looks the words up in dictionaries.

The door of the pâtisserie flew open and Kingdom Noisette stood framed in the light of a false dawn (much time had passed since I recited my poem outside Éclair de Lune's window). 'Ee oop!' he cried, his voice like the pounding of a steam-driven guillotine, his whiskers bristling. As far as I was concerned, this was a perfect ending. The man I held in higher esteem than any other had obviously come to sort things out, to right all wrongs, avenge all injustices, in the sort of patronising way (kindly but firm) we are all so used to. I rushed forward to kiss his boots, but he seized me by the collar and held me off the ground. Then, with the back of his hand, he began to slap me. His calluses were like the barnacles of a ship; they would have drawn blood had I not been a ghost. As he continued to slap me, I decided he had not come to put matters right after all; neither did it seem very likely that he had come just for the insulating-cable.

The beating went on for some hours. My memories of it are muddled. When Kingdom Noisette had exhausted himself, he passed me over to one of the others present in the pâtisserie. They all took their turn. Rosemary Gibbet-Pardoe used the complete works of her favourite writer, Bram le Fanu Maturin, to inflict the blows; her lover, Dennistoun Homunculus, used the tip of his cane; Cobalt Hugh used a bassoon; Cuneiform de Sade contented himself with calling me rude names. I was dimly aware that Éclair de Lune was vainly struggling to restrain them— their numbers were too great even for her. I felt I could stand no more. After a while Kingdom Noisette was sufficiently rested to resume where he left off. As he bore down on me again, a peculiar thing happened.

The ground opened up behind him. Part of the floor ruptured and exploded outwards, showering everyone with rubble. From the hole thus exposed, eerie figures began to emerge into the light. They wore steel helmets and carried picks; sticks of dynamite dangled from their belts. They blinked and coughed dust out of their lungs. I recognised them at once and clapped my hands for joy—they were the team of engineers from whom I had borrowed the cable. Without communications, they had indeed ventured off course and had blasted a tunnel into the pâtisserie. It took them some seconds to understand where they were. When it dawned on them that they were in the midst of some of the most renowned cakes in the city, they whooped and discarded their egg and anchovy sandwiches. Then, in a single great wave, they surged over the lip of the hole and made for the counter with vastly rumbling stomachs.

Kingdom Noisette was caught up in the relentless tide of hungry workmen; in vain he tried to assert his authority over them. The last I saw of him was a horrified visage disappearing into a sea of struggling bodies. He fixed his bloodshot eyes upon my true love and muttered the rueful words, 'Ee Claire!' and then he was gone. The engineers crashed through the pitiful barricade of overturned tables and chairs that the demi-monde hastily erected—they crushed all before them in their rush to reach the confections. Kingdom Noisette's last words had electrified my soul (which was now the whole of me) and I stood dumbfounded. But Éclair de Lune, exhibiting more fortitude, grasped me by the arm and propelled me towards the opening of the tunnel. We stumbled down into darkness. Behind us, the sounds of titanic gorging bespoke of the utter failure of the bohemians to keep the engineers at bay.

We ran for a good mile or so and then paused for breath. Éclair de Lune had wisely thought to bring a candle and a match with her. We soon had the benefit of illumination. As we wandered down the tunnel, hand in hand, she filled me in on the rest of what I needed to know. It was true that Kingdom Noisette was her father (such an absurd coincidence that I could do little but puff out my cheeks and exclaim: 'Ach!'). She had been christened Claire—Claire Louise Noisette was her real name, but she had adopted the pseudonym Éclair de Lune for a variety of reasons, some of which we have already outlined. Her father's pronunciation of her name was merely the most obvious. Others included the fact that the word 'loon' means 'harlot' and she had worked for a time in Southampton. The main reason, however, was that 'éclair' is French for 'lightning' and her family had originally come from Bolton.

Kingdom Noisette, it appeared, had been in league with Beerbohm Soames all along. He had been disappointed that his daughter had chosen a poet for a lover and persuaded Soames to keep the affair secret. In return, Noisette lent him the money to keep her in cream cakes when he imprisoned her above Udolpho's pâtisserie. But there was more to the deal than that—the bushy Grand Engineer had seen possibilities in my ghostly condition. 'The reason why his workmen accepted you so readily was because they were all ghosts as well. It was the meteorite striking the river that caused the collapse of that first tunnel and the drowning of those men. That is why you felt a calling for engineering after your own death—it was elective-magnetism; the pull of kindred spirits. My ghostly charade could not hope to compete with the real thing.' She then added that Kingdom Noisette had been investigating the potential of ghost power as a cheap source of energy. For one thing, he would not have to pay workers who were already dead.

We wandered down the tunnels for many days. It became apparent that the workers had broken into an older system of passages during their excavations. We explored caverns measureless to man (but not to woman) and eventually emerged in the cellars of the Uruguayan embassy. It was well-stocked too, with Chiantis and fruity Moselles. We were determined to start a new life together (I use the word 'life' as a mere figure of speech). And that is precisely what we did. We also attempted to find a moral of some sort in our adventures. Had they shown that love can cross all barriers and social classes, even those between living and deceased? Had they shown that lust was stronger than putrefaction? I thought they had, but Éclair de Lune disagreed. When I tried to argue, she threatened to turn me in to Canon Alberic. I have heard it said he never gives up on a case. It is a point of honour with him— he still feels he has to atone for that time he overwound the cathedral clock.

It is refreshingly cool down here in the cellar. But we are running out of wine. Éclair de Lune hints she will send me up to the surface to obtain some more. I spend my time writing short stories—I have not yet had any accepted for publication but I am hopeful. I want to write pure fantasy; I am already planning a series of tales set in an alternate world where harpies do not exist. Here is my one attempt at realism; it is not really my flask of Hock. Éclair de Lune edits all my work, she claims I am too verbose. This piece, for example, was originally nine times as long. She also edits my emotions.

My day job, of course, is much more prosaic. The digging of the underground railway system proceeds apace. Kingdom Noisette's role has been filled by his bitter rival, République Nutt, whose canals were such a sensation last year. Among the teams he employs, the band of ghosts continues as before. I wander among them trying to sell death insurance. I have to remind them that theirs is a dangerous task, that there is a very real possibility their bodies will be recovered from the bed of the river and sent to Ingolstadt for re-animation. This worries them. As ghosts, not needing to eat or drink, they can just survive on their wages. As resurrected cadavers it would mean a return to anchovy and egg sandwiches and pickled onions. My policies generally cover them against this eventuality. It is impossible to be sure. It is not easy reading small-print in total darkness.

As I roam the tunnels, I think of what lies above my head. Unless they have gone out of fashion during my subterranean exile, there must be gardens. A common garden plant used to be the one known as *Lunaria biennis*. (Yes I too can show off. Here is some more Latin: *de omni re scibili et quibusdam aliis*.) Another name for this plant, this Lunaria, is Honesty. But my Lune is not honest: the other day she told me there was no more Amontillado. She has been hoarding bottles. 'For the love of God, Joris-Karl!' she exclaimed when I pointed this out. I do not approve of such language. I do not have to put up with it. I am going to leave her. One of the workmen has a new pet; it has caught my fancy. I am conceiving a passion. It is an inanimate object, true enough. But inanimate objects are less shy with ghosts than with people.

It is a killer peruke from Wigan.

Grinding the Goblin

If a city can go mad it can also die. Our city was mad almost from the beginning: its houses tall and awry, heat-lightning playing around the chimneys like dishevelled hair; the fogs rolling incessantly down its streets like foam on cruel lips; balloons rising and setting from its parks like bulging eyes. At night, the burning buildings lit the sky a deep carnelian and licked away the stars.

I was dreaming again; my head was full of gigantic clocks tolling the centuries and vast pendulums smashing the suburbs. When I awoke, the pounding was real. My room was shaking, plaster spilled from the ceiling and settled on my forehead. I jumped out of bed; shards of chamber-pot made my feet dance. At the cracked mirror, I studied my body intently. In my dream, on the hour, a hatch had opened in my chest and my heart had wound out before me on a sort of lattice.

We were at war. Benito von Clausewitz had levered his howitzers up the mountain passes, losing half in the process, arranging the others beyond the reach of our own artillery. His men, triumphant but weary, were content to bombard us to submission before moving in for the usual rapine pleasures. Chaud-Mellé was being reduced to rubble around my ears; an irony that afforded me little amusement. I had entered the city not a month previously, on request of the Municipality, to embark upon a radical redevelopment of the cluttered city centre.

As a city planner, I was not made welcome by the populace, many of whom were inordinately attached to their crumbling dwellings. My sole friends had been my employers, the members of the City Council. Most of these were dead and my position was unenviable. Some of my neighbours even hailed me as harbinger of the evil. One polemical fellow, a minor subversive named Kropotkin Hardie, used to accost me on the stairs. 'The age of the bourgeoisie is over,' he would yell, above the roar of the guns. 'The currents of history cannot be opposed!' Unused to his accent, part Russian and part Scottish, I had difficulty gauging his meaning. Currants? What did Udolpho's pâtisserie (on the other side of town) have to do with the ideals of revolution? It is true, however, the war had affected the cake business. Plaster is a poor substitute for flour at the best of times.

Kropotkin Hardie was a true fanatic, rarely too busy to attribute every falling shell to the hypocrisy of the rich. On several occasions he invited me into his room for iced-tea. This was less an attempt to win a convert than a chance to practice his fiery oratory. He used to preach from a soap-box in Hauser Park; the shortage of detergents had ended such activity. Nonetheless, he was something of a celebrity among the *Lumpenproletariat*, handing out pamphlets on street corners, calling for the heads of the merchant classes to be arranged on the city walls, insisting that everyone address him as 'comrade' and spending much time cursing laissez-faire economics and growing his beard.

I managed to learn something of the history of Chaud-Mellé from him between political tirades and metaphysical speculations. The city was founded in 1315 by a Scottish deserter, Wraith MacDonald, who fought for the English at Bannockburn and fled to the Continent to escape the dirks of his brethren. Among the mountaineers of the Alps, he found a few who wished to sample civilisation. The original settlement had spread like gangrene, sheltered in a narrow valley between low hills. The Austrian Empire now wished to annex it—there was a rich seam of chromium below the streets—and had commissioned Benito von Clausewitz, the mercenary lens-grinder from Rotterdam, to crush all resistance.

Once, while I was perched on one of his uncomfortable chairs (made by his own hand, he proudly informed me), Kropotkin Hardie received a visit from the Secret Police. This was routine; they came at regular intervals to search for his illegal printing press. I was questioned as to my involvement with the bristling demagogue—despite my espousal of right-wing values, they saw an opportunity to try out the latest form of psychological torture, alternately snatching away and returning my glass of iced tea. 'See what they are really like!' Kropotkin declared, after they had left. I had to admit they seemed a little too enthusiastic, but I stoutly defended their basic methods.

We shared the house with two other tenants: the demure and dimpled Eliza Pippins, a cockney, and Aretino Rossetti, who claimed to be the leader of an arts and crafts movement currently sweeping the cafés and studios of the Artist's Quarter. Others I spoke to, however, denied his involvement. He was a Genoan spy, a saboteur, directly answerable to the Pope. This was a theory advanced by Kropotkin himself; it appears the Vatican had seen its own chance to seize territory. Already Papal Bulls were denouncing Vienna, that hive of sin and waltz—a poisoned bible had been sent to the Austrian Emperor. The whole of Europe stood poised on the brink of a swirling vat of greed and cream.

As I had nothing to do during the day—von Clausewitz was making a fine job of clearing the condemned buildings—I devoted myself to a little intrigue of my own. Eliza Pippins had caught my fancy; I vowed to win her over before the city surrendered. Accordingly I lingered outside her room until she emerged. She was a sweet but savage creature, dressed in corduroy, her auburn hair pinned into a bonnet, a purple umbrella in her lace-gloved hand. I introduced myself—Gropius Klee, fresh from the renowned Staatliches Cathaus in Dessau—and proposed a cup of coffee in a café on a suitable boulevard. She agreed at once —howitzers loosen mores as well as mortar—and we strolled arm in arm to the Champs-Poe. Here we settled amidst the ruined pavement, duly received our coffee (actually sand, as this was wartime) and exchanged ideas about how we might live our lives to better effect.

She worked for the Post Office; now that von Clausewitz had ringed the city with cannon, traditional methods of delivering mail had become untenable. There had been experiments with rockets—the results were disappointing. Balloons still functioned as one method of entering or leaving the city but their days were numbered. There was a shortage of ladies' undergarments, the sole material used in dirigible construction. Eliza hinted she was working on an ingenious alternative. This was vital to the defence of the town; with the demise of all our councillors, we received our instructions from England. A former inhabitant of the city had set up a Government-in-exile in Highgate. Eliza informed me he was called Mark Xeethra Samuels and kept a tea chest full of brass bones, no-one knew why. He had once been her lover but had ended the affair, declaring that kissing her was like 'biting a nectarine and discovering you've a mouth full o' ashes'.

While we chatted, a shell exploded against the side of the café, knocking us to the ground, showering us with glass and croûtons. The waiter rushed out, to ensure we paid our bill before dying; but we were uninjured. 'Apples and pears, guv'nor!' Eliza cried. My hand was on her knee; she nibbled my chin. 'Bless my crinoline socks!' We made our way back to the house and straight to bed. Her flesh tasted neither like fruit nor tobacco—there was only honey and sweat and cinnamon. After she had tickled my gambrels and I had counted her secret auburn hairs, every one of them, both fore and aft, we fell asleep. That was when I had my first strange dream. Night descended; the window rattled open, I seemed to see Eliza launching herself high over the rooftops. 'Pippins express!' she chortled, as her umbrella caught the wind. There was a demonic sort of cackle and then she was gone.

I woke and reached out for her and found that she really had gone. I closed the casement and dressed hurriedly because I was too fraught to sleep and needed to walk off my excitement. On the landing, I heard muffled sobs coming from Kropotkin Hardie's apartment. The Secret Police were ransacking his room again. The door was ajar and I stepped inside. The sobs were not emanating from the revolutionary but from the officers. Kropotkin stood watching, arms folded, smiling fiercely into his beard. The room was in total disarray; cutlery littered the floor. In the middle of the chaos, two figures in leather coats trembled.

Kropotkin noticed me and beamed. 'See? Foolish capitalist agents cannot outwit the class hero. They have looked everywhere, but still they cannot find my printing press!' I watched as one of the officers grappled with a laundry basket and tipped it over. 'Och, it is not in there gentlemen!' Kropotkin was taunting them. 'You are getting warm. Now you are hot, but not hot enough to ignite!' I decided to leave him to his entertainment. As I passed out of his room and down the stairs, my thoughts were all on the lusty motions of Eliza.

The street was full of people. Each Quarter had been organised into a sort of home-guard. We took it in turns to douse fires and tend to the injured. I made my way through a line of sour-faced cobblers and millers who were passing pails of water from a street pump to remains of the Hôtel Crowley. In the roofless Theatre de l'Orotund, I found a small gathering of artistes performing a late night cabaret. This was a misguided attempt at boosting morale. I sat in the front row—one of only a dozen people in the audience—and watched the show with a growing sense of outrage. Von Clausewitz himself could not have devised a more fiendish secret weapon. Obviously the talented performers had all been killed or badly wounded by shrapnel. There was no other explanation.

Seated on high stools, battered ukuleles in hand, a trio of faded operetta stars—Oscar Milde, Noël Novello and Ivor Timid—struggled with substandard material. They had toured Dessau while I was a student. Identical in physical appearance, it was only possible to differentiate them by their carnations. Between them, they had written one well-known song, 'Don't Put Your Somnambulist on the Stage, Dr Caligari'. I was openly contemptuous; I began to heckle, while shells rattled overhead. 'If you can't have Amontillado, you make do with Sherry,' whispered a voice in my ear. 'And if you can't have Vindaloo, you make do with a Madras.' It was a woman, as beautiful as her maxims, leaning forward over my shoulder. She introduced herself as Coppelia de Retz, wife of the Maréchal Lore de Retz, greenest of the Bluebeards and leader of the resistance. 'I've seen you wandering the ruins with a slide rule,' she crooned. 'Perhaps you'd care to extend it in my direction?'

I dribbled with anticipation. 'Gropius,' I said. She blushed and ruffled my hair with her fingers. 'By all means, but not here.' While we exchanged innuendoes, a shell arced through the open roof and exploded in the middle of the stage. When the smoke cleared, it was harder than ever to tell Oscar Milde, Noël Novello and Ivor Timid apart—their limbs were all mixed up. We stood to leave, but a sleek figure rushed from the wings and pressed us back into our seats. 'Not going so soon, M. et Mlle.?' He had a curious posture; he twirled his moustaches. 'The night is young!' With impatient gestures, he ushered on an orchestra armed with improvised instruments. 'Voilà!'

'Come, darling.' Coppelia took me by the arm and led me outside. The curious fellow was attempting to coax harmony from the collection of drainpipes, saws and egg slicers that were substitutes for tubular bells, cellos and harps respectively. There was something odd about the baton he was using. Back in the street, I confided in Coppelia. 'It looked as if he was conducting with a tail!' She laughed at my seriousness. 'Don't be silly. That was Monsieur le Purr, the famous impresario. To think that he once produced the best! Cobalt Hugh, among others!'

I remarked that war had lowered all our standards. 'Oh absolutely,' she cried, pinching my buttocks. We could not return to her house; the Maréchal had converted it into his office. Besides, he was already a jealous husband. I asked her why he seemed such a bad shot; it was his responsibility to direct our retaliatory fire, but all our shells missed their targets by an absurd distance. It was as if he was actually trying not to hit von Clausewitz. 'He takes orders from Highgate,' she informed me. 'Mark Xeethra Samuels makes those decisions.'

I thought this highly unsatisfactory. What would my Masters back in Dessau have said of such lack of co-ordination? Industry and Reason must merge into one substance; a thorough grounding in all disciplines of an art (and war is an art) is necessary in our tarnished age. I do not look back to the past—as Aretino Rossetti claimed to do—to find answers to the problems of the present. I find them in the idea of the Universal artwork, the *Gesamt-kunstwerk*, in which all is in accordance with Nature, Spirit and Lust. I tried to show all this in an early architectural work entitled 'Brickhouse in Cheese', but it fell down.

Back in my room, I took off my morals with my coat and hung them both on the back of my door. The house was alive with sounds. Kropotkin was shouting downstairs; the very walls seemed to be revolving. Before she could loosen her stays, I had Coppelia around the waist. 'How now, gnädige Frau?' I cried. She yielded to my lips. 'But you must extinguish the light!' she insisted. I was sorely disappointed by this; I was keen to view her naked flesh. 'Shy, eh? But I wish to taste your mettle!' At this, she proffered me a highly suspicious look.

In the end, she had her way—we made love in a darkness punctuated only by the bursting of enemy shells. She was savage; cold to the touch, mechanical in her thrusts. It did not matter—I was having an excellent siege. We embraced and talked. She made toys for a living—automatons and suchlike. The business had been in her family for generations. She was a descendant of Coppelia Coppelius, who had sent a mechanical set of false teeth to George Washington. I knew nothing of such devices; I was too enamoured of glass and tubular steel. While she played raconteur, I drifted into sleep.

Thus it was that I had the dream of gigantic clocks and pendulums that dangled from the Pole Star. When I awoke, Coppelia had gone; I was doing a poor job of keeping my women. I was stiff. Rods of iron had been inserted into my bones. My heart really did feel like the spring of an overwound watch. At the mirror, I inspected my chest. When I turned, Eliza Pippins was standing by the bed, hair loose around her shoulders, as if she too had been buffeted on waves of lust. I was both happy and fearful. 'But how did you enter?' I cried. 'I always keep the door locked.' She folded her umbrella and closed the window behind her. I could not fathom it. She must have sneaked past while I was intent on my body. 'Recorded deliv'ry,' she announced.

She reached into her bodice and pulled out a letter. I was aghast. Recorded deviltry? Did a bureaucratic demon lurk in her cleavage? I was obviously still having problems with her language. I opened the letter and found a note signed by Mark Xeethra Samuels himself. 'Welcome to the Commune,' it said. That was all. I cast it aside and hugged

Eliza; she could smell another woman on my skin, but returned my caresses nevertheless. 'A right ol' parvenu, God bless 'im,' was her comment. I wondered at the cryptic message. Commune? Did Samuels mistake me for one of Kropotkin's accomplices? And what had this to do with the legitimate Government? Was the exile expressing anarchist sympathies?

There were too many questions. My body still felt strange; I needed coffee and muffins, and to oil my insides with marmalade. I asked Eliza to join me for breakfast. 'Absolutely knackered, guv'nor,' was her characteristic reply. She climbed into bed and told me she would await my return. The door was still locked (so how did Coppelia depart?) and I turned the key and descended the stairs. Kropotkin Hardie was coming up to see me. He grasped my arm and gazed at me with sparkling eyes. 'Well done, young laddie! I knew you'd join us sooner or later.' He pressed a book into my hand. 'My latest treatise, fresh off the press!' I was now utterly dumbfounded. I took the volume, bade him good-day and headed towards the Champs-Poe. What was going on?

While I was passing the shell of the Cathedral, two figures blocked my path. They were the officers who had tormented me with the iced tea. 'What is the meaning of this?' I cried, as they laid rough hands on me. Somebody must have been telling lies, for they guided me down a myriad of little lanes towards the ruins of the Police Station. Inside, I was blindfolded and led up stairways and along corridors. Finally, I was thrust into a room and the blindfold was removed.

A swarthy man sat before me, stroking his corrugated beard with a hand heavy with ornate rings. His desk was strewn with papers and clay tablets. 'Do you know who I am?' The ringlets on his forehead danced as he stood and leaned forward. The two officers were behind me; I could smell the unwashed leather of their coats. I shook my head—it seemed to rattle as I did so—and regarded him more closely. He toyed with a copper paper-knife and smiled. 'I am Cuneiform de Sade, the new Chief of Secret Police. Do you know why you are here?'

I shrugged. 'I can only assume it has something to do with one of my neighbours. He is a well-known subversive.' I was aware of the book Kropotkin Hardie had given me which I had thrust into a pocket. What should I do? Reveal it and claim it was forced on me unwillingly? Cuneiform de Sade opened his mouth to laugh; the room was suddenly heavy with the scent of lavender. 'Ur! Ur! Ur!' he chortled. He continued in this mode for some time. I was tempted to join in. Abruptly he stopped and slammed his fist on the desk. 'Oh yes! And you shall net him for us!'

What followed can best be described as diabolical cruelty on his part and understandable cowardice on mine. Needless to say, after the feather had been put away, and my socks had been returned, I was no more than a pawn in the sweaty palms of a malevolent grandmaster, dancing on a checkerboard of nights and days (but the nights so bleached by burning buildings, and the days so blackened by the smoke of those buildings, that it might as well have been all of one colour).

Cuneiform de Sade cleared his desk with a sweep of his arm and placed maps on the surface. The plan was that I would try to gain the confidence of Kropotkin and persuade him to reveal the location of the printing press. If, however, this did not work, I was to lead him to a predetermined place, where agents would leap out of the shadows and give him a fatal beating. 'We must find that press, or else pulp the printer!' Cuneiform de Sade explained. He added that the latest work from the press—the one Kropotkin had given me—was the most dangerous yet. The arguments were so persuasive that even he—the fiendish Chief of Secret Police—had been tempted to pack it in and join the Commune. 'Appealing sophistries!' he avowed.

The maps showed Chaud-Mellé in as much detail as could be expected from a city designed along the principles of chaos. One set proved more interesting to me than the others. They were plans of the underground network of tunnels carved out by Kingdom Noisette some years previously. I did my best to memorise the main routes. The underground railway, of course, had never been completed: inflammable gas had leaked into the system. The whole city now rested on veins and arteries of methane that presumably broiled from station to station.

'If he will not reveal the location of the press,' Cuneiform de Sade repeated, 'you will lead him to the junction of Machen Street and the Rue Rogêt. There we shall pounce with cudgels and staves!' He rubbed his hands together. 'We shall swallow this foolish Anarchist! Then we shall swallow all his fellow conspirators! I shall swallow them whole and do honour to my regal ancestors!' He sat back in his chair and made a ziggurat with his fingers. I could hardly resist a parting thrust as I was led out: 'Two swallows do not make a Sumer.'

Back on the street, I sighed and held my head in my hands. What was I to do? If I did not comply with their demands, they would consider me a sympathiser and tear me to pieces. I had no love for Kropotkin, but he seemed more decent than de Sade. It was no longer possible to remain neutral. Yet I had a plan of my own and I rushed towards home to put it into operation. Eliza, Coppelia and I would escape from the city by means of the tunnels. I paused at a café, ordered an absinthe (actually bile from the mortuary vats) and a napkin, and drew on its crumpled surface a good likeness of what I remembered of the map. Then I folded the napkin in my pocket, paid for the drink and resumed my rushing.

When I reached the house, Eliza was up. She was coming down the stairs. I gripped her ankles and kissed her crinoline socks. Unable to contain myself, I blurted out all my hopes. I waved the napkin under her retroussé nose. 'Lordy!' she exclaimed. My hysterical monologue was interrupted by a laugh. I looked up to see Aretino Rossetti peering at us over the balcony on the next floor. 'Hush darlin',' Eliza cautioned. She gently directed me into her room, which was next to Kropotkin's. It was as sparsely furnished as mine. While she drew the blinds, I had a very quick rummage through her chest of drawers for black stockings. I was not to be disappointed—seamed ones at that.

She sat next to me on the bed. I told her that although the tunnels were full of inflammable gas, I had developed at the Staatliches Cathaus a new form of portable lighting called the electric torch. There was no doubt I could make another one out of available materials. The electric light would not ignite the gas. The longest tunnel stretched far beyond the city walls—further than Benito von Clausewitz's guns. The three of us (I told her all about Coppelia) could be out of Chaud-Mellé by this time tomorrow and well on our way to the safety of the Forest Cantons. I had contacts in Unterwalden where the Habsburgs (and all Austrians) were uniformly despised, and where good modern architecture was much needed. If we could survive the gas, we had nothing to fear.

Eliza sighed. 'It's not the gas, guv'nor. It's the 'arpies!' I asked her to elaborate. Apparently there had been a fashion for keeping young harpies as pets; when they had grown big, and more unmanageable, many had been flushed into the sewers. They had dug their way into the railway network—within a generation, their wings had withered. They were blind albinos, fierce and eager to rend any who ventured into their domain. 'Already thought o' that,' she said, plastering my deflated ego and pumping me back up with a comment that, despite being unworkable, it was a good plan. 'Vicious blighters!'

So now I knew that methane had no adverse effect on harpies. It was small consolation for the loss of my freedom and the love of two fine auburn haired women. We tumbled together on her bed; it was hard and lumpy. They were so similar in their reactions and needs, Eliza and Coppelia, it was as if they were two aspects of the same being. I could not choose between them—partly because I desired them with equal intensity and partly because I was as greedy and selfish as any man in my position (which was cuissade moving to missionary). I brought her to climax with tongue and toe—a trick I had learned in Munich. 'Jellied eels!' she declared, writhing in delight.

That night, my dreams underwent a radical shift in character. They had previously consisted mainly of steel and glass edifices, geometric patterns and ergonomic chairs. Then had come a transitionary period: my dream that Eliza had flown from my window; the clocks and pendulums. Now I bathed in Mediterranean climes. I was a restaurant owner, somewhere in Sardinia. My customers were roughnecks. I could not account for such a ridiculous scenario. I was Gropius Klee, square of jaw and blond of fringe, who had never ventured below 45°N. Furthermore, my knowledge of Italian was very poor: *Chi tace confessa!*

I had no option but to accede to Cuneiform de Sade's wishes. (I did have an option, but this is mere pedantry). To prepare for winning over Kropotkin's confidence, I decided to study his book. In the evenings, Eliza was engaged on Post Office business. It was not possible to meet Coppelia. So I had little to do but read. The book was indeed accessible; the author rarely resorted to jargon to describe bourgeois tyranny. By the end, I was in danger of subscribing to his views.

Kropotkin was producing new works at an alarming rate. These urged the populace to regard the Chaud-Mellé authorities with as much contempt as Benito von Clause-witz. 'At least the Austrians are honest about their oppressive agenda,' he told me. The Mediterranean dreams had started to impinge on my waking life. It was a form of escape, I suppose. Now my hopes of fleeing through the tunnels were dashed, my brain was trying to present alternative relief from the horrors of the bombardment. I sipped iced-tea in his room; the Secret Police no longer bothered him. He was mildly disappointed by this. 'They have given up searching,' I remarked. 'Perhaps they believe they will never find the press?'

He grinned. 'With good reason!' Though I tried, by ever less subtle means, to trick him into revealing its location, he said not a word. Yet he treated me as a genuine convert to his cause. 'The Commune will need architects like you,' he enthused. 'People who know how to justify the existence of cheap, ugly buildings by citing the ideals of progress!' I told him there was more to it than that—the Staatliches Cathaus did not always recommend second-rate building materials. Besides, it was a free market. At this, his brow darkened. 'Mind your language!'

Finally, I knew I would have to fall back on the second plan. If I did not act quickly, Cuneiform de Sade's men would arrest me. I informed Kropotkin that I had met someone who wanted to join the Commune. They were extremely shy and did not wish to come to his house. 'Perhaps we can go out to meet this person?' I ventured. Kropotkin nodded assent. I led him to the junction of Machen Street and the Rue Rogêt and took to my heels as the agents pounced on him and wrestled him into the shadows. Even as I ran, I could hear the sounds of the beating.

I made my way back towards the Champs-Poe by a complicated route, in which I attempted to shake off the conscience that was yapping at my ankles. The sense of desolation was profoundly affecting; about a third of the city had been completely reduced to ashes. By the end of the week it would be closer to half. As I picked my way over the broken Uruguayan Embassy, the hallucinations dizzied my head again. I was boiling pasta in one huge pot; tomato and oregano sauce bubbled in a second. I blinked these absurdities from my lashes and continued my careful progress. I was almost back onto the street proper when I spied two figures walking towards me. It was Eliza and Coppelia, arm in arm. I hid myself in an outcrop of tumbled statues, mostly of Uruguayan heroes thumbing their noses at the Spanish Embassy opposite.

Eliza and Coppelia were both laughing, though I could not make out their words. They stopped for an instant, kissed each other farewell (on the lips!) and Eliza moved off. Dusk was drawing near; it was time for her to start work. As Coppelia passed, I jumped out. 'We meet again!' I cried. She did not flinch. I joined her and we sauntered off at a scenic tangent. I did not mention Eliza directly. I was subtle. I said: 'I hear that the last balloon left Chaud-Mellé this morning. What will the Post Office do now, I wonder?' She confirmed my observation. There were no more ladies' undergarments to be had in the whole city. 'We have given up our knickers for the cause,' she added. This distracted me from the more taxing problems on my mind. Women no longer wore undergarments? Then the gates of Heaven were always open!

I made a mental note to myself always to linger at the bottom of stairwells in future—not that there were too many of them left. 'Thus are we trapped for good in this stink,' I murmured. She smiled and eyed me curiously. I wanted to take her around the waist, but a gulf had opened between us. I dared not inhale the scent of her hair. Once more the vision of the restaurant troubled my mind. It threatened to subsume my consciousness. I reached out for a cleaver; it was Coppelia's hand, as cold as tempered steel. 'Careful. My husband often lurks in the bars around here.'

She prised my fingers apart from hers. I told her I loved her. She was amused. 'Nonsense, my sweet.'

We walked without direction, struggling to identify a single star in the bruised sky. In what capacity did she know Eliza? This question returned to burn my tongue like vinegar; every time I was about to try it out, a mirage of the restaurant knocked it loose. 'I know this sounds silly,' I mumbled, 'but I keep thinking of Sardinia.' She did not reply. Evidently she was not impressed. 'And my heart feels like a cuckoo in a clock.' I wanted to touch her hair; my fingers would not move. On her lips, Eliza's scarlet lipstick mingled with her own blue shade to colour her kisses crimson—but those kisses were not for me. 'Something is amiss,' I persisted. 'Something fundamental.'

She matched my gaze and tightened those lips. 'You're a lovely boy. A bit stupid perhaps, but lovely all the same. I'd really like to stay and talk, but I have to get home.' She blew me a kiss—the best I could expect. I caught it in the palm of my hand, smeared it over my forehead, cheeks and mouth and then put it in a pocket for later use. She slipped into the night like a trickle of oil; I was alone with my conscience. My life had become a pimple on the nose of the ineffable; my emotions were about to burst. I promptly sat down in the dust and remained there for the best part of the night.

While I sat, my thoughts alternated between the escapism of my Mediterranean fantasy and the harsh reality of the spinning shells. In its own way, I knew, the siege was a beautiful thing. I had seen all manner of wonders in Dessau—chairs that folded into tables, doors that doubled as ladders, ironing boards that descended from the ceiling. But the destructive fury of total war made all our craft obsolete. Here was a more perfect blend than that of Industry and Reason—here was the illegitimate offspring of Industry and Unreason. Von Clausewitz's guns were not just an extension of his loins (sowing seed that reaped) but

217

also struts of Truth. The fist is a most effective syllogism; knuckles, chin, necessary conclusion. Or more aptly: the howitzers were fingers; our civic craters, sockets of the gouged.

Destiny? We had chosen this outcome as surely as my alter ego in Sardinia chose Parmesan over Cheddar. Thus it was, veering between the twin tastes of philosophy and pizza, and skipping through the twisted metal and blackened stone, I returned to the house. I hoped de Sade would expect no more of me. I was filthy, tired and hungry. I was fully prepared to abandon myself to a quietism of despair; indeed, I was keen to begin such abandonment at once. But first I required a pillow and my last chocolate biscuit— cunningly concealed in a bar of soap over my washstand. '*I gran dolori sono muti*,' I counselled myself. But this was not honest German. It was the sunny tongue!

There was oil on the stairs. I followed it to Kropotkin Hardie's room—the door was wide open. The anarchist himself was kneeling in front of the hearth, feeding papers into the grate. But there was no fire to receive them. The leaves were sucked up the chimney with great force. I rushed to his side. 'But these pages are blank!' I protested. He was in a terrible state; his blood was strangely dark. 'Don't blame you for running, laddie,' he said. 'Capitalist swine!' he shook off my attempts to carry him to the bed. 'Work to be done!' He told me that a shell had struck the junction of Machen Street and the Rue Rogêt while the beating was taking place. The officers had been killed instantly; he had crawled back on his hands and knees.

'But what are you doing?' My impatience was greater than any feelings of sympathy. He continued to feed in the blank sheets. They disappeared up the flue with extraordinary speed. 'Don't you understand?' he grumbled. 'It's the house. The house is the printing press! The entire house!' He giggled with childish delight. This explained the noises I often heard at night—whirring of machinery, as if the walls of rooms were rotating and the banisters tapping. It also explained why my bedsheets were always covered in black ink.

The system was a delight. After inserting the pages in the grate, the mechanism took over, printing text, binding the books and ejecting them from the highest chimney. The finished product flew in a calculated arc towards his distributor. ('I won't give his name, but he's a famous impresario.') Anyone seeing the tomes racing across the sky would take them for enemy shells. All along, the officers of the Secret Police had been standing within what they had sought! I felt an enormous affection for the clever revolutionary—and an extreme hatred for Cuneiform de Sade. However misguided, Kropotkin's resourcefulness was vastly superior to the Police Chief's Assyrian cynicism.

His wounds were severe. He was obliged to rest from his work and look at me with glazed eyes. 'I'm not much longer for this city,' he said. 'But the fight will continue. Take this, laddie.' He reached into his pocket and handed me an object wrapped in old newspaper. I thanked him and offered to treat his injuries with bandages from my own supply. He continued inserting papers into the grate. I jumped up the stairs to my room. It had been ransacked. In red paint, daubed above the bed, a dripping crucifix showed me this was the work of Aretino Rossetti. I checked my belongings—the only thing missing was the napkin with the map of the underground tunnels. I suddenly wanted nothing more than to nestle into Eliza's arms. It was almost dawn. She would be back soon. I found the bandages and raced down.

I was halted on the stairs by Rossetti himself. He was dressed in the robes of a Cardinal—he had decided to show his true colours. There was a menacing light in his dark eyes. 'Ha, ha! I shall be beatified for this!' He reached out and snatched the newspaper parcel from my grasp. 'So this is the printing press, eh? A little smaller than I would have imagined. But I have what I came for—I have also your map. In a week I shall be in Rome, sipping sherbet with the Pope! Without the press the resistance shall crumble. We shall let von Clausewitz take Chaud-Mellé and then wrest it from his weary hands! After we have defeated Austria we will turn on Turkey, Serbia and Wales!'

I shook with loathing. *'Il meglio è i'inimico del bene!'* He was as stupefied by my knowledge of his language as was I. I pointed out that the tunnels were dark—he would not be able to use a flame because of the methane. He held up a green glass jar within which glowed a circular object. 'His Holiness has leant me a halo. I am well served.' He turned and fled before me. I ran after him. The sky was lightening in the east. He was much fitter than I. Pausing to catch my breath, I glanced up. A tiny dot was spiralling towards the ground. At first I thought it was another shell, but it resolved itself into a figure carrying a purple umbrella. 'Eliza Pippins!' I roared.

Behind me, Kropotkin's books were still firing out of the chimney. I waved to Eliza. She noticed me and waved back. This was her mistake. She drifted into the path of one of the flying volumes—it struck the umbrella from her hand. At once she began a steep descent—a sickening dégringoler—flapping helplessly to arrest her motion. I ran forward, holding my arms out, desperately hoping to catch her. Needless to say, I was unsuccessful. She hit the ground and broke into a million pieces. I hastened to her side—her many sides—but stopped in some confusion. There was no blood. Cogs and little wires lay scattered in profusion at my feet. Her head and torso were still joined together. I cradled them in my arms. 'I'm so sorry!' I blabbed.

She winked at me. A change had come over von Clausewitz's guns. It was as if he had filed them down, to alter their pitch. I recognised the melody of the Austrian National Anthem. Eliza coughed and oil poured out of her nose. 'The hills are alive with the sounds of gor' blimey music,' she gasped. I closed her eyes. My true love had been a puppet! I had no doubts as to who was behind this outrage. With decisive steps, I made my way towards the toyshop of Coppelia de Retz.

I wanted to know about Eliza and my own watch-like heart. I would no longer be fobbed off with evasive replies about the latter. I also wanted to know about Sardinia. It did not take long to reach the shop in question. It was completely undamaged—one of the few structures in Chaud-Mellé that could claim the distinction. I stepped inside, pushed my way past the simpering assistant and emerged into a dim chamber. At a long table sat a host of assorted characters. I recognised Coppelia at the head, Maréchal Lore next to her, the impresario known as Monsieur le Purr. They did not seem surprised to see me. Coppelia rolled her eyes in exasperation and clucked her tongue.

'At last! We thought you were never coming, darling. Really, you have been most obtuse about all this. Take a seat and I'll introduce you to the others.' I collapsed into a chair and returned the greetings of those I did not know. One by one, we were introduced. There was Alfred Carnacki, the reformed bank manager; Jilly Tolkien-Twigge, the mountain climber; the Reverend Douglas Delves, heretical vicar and possessor of an eldritch pickling jar (which he carried at all times); the sardonic Caspar Nefandous, pockmarked and sensitive; Xelucha Dowson Laocoön, a withered noxious sage; Rodin Guignol, sculptor and acrobat. Two places at the table were empty. I nodded at them.

'Those are reserved for Kropotkin Hardie and Eliza Pippins.' It was Monsieur le Purr who spoke. I told them that Eliza was dead (or broken!) and that Kropotkin was in almost as bad a condition. They seemed to take this well; they inclined their heads, a simple mark of respect. 'They are not dead, as such,' the impresario continued. 'Eliza is in London and Kropotkin is living in Kiev. Do not grieve for them, Monsieur.' When I responded that I was weary of metaphysics, he shook his head. 'These are solid facts. They left Chaud-Mellé a week ago.'

Coppelia took pity on my confusion. 'Listen, darling. It was Mark Xeethra Samuels' idea. In Highgate, he discovered all the lost secrets of analytic philosophy. He formulated the idea of the Commune. When von Clausewitz blockaded the town, he devised a plan of escape for members of the movement. He enlisted my services—I have been replacing chosen citizens with automatons. The real members have been smuggled out of the city by cannon. That is why the Maréchal was such a bad shot. Really he was firing comrades into the safety of the hills.'

This seemed such a far-fetched idea that I burst into hysterical laughter. The mirage of Sardinia shimmered before my eyes again: I was preparing spaghetti. I resisted the temptation to give myself up to this stringy illusion. Coppelia did not heed my disbelief. She continued: 'So now there are no real members of the Commune left in the city. They have all been blasted clear in protective hollow shells. Parachutes ensured they landed softly—one of the reasons for the acute shortage of ladies' undergarments. Eliza was replaced before she ever met you; this is also true of myself. Do you really think we would have gone to bed with you in the flesh? You have nothing to offer a woman!'

This rang true. Yet why had I been adopted into the Commune? All my values were right wing. I did not think Mark Xeethra Samuels would have listed me among those to be saved. Unless, of course, he was in need of a new bathroom. Coppelia explained this also: 'The simulacrum of Eliza fell in love with you despite her better judgment. She gave herself to you. However, being of a highly conventional upbringing, she could not accept the idea of a puppet-human relationship. The only option was to convert you also into an automaton. She has been an active Communard for longer than almost anyone; I owed her a favour. I followed you to the Theatre de l'Orotund and seduced you. I performed the operation when you fell asleep. Your real self was fired into the hills that same night, together with Monsieur le Purr. You both travelled south and started a new life in Sardinia, or so I believe.'

I clutched my chest. 'An automaton! This is impossible! The real me is in Sardinia, you say? Then why has my consciousness remained behind?' At the same time, I knew she spoke the truth. She suggested that, being of a prosaic turn of mind, my identity had fixed itself too firmly to my new body. 'When you are destroyed,' she said, 'your consciousness will leap back into your real self.' This was an utterly astounding concept. I could do little but dribble for a score of minutes. 'We have scattered the members over Europe,' she added. 'We have new names and identities. You are no longer Gropius Klee; you are Giovanni Ciao. One day, when we are stronger, we shall reunite and rebuild Chaud-Mellé as a Utopia, full of crystal towers and citizens in togas. There will be aeolian harps on every street corner!'

Monsieur le Purr patted my hand. His touch was soft and velvety, but hinted of power. 'The whole charade was carried out for the benefit of the Secret Police, mon ami. Had they discovered our escape method, they would have followed our example. We wanted them to remain behind to be butchered by von Clausewitz. That way, they are removed without any danger to us.' He narrowed his eyes. 'It is a good life in Sardinia. We are partners in business, you and I.'

Coppelia grinned feverishly. 'It does not matter what happens to us here. This is because we are really elsewhere! The real Eliza does not know you, nor would she want to. I am living in Paris and have never met you either. But you are certainly not my type. If you were less ugly and less stupid then perhaps . . .' I gave way before her wisdom. We burst into peals of laughter. When I had recovered, I told them about the newspaper parcel Kropotkin had entrusted to me.

'Oh, you mean the bomb?' Monsieur le Purr yawned, reached into his pocket and produced an identical package. 'We all carry one of these. If any of us feel like ending it here and now, we simply unwrap the device and bite off the fulminating cap. The explosion is identical to that of one of von Clausewitz's shells. Why do you ask?' I stood up and knocked over my chair. 'Aretino Rossetti! The fool has taken it down into the tunnels! The methane! If one of the harpies bites him . . .'

There was a tremendous explosion, greater by far than anything I had yet experienced. The four walls of the room were drawn up around us. The world turned white and deaf. I was pounding peppercorns with a mortar and pestle; I was whisking white wine sauce. I picked myself up and gazed around. The entire city had vanished. A huge scoop had been wrested from the earth. Chaud-Mellé was high in the air, falling towards von Clausewitz and his men. As I watched, the first houses crushed his guns, crumpling on the hillside into dust. I recognised my own house, the printing-press, exploding like an ink-blot on the horrified heads of his lieutenants. A typographical terror?

The whole network of Kingdom Noisette's tunnels had been exposed, like trenches in a ludicrous new game of war. Blind harpies struggled to take flight from the pits. Despite their withered wings, some managed to spiral upwards in a pale cloud, colliding with each other and screeching wildly. I looked around. Coppelia was lying some yards away in a heap. The others had been vaporised. I spotted a splinter of Xelucha Dowson Laocoön, noxious sage no longer—merely a noxious fragment. I watched Coppelia open her eyes. 'There are two things I do not grasp,' I cried. 'How did you leave my room when the door was locked? And how did Eliza fly? Was she full of helium?'

She spluttered. Her mouth attempted to form words. I picked it up and fixed it to her face. 'You left the key in the lock,' she replied. 'I am squeamish about keys, being a mechanical puppet. So I dismantled myself, piece by piece, passed myself under your door and reassembled myself on the other side. As for Eliza, I made her with hollow bones. Her dimples were designed to reduce drag.' There was nothing more to be said. I turned and watched the rest of the city fall.

Something extraordinary started to happen. A ghost City began to rise up from the bare earth. First the foundations shimmered into view and then the buildings followed. I suppose if a city can go mad, it can also die. And if it can die, it can turn into a ghost. 'Chaud-Mellé is saved!' I shouted. Although more tenuous of substance, it was the same place I had come to love and despise. 'It will make no real difference,' Coppelia pointed out. 'Ghost houses may be impervious to shells, but the Austrians will simply send to Rotterdam for ghost-cannon. The siege will begin all over again. Life is a disappointment.'

I ignored her and skipped down the phantom boulevards, over the spirit bridges, weaving in and out of the misty arcades. Everything was as good as new—though considerably more eerie. I danced past cafés, through graveyards (are ghost graveyards full of the living?) and towards my old house. Would Eliza's room be replicated in ectoplasm? Would there be ghost stockings in her ghost drawers? I was so eager to find out, I burst into her room without knocking.

Cuneiform de Sade, battered and bruised, was waiting for me on the bed. His eyes were like tarnished coins. He spoke with some difficulty, teeth like chisels on the clay of his tongue. Eliza's ghost underwear did not suit him. 'At last I will have some satisfaction!' He took hold of the copper paper-knife in his belt and advanced towards me. I fell back and tripped over a purple umbrella. The next thing I knew he had inserted the blade between my artificial ribs and had severed the roll of paper tape that determined my actions. I screamed and screamed; the pain was unbearable. It was a burning sensation. . . .

I winced and licked my fingers. Red wine sauce had spattered onto my shirt. I sighed. The pirates in the restaurant were clamouring for their pasta. I was Giovanni Ciao, recently arrived in Sardinia—running this establishment was a thankless task. The harbour waters slapped the walls of my kitchen. Why did I have to do all the hard work? Where was Monsieur le Purr? We were supposed to be in business together. I had been awaiting his arrival for a week. I wondered if, like me, he had been given a new identity. How would I recognise him?

A year later, I am still waiting. At least I am not entirely devoid of company. In the evenings, an old grey cat comes to visit. I feed him milk and cheese and ground goblin, which is a popular local dish. There are many goblins around these parts. They are very powdery and easy to grind, but too highly flavoured for my taste. The old grey cat helps to catch them; we often see them peering at us from holes in the wall. One day, when business is booming, I will sell up and go in search of Eliza and Coppelia. We shall set up house back in Dessau. The old grey cat laughs at this. He is a cynical sort of feline, but I am fond of him. His name is Herodotus and he has a mouth full of stories.

Afterword
E.F. Bleiler

Afterword
E.F. Bleiler

Writing an afterword or postscript for you is either pointless or thankless, for you have already read Rhys Hughes's *Worming the Harpy* and have your own ideas about it. If this were a conversation, we could talk about them. But it isn't, and to point out brilliancies would be insolent and supererogatory.

As an epilogist I cannot prepare you for Rhys Hughes. In any case no-one reads epilogues, and I need not go into the strange and wonderful things to be found in his work, for you are already certain of them. Nor can I soothe you if you found Hughes too ferocious on occasion. But I can give you a very few biographical facts (hoping that you belong to the critical school that believes that authors really exist) and describe my own appreciation of his stories.

In an earlier paper (in *Supernatural Fiction Writers*, edited by my son Richard) I gave Hughes's ideal biography in fanciful terms: his saturation in philosophy and history, his linkage to Borges, his connection with Celtic myth and folklore, his awareness of the Welsh literary tradition from Taliesin to Caradoc Evans (whose name should not be mentioned to loyal Welshmen), and his amused saturation in the fantasy worlds of the nineteenth and twentieth centuries.

For those of you who prefer a materialistic alternate world: Rhys Henry Hughes was born in Cardiff, Wales, on

24th September 1966; studied engineering in university; worked in a variety of jobs in a variety of places; travelled to many distant lands.

That is the formality: For us, his more significant education lies in thousands of hours reading hundreds of books that gloom in the shadowy side of Western culture: eccentrica, mythology, folklore, comparative religions, alchemy, Renaissance and modern occultism, abnormal psychology, *psychopathica sexualis*, fantastic fiction, and whatever else.

As you may have gathered from other sources, Hughes is a prolific writer, whose avowed intention is to create a matrix of one thousand interlocked stories that do—what? Perhaps serve as a mosaic of human strangeness? Perhaps develop a web in which motifs slide from strand to strand. Either, or not, this is worth waiting for. Will there be, after a thousand are completed, a thousand and first, an *alf lailah wa lailah*, a master document freezing the others in place?

What do I like about Rhys Hughes's work? Fun. Hughes sees and precipitates in words the latent humour in almost anything. Ranging from what our culture considers pleasing and smilingly ridiculous to horrors that have to be laughed at if they are faceable at all. Hughes is a laughing observer, both inside and outside. With Hughes you get humour that is white, various shades of grey, black—and I don't know why humour cannot be characterised by other colours. Is 'One Man's Meat' green humour as the chlorophyll sputters out?

I am also enormously impressed by Hughes's stylistic brilliance. The richness of language, the occasional Cambrianisms, the inexhaustible array of puns, weird metaphors that form the point of a story. And I envy him his netted imagination. As a man who sees connections where others do not, he offers enough ideas, if parcelled out, to fill a catalogue of fantasy for a generation of writers.

Most of all, I think, I delight in Hughes's madness. (Since reviewers agree in calling him mad, he must be used to the term by now.) By madness, I don't mean the pathology of a scarecrow numbed out of sensation by electric shock or dubious drugs. I mean what the early nineteenth-century Romantic, like E.T.A. Hoffmann, meant. Sensitivity to the weirdness of life, so that his world, though hyperbolically strange, is more profound and esoterically true than the world of two and two makes four. Hoffmann himself was one of these men, as are several of his characters. Hieronymus Bosch, William Blake, Odilon Redon, Salvador Dali, George MacDonald, David Lindsay. Some call them visionary. I respond to these men. I usually write stodgy textbooks, pedantic book reviews, stuffy academic introductions in the opposite structuring, but within me, I like to think, is something of Rhys Hughes's madness that awakens me.

I could be wrong, but I think that much of Hughes's work appears spontaneously from his unconscious; what might be dream in others, in Hughes is material accessible to his waking mind. Some of his stories are obviously closely planned, but others leap together unexpectedly as bizarre associations link out. I find this profound haphazardness attractive. If Edgar Allan Poe were living, he could probably analyse it and tell us something about the Rhys Hughes who amazes us.